A Love Foretold

all the best,

Suzanne DelYoung

A Love Foretold

SUZANNE DEYOUNG

THE HIGH ROAD

CHICAGO, ILLINOIS

"Better is the scanty store of the just
Than the great wealth of the wicked
For the power of the wicked shall be broken
but the Lord supports the just."

—Psalm 37

Thank you, God, for being by my side every
day of my life!

Acknowledgements

Many people in my life need to be thanked and acknowledged for their love and support.

I met my husband Dennis when I was fifteen and a half years old; he was seventeen. The half year is important because I was not allowed to date until I turned sixteen. That night he flirted and charmed like no one I'd ever known. I was so smitten I begged my parents to let me go out with him. He was my first date, my first kiss and the only man I am proud to say that I have shared my body with. I believe that is why our love making is still so wonderful and meaningful to us both after all these years. We had great fun making sure my sex scenes were accurate.

Dennis lovingly appointed himself my logic police for my book. His encouragement, input, and dedication were advantageous during my writing process. He made sure I stopped to eat and sleep whenever I became obsessed with completing this novel.

CarrieAnn, our daughter, is one of the two special gifts from God who were born out of the exceptional love Dennis and I have for each other. She is my best friend who encouraged me and shared many of her young adult life experiences that helped inspire my characters. CarrieAnn is a publicist and marketing expert with two college degrees in Broadcasting, Journalism, and Psychology. Our son Matthew, our second special gift of love, took on additional responsibilities, giving me more time to work on my book. He also kept up his 3.0 grade point average in college, jobbed out with his band Mama Green and worked with his lighting company "Above the Stage."

My parents, Connie and Jim Feusi, offered their unconditional love and support throughout my entire life. It is by their example that I've learned the meaning of true love. My father worked seven days a week to put me and my four siblings through Catholic grade school and high school. We were also fortunate to have piano, voice, dance, baton, and any other lessons my mother could take us to on the bus. There are not enough words to express my gratitude for all the incredible sacrifices they made for me.

My beloved Grandmother, Susie Espostio, showed great strength as a woman while always conducting herself like a *lady*. She has been my role model. My Grandmother was the first person who encouraged me to talk to my relatives who had passed on. I learned not to fear them as she lovingly conversed with them. She is the inspiration for my book.

My Grandfather Dominic Esposito took me every week end to the games my uncle Frank coached. As a little girl, I got to sit in the boys' locker rooms. As a young teenager, I was the envy of all my girlfriends.

My grandparents' neighbors, Little Grandma and Little Grandpa Davidson, were two special people who always had a penny for a gum ball at my grandparents' grocery store and time for this inquisitive little girl.

My godparents, Dorothy and Ben Davia, set an important example for Dennis and myself. As a traveling salesman for Anheuser Busch, he and my godmother always traveled together. Their successful marriage made the difficult decisions about separation that Dennis's profession presented to our family much easier. We followed in their footsteps and decided to travel together. Each city and hotel room became our home on the road, touring with his rock group Styx. It was not always easy, but I have two wonderful children, and as this book was being completed, Dennis and I celebrated our thirty-third wedding anniversary. I feel blessed to have such a wonderful family.

Other people who encouraged and supported me are listed in no specific order: Laura Fisher, Denise Arkus, Deana Olson, Pam Lofrano, Chuck Lofrano, Lori Alexander, Rick Kogan, Coleen Kogan, Lisa Kikkert, Prudy Pierce, Allison Lofrano, Dawn Feusi, Beverly, Jim and Ben Feusi, Peggy Mailborki, Lynn Rowlands, Bill and Deana Vincent, Aunt Jenny, Aunt Emily Greenwell, Aunt Jo Delore, Aunt Eleanor, Uncle Frank Esposito, Aunt Eva, Uncle Tom, Aunt Raphline, Aunt Helen, Pat Kohl, Diana Jay, Tim Orchard, Tom and Joyce Short, Donna and Dave Heaster, Noreen and Glen Stell, Dan Jesslus, Tony Cozzi, Murial Cozzi, Laura Zuawick, Les and Ellen Zurawicki, Laura Koch, Dawn Lara, Joyce Griffith, Linda Lewis, David MacKinnon, Jody Blanco, Michael Minton, Darcy, Jim, Jamie and Mark Corte, Liz and Bob Sayad, Kirk Lindquist, Robert Grunsten, Linda Griffith, Michael

Lynch, Dorothy and Ben Davia, John Touhy, Carl Flanders, Courtney From, Jackie Crum, Jim Majors.

Last but not least I would like to thank all the millions of fans who have supported Dennis, his special talents, our marriage and his career as a rock star with the group Styx. Our diverse journeys throughout his career made it possible to experience the many highs of such a privileged lifestyle. Inevitably we also were exposed to the small subset of low life, who in my mother's day were called floozies; in my day the guys in bands called them star f***kers, and in the movie *Almost Famous,* they were described as band-aids. To these women I say, "You should have taken the high road. True love is worth waiting for!"

Suzanne DeYoung

*F*ather Wind whipped viciously through the mighty oaks with no thought to the damage his anger wrought! Mother Rain cried tears of frustration over the destruction about to befall the ancient Waushanee tribe. Nestled deep in the heavily wooded forest, a secluded wigwam stood hidden among the trees. As storm clouds approached, two lovers lay spent, secure beneath a buffalo skin rug, basking in the afterglow of their passion.

"Heart of my heart," Napayshni whispered to his beloved. "I promise tonight will be the last time we meet in secret. Tomorrow, when we return to my village, I shall proclaim my love for you and take you as my wife. In the spirit of the Orenda, I shall convince the elders of my tribe that the mixing of our blood will bring strength, not weakness to my people." Taking the feather from his hair, Napayshni continued, "According to the Orenda, our tribes believe the ancestry of the family is passed on through the blood of the mother's descendants. As my one true love, I give you this to seal our union."

Larken wept silent tears of joy, overcome by the beauty of his gift. She knew the giving of a feather signified Napayshni's everlasting love. She reached out and traced her fingers over the sharp contours of his ruggedly handsome face. Tenderly she kissed each battle scar. Until this night Larken had never lain with a man, and though their love presented many problems, Larken knew she could love no other.

"My darling, you are the Keeper of the Mystic Healing Shield and the bravest of the Waushanee warriors. Your people will never accept a white woman as your wife," she sighed in her soft Irish brogue.

1

"My sweet Lark, I will invoke the spirit of Dengana-wodah, ancient mystic and prophet of my forefathers to come to our aid. His vision of virtue and fairness brought peace to our people by uniting the Five Tribes. I know he will champion our cause." Napayshni branded Larken with his touch as he continued a path of scorching kisses along the curves of her young, graceful body.

"How can you make this great sacrifice for me when I have already caused such dissension within your tribe?"

Without warning, a fierce gust of wind propelled the flap of the wigwam open. There, illuminated by the glow of the campfire, stood the raging savage warrior Inteus. His twisted face was filled with anger and jealousy for his half-brother Napayshni. Black and white lines slashed across his forehead and cheeks. His body was smeared with the color of red clay. Napayshni knew what Larkin did not: these marking symbolized a fight to the death. As he burst into their private sanctuary, his thunderous voice roared, "This woman has bewitched you, my brother, and you have brought dishonor to our tribe. The ancient shield that you proudly claim as your own has been soiled by the touch of this white devil!"

Suddenly, like a violent bolt of lightning, Inteus thrust his spear into Napayshni's chest, inflicting a mortal wound. Larken screamed in despair. With no thought to her own safety, she fell to the ground and cradled Napayshni's head in her lap. She watched helplessly as life's blood flowed from his body.

"Your tears will not bring honor back to my tribe!" Inteus roared as he reached into his boot and withdrew his knife. Sensing his intent, Larken threw herself across her beloved's body to protect him from this final act of depravity.

"No!" she shrieked.

Inteus viciously pushed Larken aside and slashed Napayshni's scalp as his final coup! He dragged Larken into the raging wind and summoned his gods.

"This woman and the Shield are now mine!" Inteus bellowed into the dark tomb of night.

2

Father Wind and Mother Rain lashed out at the injustice of this vile act, knowing that violence only begets violence. Inside, lying in a pool of his blood, the other half of Larken's heart beat one last time, never to learn of the seed planted in her womb.

ONE

*R*ose, what happened to that Indian?" Kady yelled to her sister.

"Indian, what Indian?" Rose questioned, waving her hand in exasperation. She was ready to call it a day and couldn't be bothered with any of her sister's nonsense.

"Come on Rose—the one that was sitting in the back for the last hour." Suddenly a sense of unease washed over Kady as she realized she hadn't seen him get off their bus.

"Indian like Gandhi, or Indian like Tonto?" a perplexed Rose asked as she gathered up the remaining tour pamphlets left by the last group of passengers.

"American Indian. You must have seen him. He was wearing an outfit that fit him like a glove, tight buckskin pants, suede fringed vest, and muscles to die for."

"Oh, no. Don't tell me I missed a chance to see how the West was really won. I must be slipping. Describe this guy again," Rose asked.

"Well, he was quite handsome, in a dark and mysterious way. You couldn't miss him."

"Sis, if you've put your contacts in backwards again, I swear I'm jumping off this bus and hitch hiking back to the Pier," Rose exclaimed.

Kady, the more sensible of the two, was not prone to fantasy. Whoever he was, she was sure that he had been sitting on their bus!

Kady stopped at the next traffic light and turned to her sister in a huff. "Look, I know what I just saw! As a matter of fact, he got on the bus with the group of senior citizens we picked up at La Salle Towers."

Kady remembered feeling strange when she caught him staring at her in the rear view mirror. She felt as though he was trying to tell her something. Just remembering the glare of his deep, dark-set eyes gave her the creeps. She gave herself a quick shake to block him from her mind, a trick she had mastered in her youth when trying to avoid unpleasant thoughts.

The light changed, and Kady accelerated back into the heavy traffic that was typical of a downtown Chicago afternoon. She tried to focus on the erratic movement in the streets, ignoring the blare of horns and the constant shuffle of people as they crossed haphazardly in front of cars. They had just dropped off their last group of tourists for the day, and Kady continued to drive toward their home office at Navy Pier. She desperately wanted to discuss the mysterious man but was convinced her sister would think she was nutty. Kady knew what would happen once Rose started in on a subject—there would be no end! She decided to keep quiet, determined not to add more fuel to her sister's fire.

With one hand on the metal bar above and the other filled with the discarded pamphlets, Rose made her way to the front of the bus to continue the crazy conversation she'd just had with her sister.

"You know, I'm beginning to think you need to see a shrink, or better yet a medicine man. I hope you know that you're starting to sound like Aunt Willa, always talking to Uncle Danny as if he were still alive. All I ask is that you let me know the next time you see the handsome Mr. Tonto. If he wants you to join him in his tepee, and you're not interested, remember you do have a twin sister. This little squaw will make sure the 'buck' stops here!"

"Good grief, Rose. It's nothing like that!" Many times Kady had been the unfortunate object of her sister's wicked sense of humor, but this time she couldn't help but chuckle at the picture Rose's remarks had so vividly conjured up.

At the age of twenty-seven, fraternal twins Kady and Rose Dailey worked full time during the summer for their family-owned business, appropriately called Dailey City Tours. Kady had graduated from the University of Illinois with a Masters Degree in education and a minor in history. For the last two years she had been teaching American history at the Latin School in the city. Rose was still working toward her Master's Degree in business marketing and hoped to someday open her own public relations firm.

Recently, their brother Seth had taken over the day-to-day management of the company when their father Ignatius retired early due to his declining health. Much to their dismay, one of Seth's changes in company policy required them to dress in identical uniforms. Both sisters were fiercely independent and had rebelled against this common twin ritual of dressing alike. During one of their many lengthy arguments over the wearing of the unfashionable navy blue attire, Rose was heard to exclaim, "Oh, Seth, I love these outfits. I feel like the female warden in 'Prison Girl Sluts.' "

"Oh, and by the way," Kady chimed in, "Where are the matching Dr. Scholl's pumps?"

Although they finally gave in, they continued to give Seth a hard time and vowed never again to be coerced into wearing identical clothing.

Driving with the hot afternoon sun glaring through the window had taken its toll. Both girls were wilting in their cumbersome uniforms. As they approached another stoplight, Kady searched her purse for a quick sugar pick-me-up. She pulled out a silver hair clip and a melted chocolate Hershey Kiss. Popping the treat into her mouth, Kady turned to her sister.

"Rose, would you please help me tie this mop up? I swear one day I'm gonna cut it all off."

"Don't you dare, Raggedy Ann! Women would die for hair like yours." Rose reached up, grabbed the barrette, and pushed Kady's hair away from her heart-shaped face. Her curly auburn locks were worn in a natural free flowing style that only enhanced her flawless complexion. Kady did not think it was necessary to spend more than a few minutes in front of a mirror just to get up and drive a bus. It was a good thing, too, since Kady and Rose shared a downtown Loop apartment that had only one bathroom.

Rose, on the other hand, teased and lacquered her long blonde hair so that it never seemed to move. Her glamorous look was the result of a nightly procedure that involved gooey styling gels and the always torturous ritual of sleeping on large rollers. Rose would sooner face a firing squad than leave the apartment without her makeup picture perfect.

She was always chiding Kady about her penchant for going *au natural*. Kady wore makeup for only the most special occasions. It annoyed her to no end to hear Rose's lectures on skin care and daily workouts. Kady was, for the most part, satisfied with her body. However, she had always been a little embarrassed by the ample size of her breasts. When she began to fill out in the fifth grade, Kady was mortified by her male classmates' reactions.

Always shy, she absolutely dreaded the unwanted attention. As Kady matured, she became aware of their advantages and the amount of attention she drew from the opposite sex. They still, however, made her feel self-conscious.

Kady was five foot six, one hundred and twenty-seven pounds. She was fortunate to have the shape and high metabolism of her paternal grandmother, Katherine Dailey, who cooked like a gourmet chef and enjoyed eating and sharing every calorie with her beloved family. Kady also loved to eat. Kady knew at some point that her fat-filled diet and obsession with chocolate would eventually catch up with her, but for the time being she was going to enjoy life and the body she was blessed with.

Kady would sooner spend her free time with a box of Fannie May assorted creams than walking on a treadmill going nowhere. She could not understand the nineties fixation where women toned their bodies to the point that their features looked like they were chiseled out of stone. It reminded her of the photos she'd seen of women in the seventies with bouffant flipped hair, thin masculine square-jawed faces, trying desperately to imitate Farrah Fawcett. Air heads, thought Kady. "No individuality." She firmly believed that men still secretly preferred women who were soft and comforting. She was proud that none of her body parts were man-made, but gifts from God, and good family genes. Kady's only claim to vanity was the repair of chipped front teeth she'd gotten learning to ride a bike.

She came into the world only five minutes earlier than her sister, yet Kady had always been more mature and responsible than Rose. Devoted to her family and students, she was the kind of person others turned to for support and guidance. She was a friendly face, always there to motivate, brush away a tear, or lend an ear whenever needed. Kady was considered a softy for every sad story, charity case and stray animal that crossed her path. She was strong in her faith and tried to live her life as a God-fearing Christian woman.

Rose was more self-absorbed. Her life centered on her studies, friends, figure and dating as wide a variety of men as her busy schedule would allow. While she loved her family dearly, her goal-oriented life style did not include time for love, marriage, or children. She was a stereo-typical female GenXer while her sister was a throwback to more traditional times. Kady chalked up their differences to the fact that they were after all fraternal twins, not even remotely identical.

It was the middle of a very busy week for the Dailey City Tours bus company. In the city of big shoulders, tourist season began with the onset of summer vacation for the sub-urban schools. Downtown hotels were filled to capacity with travelers from all over the world, and the streets were alive with teenagers in search of a big city adventure.

Kady and Rose pulled into the underground parking lot that housed their tour buses during the night. After parking, they proceeded to get the bus ready for the next day. Rose pit-ied the frantic teachers whose job it had been all day to keep twenty-six fourth graders under control. Kady's dedication to her career of teaching sniveling prepubescent brats five days a week made Rose think her sister was either nuts or applying for sainthood!

Looking at all the sticky fingerprints left by the school children gave Rose an idea. "Sis, let's flip a coin to see who gets to clean the inside of the bus! Heads I win, tails you lose!"

As the coin spun in the air, Rose yelled, before Kady had a chance to respond, "Tails you lose!" With a saucy flick of her wrist, Rose smacked Kady a high five and sauntered off of the bus.

Kady's good nature allowed her to go along with her sister's ploy to get out of the unpleasant task. Joining Rose in the confined quarters of the janitors' supply room, they gathered rags, buckets and disinfectants.

Kady had just begun cleaning the last rows of seats when she heard a loud whooshing noise. She glanced up, and there was Rose aiming the garden hose at the window, pretending to spray Kady's head. She shook her finger, scolding her sister's latest antics.

As Kady continued her cleaning, she reached down and saw something sticking out from under a worn gray vinyl seat. It was stuck in a mess of sticky goo that she'd tried to pick up with her rag. It wouldn't budge. She got down on her knees and stretched out her hand. Kady strained to get under the seat, reaching blindly as her fingers touched upon something soft. An unexpected chill passed through her. Gingerly pulling out the object, she could hardly believe her eyes.

"Oh, no!" she gasped, making an immediate connection to her mysterious Mr. Tonto. She stared at a white feather tipped in black. Not the kind of thing you would find just anywhere.

Kady quickly shoved the feather into her pocket. For a second, she thought she might be hallucinating.

A few moments later, she reached back into her pocket to check for the feather. With a feeling of dread, Kady remembered the numerous visions and premonitions she'd had as a child. Could they be starting up again? Had there actually been an American Indian on the bus?

As these thoughts bombarded her brain, she recalled a little girl struggling with visions she couldn't understand, and a family who regarded them with skepticism and disbelief. Even when her forewarnings became a reality, everyone seemed to regard them as mere coincidence. Because she was a twin, her parents assumed she was simply struggling with her own identity. Nevertheless, a series of incidents eventually convinced Kady's family that there was more to her imagination than met the eye.

Kady was eleven when she had a premonition that would change her family's thinking forever. It was her father's fortieth birthday, and her mother Eileen had planned a surprise party. While cleaning out their attic one afternoon Eileen had discovered an old suitcase tucked away in a corner. Inside some clothing was an antique pocket watch that had belonged to Ignatius' father. Kady's mother was having the watch repaired at Ima Cousin's Jewelry store on Michigan Avenue. On their way to the jewelers, Kady unexpectedly knew something strange had happened. She remembered feeling uneasy, sensing that a disaster was about to occur. The feeling was so strong Kady knew that she had to warn her mother.

"Mom, you can't go into Cousin's. It's being robbed!" she said, assuming her mother was aware of the robbery in progress.

"Honey, I don't know what you're talking about. Stay in the car with your sisters, and I'll be right back. Dad's party is in a few hours, and I have to pick up his gift."

Kady jumped out of the car and screamed, "No!" and grabbed her mother's arm refusing to let go.

Shocked by her daughter's behavior, Eileen became angry. "Now, Kady, that's just about enough of this nonsense. Let go of me and get back in the car." Pulling away, Eileen began to walk toward the store's entrance.

Suddenly police cars with sirens blaring pulled up in front of the jewelry store. Kady's mother watched, stunned, as the police rushed into the shop and dragged a man out, still wearing a black nylon stocking pulled over his head. Sneering, he was ushered into the police car. Eileen was stunned; she'd nearly walked right into a very dangerous situation, not only for herself, but for her children. But even more astonishing was Kady's premonition.

"Kady, I don't know how you knew Ima Cousin's was being robbed, but I'm glad that you did. She hugged Kady and gave her a kiss on the cheek. "Thank God you stopped me from going into that store." Eileen made the sign of the cross, grateful for her lucky escape. On the way home they stopped at their church and lit a candle for Kady's intuition.

That night after the celebration, the Dailey family eagerly awaited the evening news for complete details. Her father called her his little heroine. When the photograph shown on the television had matched Kady's physical description of the robber, including details she had concealed from her family, Kady felt very uneasy. She had even known that the jewel thief had a triangular chip out of his two front teeth, similar to her own.

In typical sibling fashion her brothers and sisters did not let her heroic act go to her head. They teased her unmercifully especially her brothers. They stopped just short of calling her a freak. Just the same, she'd certainly felt like one.

Later that same year Kady was at a slumber party with her sister and some of her high school chums. It was around midnight when her best friend Denise Applebee pulled out her Ouija board.

"Hey, everyone. Let's see if we can conjure up some ghosts. Kady, you're good at this. Who should we try to talk to?" Denise questioned.

"Oh, I don't know, how about Mr. O'Riley? He was always such a nice old man," Kady said.

"What are you talking about? Mr. O'Riley isn't dead. I walked by his house this afternoon, and he was out mowing his lawn," Carrie Finn exclaimed.

"No, he died. He fell down his porch steps and cracked his head open!" Kady argued, feeling a little shaken. She decided to quickly change the subject. "How about if we try to contact Mrs. Murphy? You know—that woman who used to live in the old haunted house?"

She knew that this would divert the attention of her friends. The girls would try to top each other with stories of how often they had tried to sneak into her abandoned house. Kady breathed a sigh of relief as the conversation about Mr. O'Riley was immediately forgotten.

The next day as the four girls were walking home from school, they saw an unusual flurry of activity at the end of the block. Curious, all the girls ran to see what was going on. As they approached Kady felt her stomach turn completely over. An ambulance was parked on the side driveway of Mr. O'Riley's house. The paramedics carried the poor old man out on a stretcher. He had a two-inch gash on his forehead caked with dried blood, exactly as she had envisioned it the night before.

"Oh my God," Rose whispered. "It's Mr. O'Riley. Wow, sis. Do you have a crystal ball or something?"

Kady stood bewildered and slowly realized that none of her friends would look her in the eye. After that day, no one ever mentioned the incident again, and it was the last time they ever played with a Ouija board. She felt like a freak of nature and no longer doubted her strange perceptive skills. Kady went to the library and read every book she could get her hands on that dealt with the paranormal. The more she learned the less she wanted to know. It was then she decided she didn't want to be the recipient of these dubious gifts. Kady armed herself with knowledge so that she could recognize when a precognitive event was about to take place.

It was after these incidents that she decided to work on suppressing any further premonitions. She dampened her creative imagination, not wanting to walk beyond the corridors of life that she did not understand.

Kady did not want to stand out or be different, so she made a conscious effort to block her psychic abilities from her mind. With time, her premonitions became less and less clear.

Kady reluctantly looked down at the feather. It was real all right, and the prospect of her intuitive powers returning filled her with a sense of dread! Please, she thought, not again!

"Hurry up, Kady. I'm done. I'll meet you in the supply room," Rose announced.

"Just give me a few minutes to finish," Kady explained and quickly completed her task, returning the bags of garbage and dirty rags to the maintenance room. Rose waited, impatient to go home.

Kady was glad that her sister was waiting for her. Years ago the girls had made a pact never to walk through the dark underground parking lot alone, believing there was safety in numbers. After six p.m. most of the fast food restaurants and shops closed for the night due to a recent outbreak of robberies in the parking lot adjacent to the Pier. Kady and Rose had friends who lived in the North Pier building that the thieves had targeted. Since then, they were very cautious and alert when walking from the parking garage to their offices.

Every employee who worked for Dailey City Tours had to complete classes in CPR. It was a mandatory rule, set down by their father Ignatius. Kady and Rose learned self-defense at an early age from their Aunt Eva and Uncle Tom O'Connor. They were retired police officers who ran classes for senior citizens. Their years on the police force taught them that a little knowledge could make the difference between being the victim or being the victor when personal safety was threatened. Ever vigilant, Kady and Rose had taken their lessons to heart!

Picking up the pace, they headed for the entrance marked Pier Personnel Only and rode the elevator up to the top floor. Dailey City Tours leased the entire third floor of office space. From the time their brother Seth took over management, the company had expanded its growth. Dailey City Tours was well on the way to becoming a Fortune 500 company.

As they entered the reception area, their younger sister Patti greeted them. Eighteen months their junior, Chatty Patti, one of the many nicknames she was affectionately called, was a typical freckle-faced redheaded Irish lass.

"Hi, kids. Boy, do you two look like worn-out clones the wind blew in! Been a long day, huh?" Following in the family tradition, she worked for Dailey City Tours during the summer months. In the fall she was a marketing-communications student at DePaul University. Talking nonstop, Patti continued, "You both have messages in your boxes. Rose, Kevin called and he wants you to meet him at Café Iberico around eight-thirty. I told him you'd be there. Kady, Aunt Willa phoned and she wants you to stop by before you leave today. She said it was very important."

"Is nothing sacred? I've just had my social calendar for the evening filled out by my baby sister. No sense in wasting time checking out our messages! Patti the snoop just told us all we needed to know!" said Rose.

"Younger sister privileges," Patti quipped with a grin.

Kady's ever hungry stomach growled, giving her an excuse to quickly change the subject. "Hey, Patti, did you eat all those chocolate covered bananas I left in the refrigerator?"

"There was only one left. Anyway how long did you expect it to stay fresh? I left you the tangerine. It's way healthier."

"Gee, thanks. You're all heart! Rose, I'm going to stop by and visit Aunt Willa. How soon will you be ready to leave?"

"I'll be a while yet. I have about forty-five minutes of paper work to wind up," Rose answered.

One advantage to driving the tour bus was that it involved no paperwork. It was the job of the tour guide to fill out the time sheets and complete all the forms. Making a hasty retreat, Kady shouted on her way out the door, "I'll be back in thirty minutes!"

As Kady punched the elevator button going down, she unconsciously reached into her pocket. Her fingers tingled as she felt the heat that radiated from the feather. Kady held it in the palm of her hand and reassured herself, "I know there's a logical explanation for this. I'll bet Aunt Willa saw Mr. Tonto getting off our bus!"

Wilhelmina Newton's offices were on the ground floor, adjacent to her famous restaurant, Widow Newton's. The rich dark mahogany door was slightly ajar as Kady peered in.

"Hi, Rita. Is Aunt Willa still here?"

"Hey, Kady. Come on in. She's expecting you!" said Rita Flynn, the receptionist. She was a distant cousin and a dear friend of Aunt Willa's.

"Thanks, Rita. How is your family?" Kady asked as she walked toward her aunt's office.

"They're just fine, thanks. You better go right in. Willa's on the war path today, and I'm hoping your visit will calm her!"

Dressed in an elegant Oleg Cassini business suit, Willa Newton greeted her niece with a big hug. The dark circles under her eyes were evidence of a recent bout with a migraine.

"Hi, honey. I was hoping you'd have time for a visit today."

"I always have time for my favorite aunt!" Kady replied, still clutching the feather in her hand.

Willa motioned toward the feather with bent fingers and said, "I see he's made contact with you."

"What do you mean?" Kady asked, startled.

"Sit down, honey. I think we need to talk." Willa slowly lowered her petite frame into her burgundy leather office chair. Her arthritis bothered her today, and she felt every bit of her seventy-two years.

"I'm all ears," Kady said, placing the feather back into her pocket.

"Do you remember the story surrounding the opening of my restaurant?" Willa questioned.

"Yes, of course I do. Just before Uncle Danny died you were planning on opening a restaurant here at Navy Pier. When he unexpectedly passed away, you had all but given up the idea. Then, one night he came to you in a dream and insisted that you allow nothing to deter you from building Widow Newton's. The rest, as they say, is history."

Willa had spoken to Kady many times about her life with Uncle Danny and how their restaurant came to be. For most of his life, Daniel Newton had been a successful building contractor whose company specialized in boiler installations. A tragic accident destroyed his business and forever changed their lives. Daniel never did fully recover from the incident. To this day, Willa was still sensitive about the accusations of negligence surrounding her husband's company. Kady knew they had shared a great love for each other, one that even death could not diminish! Aunt Willa was convinced that they were soul mates who had met in a previous life, ordained as it were by destiny to be together. Theirs was the kind of love that Kady had always dreamed of. Willa told Kady that when the time was right, she would find the one love that would be hers and hers alone. Kady was well aware of her aunt's devotion to the memory of her husband, and her eccentricities were legendary, but nothing could have prepared Kady for what followed.

"Well, honey, it seems as though your Uncle Dan's on a mission. I sense his spirit is restless."

"A mission? What kind of mission?" Kady asked curiously.

"Dan spoke to me again in a dream and asked for our help," replied Willa, closing her eyes to vividly recall the night before. "I did a foolish thing last night. I had a glass of

Merlot with dinner. I know, I know. Red wine is taboo for migraine sufferers. But sometimes I can't resist. I tried to sleep, but couldn't so I got up and took some Vicodin for the pain. I even tried the blue gel face pack—anything to stop the pounding in my head. About fifteen minutes later the medication began to take effect. I started to nod off when somewhere in the distance I heard your uncle Danny.

"At first his voice was unclear, but as I crossed the threshold between reality and dreams, I could feel a spiritual force calling to me. It was Daniel's voice I heard. But the physical form was not your uncle's. What I saw was an American Indian, resplendent in a full-feathered ceremonial headdress—a character directly out of the old West. I must admit that he was quite handsome and regal. The vision soon faded. When I awoke, all I could remember was Daniel's voice repeating, 'With Kady's help, all will be revealed when the lark sings.' What does it all mean, honey? I don't understand your Uncle Daniel's message."

Kady could hardly believe what she had just heard. She slowly removed the feather from her pocket. "Aunt Willa, there was a man…at least I think there was…on our bus today…he was an American Indian…Aunt Willa I don't think I can do this." Kady lowered her eyes and stared at the feather, her hand trembling.

"OK, sweetheart, I'm as confused about this as you are, but please reconsider. Your uncle and I need you."

"Why me, Aunt Willa? What could I possibly know about Indians?"

"Look, sweetheart, I know you have always been uncomfortable with your psychic abilities, but I think I know someone who might be able to help us. This Thursday our Twilight Club is having a guest speaker who interprets dreams and speaks to our loved ones that have crossed over. I'd like you to meet with him; maybe he can help us. Please say you'll come."

Feeling pressured, Kady hesitated for a few seconds. For her, confronting repressed psychic feelings was always difficult. Suddenly she heard herself blurt out, "Well, OK, I'll try to make the meeting…but that's all I can promise!" Getting up, Kady leaned over the desk and gave her aunt a quick hug.

"Bye, Aunt Willa. Rose is waiting for me. You know how impatient she is. See you Thursday," Kady stuttered as she dashed out the door.

Dazed by her aunt's revelations, she walked trance-like out of the office, wondering what had possessed her to agree to help. She tried to convince herself that she didn't have enough evidence to prove a connection between the man on the bus and her aunt's dream, but there it was. The foreboding of dealing with her premonitions again gave her a feeling of tremendous unease. It settled in the pit of her stomach and fueled her anxiety. Kady nodded to Rita and headed toward the door.

"Wait!" Rita yelled and motioned Kady over to her desk. Rita held her hand over the telephone mouthpiece and whispered, "Your sister Patti is on the line. Rose is on a rampage. She's in a hurry to get home for her date. She's waiting for you on the ground floor."

"Thanks," Kady mumbled as she headed toward the elevator.

Willa glanced wistfully at the photo of her beloved husband, "Be patient, Dan." She reached for the phone and dialed the office of Colin O'Dannaher, the grandson of her best friend Edna O'Dannaher. Willa and Edna were childhood friends who'd grown up together in Bridgeport. Of all her friends and family, Edna was the only one who felt Willa's dreams of Daniel were real. Having suffered a terrible loss herself, Edna came to believe in the existence of communication with the spiritual world. Some twenty years earlier, on a bright October Saturday, tragedy struck her life. Her husband Peter, son Brent, daughter-in-law Lilly, and grandson Colin were out for a drive in Peter's brand new Buick, when a drunk driver blew a red light and crashed into their car. The accident was pure devastation. The only survivor was twelve-year-old Colin. He was rescued from the crash with multiple head and leg injuries, which left him with many painful months of rehabilitation. It was during this time that he began receiving spiritual messages from his deceased mother and father.

Edna, who had been completely despondent with her loss, had focused all her attention on Colin's recovery. Night after night she kept vigil over her grandson until he was released from the hospital. At first Colin's psychic abilities shocked Edna, but over time she not only accepted but encouraged him to explore his newfound communication with those who had crossed over. She was in great need of any contact with her departed loved ones. With Edna's constant reinforcement, Colin grew to become a man who not only accepted the passing of his parents, but of his own special psychic gifts. His understanding and belief in life after death ignited an interest in the spiritual world that transformed into a lifelong passion. With the great loss they both had shared, Edna and Colin had bonded into a complete, loving family.

Edna had inherited the O'Dannaher Construction Company from her late husband Peter, who had made the transition from carpenter to contractor. What began as a simple addition and rehabbing business Edna had transformed into the most respected and lucrative historic renovation firm in the city.

While in high school Colin had earned his stripes as an apprentice carpenter and had worked full time during the summer, for the company during his junior and senior years. After graduating college, he had gone to work for his grandmother as chief foreman. Together they pioneered many innovative techniques for restoring and renovating period architecture. Preserving old buildings allowed them the chance to do what they loved most, enhancing and cherishing the past.

After four rings, Colin's answering machine clicked on. "Hello, this is O'Dannaher Construction Company. We are unable to take your call at this time. Please leave a message at the sound of the tone. Beep, beep, beep..."

"Colin, this is Willa Newton, and I'm calling to confirm your appointment as our guest speaker on Thursday, June 24, at seven-thirty p.m. I'm looking forward to our meeting. Love to Edna," Willa replied self-consciously, wondering if she would ever get used to speaking into a machine!

Two

*W*hat took you so long? You know I have to meet Kevin at eight-thirty. If we don't hurry I won't have enough time to get ready! Here, I brought you your purse. Now, let's get going!" Rose dragged her sister toward their new fire engine red Toyota Camry. She knew her sister was tired after a long day of driving, so when they went home, Rose appointed herself the designated driver. Moving faster than the speed of light, Rose flashed her parking permit at the uniformed guard behind the plate glass window. Making a quick left turn out of the parking garage, she continued toward the yellow, changing stop light.

"Rose, stop! There's a cop! Don't blow this light!" Kady admonished grabbing on to the 'oh my God bar' above the side door window to keep herself from falling out! Kady glanced out of the window toward the Pier. From the corner of her eye she caught sight of a flurry of buckskin. Kady did a double take as she recognized the apparition. It was him.

"It can't be!" Kady said out loud. She shook her head hoping the phantom would disappear.

"What now?" Rose questioned her sister.

"Oh, nothing, just get me home. I'm exhausted and hungry!"

Sighing, Kady leaned back into her seat, suddenly feeling small and helpless. Kady's well ordered world was unwinding out of control. She wondered how she was going to explain another Mr. Tonto sighting to her sister.

Rose stepped on the gas pedal and sped away from the turning light as Kady glanced back one more time, expecting Mr. Tonto to vanish. Instead, he gave her a quick nod of recognition. Kady cringed, sinking down further into her seat, and remained quiet for the duration of their short ride home.

It was after seven p.m., and the traffic had dwindled to a few cars. A dusky light veiled the city streets.

They pulled up in front of their Adamesque apartment building in record time. It was located on the corner of LaSalle and Goethe. Quickly, Kady came out of her trance as Rose slid into an illegal parking spot. Sarcastically she asked, "Rose, if you keep this up I know I'm gonna see you on America's most wanted list!" Recently Kady discovered a four-inch stack of unpaid parking tickets in the bottom drawer of their grandmother's antique pine desk.

"You know I'm a rebel, and I'm never ever gonna be any good!" Rose sang off key as she tossed her long blonde hair over her shoulder and darted from their car. Huffing and puffing hard, Kady tried to match her sister's stride as she made her way up the stairs toward their two-story apartment. Briefly Kady wondered if she should try working out. She was out of breath trying to keep up with her sprinting sister! Nah, thought Kady. I'll live longer at my own pace!

Kady's black cat Midnight greeted her at the front door. As she bent down to pick up her feline friend, Kady felt comforted by the warmth of her beloved pet.

"Get that animal out of here. I'm going to wear my white DKNY pantsuit and I don't want her hair all over my outfit!" Rose exclaimed, dashing into their only bathroom.

"Awe, Rose. She only came near you because she loves you," Kady said with a grin. She knew that Rose and Midnight had a love-hate relationship. It seemed as if Midnight went out of her way just to annoy Rose. Rose had threatened the cat many times with bodily harm. Midnight counted on Rose's sisterly love to save her from being thrown out the window. In retaliation, Midnight continued to leave hair all over Rose's clothing. She constantly jumped on Rose's bed and disturbed the pillows. Midnight would do anything to cause havoc in Rose's well-ordered life. She had no affinity toward animals, especially stray alley cats!

Three years before, Midnight had the good sense to show up at twelve p.m. on Kady's bedroom windowsill instead of Rose's. For weeks, Kady advertised in the newspaper, and inquired around the neighborhood to see if anyone was missing a black cat. No one answered her ad or came forward to claim the lost animal! Kady fell in love with her stray and decided to adopt the cat. She appropriately named her Midnight. It was no surprise to Kady when her sister announced to their family that Kady had found her *familiar*!

"I'll take her out on the patio just as soon as I order that deep dish, double cheese pizza I've been dreaming about." Kady, who loved to eat, knew it would take at least thirty minutes to deliver her dinner. To appease her growling stomach, she grabbed a hand full of chocolate Hershey Kisses from the bowl sitting on the kitchen table. She ignored the electronic beeping and the red light reminding her that she should check their messages. Still holding Midnight, Kady slipped out of her blazer, trying to get comfortable. As she threw her jacket over the back of a kitchen chair, the pocket of her blazer brushed up against the buttons of their answering machine. The feather fell out, gliding to the floor, and the answering machine suddenly engaged.

"Hello, this is—" Unexpectedly, Midnight jumped out of Kady's arms. Then she ran and hid under the kitchen table. When Kady reached down to console her, she darted under the living room sofa. The cat acted as if she was afraid. Kady was startled by Midnight's unusual behavior.

"Midnight, come here, girl. Come on out. You know I can't reach you under there!" she coaxed. As the unheard message played, Kady crouched down and made one last plea. "Midnight, please come out. I'll fix your favorite Fancy Feast cat food for dinner tonight."

Kady gave up and returned to the kitchen. She hoped the smell of food would draw Midnight out from her hiding place. In the background the answering machine continued as Kady missed the first two messages. A familiar voice finally drew Kady's attention. "Kady, dear, it's Mom. I just had a call from

Aunt Willa, and she wanted me to remind you about the Twilight meeting this Thursday at seven-thirty. She has someone she'd like you to meet. He sounds very interesting honey. Love to both my girls. See you at church on Sunday."

Kady was not looking forward to seeing her family at Sunday's Mass. Following the service it was their custom to gather for a brunch at their parents' home. Frequently this invitation included many of their relatives and friends. The girls affectionately referred to their parents' home as the Dailey Compound.

The conversations at brunch always led to the discussion of the Dailey's desire for more grandchildren. Two of the older Dailey children had presented Eileen and Ignatius Dailey with six beautiful grandchildren. Their older brother and sister loved to remind Kady that time was running out on her biological clock. Usually Kady took their good-natured teasing in stride, but today Kady was on edge and her mother was an expert at reading her children's moods.

Kady loved her family and appreciated growing up in a loving, two-parent atmosphere. Eileen and Iggy had just celebrated their fortieth wedding anniversary. Kady was proud of her parent's lifelong commitment to marriage. Her own experiences with her single-parent students reinforced her belief that it was important for children to be raised in a two-parent family—no "Murphy Brown" for her. Kady's faith, as a result of her growing up an Irish Catholic, was of the utmost importance to her. Her parents' motto was, "A family that prays together stays together." Both Kady and Rose were raised to believe that the sexual revolution of the sixties and seventies was destructive to society as a whole and that free love was anything but free. There was always a price to pay! Having higher moral standards, Kady was mature enough to realize that an impulsive decision could lead to dire consequences. She hoped one day to find a man who would share her values and be committed to a faithful relationship. She yearned for a knight in shining armor to sweep her off her feet. With so many important goals to accomplish, Kady had vowed to never be tempted to fall into the "Tramp Trap." Kady had always believed that she could never be duped by any man—that is, until she met the number one don Juan on campus and fell like a ton of bricks, figuratively and literally.

During her senior year at grad school, Kady thought she'd met the man of her dreams. Brick Jackson was a sexy, struggling author and playwright who hoped someday to pen the next *Gone with the Wind*. For the first few months of their relationship he was a perfect gentleman, attentive and content to follow her lead, letting romance take its natural course. Brick wove a spell around Kady, using his charm and whit. Lost in the fantasy Brick created, Kady thought they were soul mates. He seemed to know what was important to her, telling her exactly what she needed to hear, making her believe that they shared the same hopes and dreams for the future. Brick had very little family of his own, and he appeared to revel in her large family gatherings, even going so far as to attend church with them every Sunday. After two months of steady dating, Brick suddenly brought up the "L" word! It was a conversation Kady would never forget. Ever the smooth talker, Brick cornered Kady one quiet night while watching a video in her dorm. As they sat, side by side with their arms around each other watching the end of *It Happened One Night* starring Clark Gable and Claudette Colbert, Brick pulled her into his arms, kissing her passionately, whispering into her ear, "Kady, I've fallen in love with you. Honey, let's get engaged."

While Kady never lacked for male attention, she never been in love before, and throughout college she had concentrated more on her studies and achieving her scholastic goals than earning an MRS degree. When Brick pursued her, Kady was not only flattered, but thought she was the luckiest girl on earth, because of his popularity.

Rose tried to tell her that she was in way over her head, but Kady had never been the center of one man's undivided attention before and fell quickly under Brick's spell. Kady's only experience with love was the unconditional love of her family. But Brick's attentiveness and declaration of love made her feel so special that she quickly responded, "Oh yes, Brick, I love you, too, but my parents will insist I finish school first!"

"Hey, a long engagement is fine with me," replied Brick. "Why don't we keep this our little secret for a while?"

Although Kady longed to share this happiness with her family, she reluctantly agreed. Soon after she consented to their secret engagement, Brick began to make strong sexual demands. His new mantra became, "Being engaged is just like being married," followed by, "I only want to show you how much I love you, honey!"

Kady believed that the ultimate giving of her body was a gift that should be shared with the man she would marry. Kady wasn't sure if she was ready for that final commitment, so she begged Brick to wait and give her more time. His charismatic charm and personality were hard for someone with Kady's shy personality to resist. But there was something that just did not feel right.

He was a writer; his specialty was fantasy and fiction. The story he initially created to lure Kady was almost irresistible, promising marriage, children and a happily-ever-after future. Then suddenly, when Kady wouldn't give in sexually, he became a Jekyll and Hyde, playing into her insecurities. One minute he would make her feel like she was the most important thing in his life, the next he made her feel she should be grateful that she was the "chosen one." After all he would pompously claim, "I can have any girl on campus!"

He would then reinforce his ego by outrageously flirting with anything wearing a skirt and tight sweater, while a shy Kady stood by helplessly watching. Even though Kady knew she was attractive, these displays made her feel insecure. Little by little, Brick became more insistent with his sexual demands. Angry at her refusal to have sex with him, he used other women as a tool to get even. Kady suspected he'd cheated on her when she wouldn't give in, but he'd always denied her accusation, making her feel the arguments were all her fault and telling her she was crazy. Then Jekyll would return, and Kady would feel the full force of his charm again. This went on for months, and Kady's confidence suffered as well as her grades. She felt like her life was one big roller coast ride spinning out of control. Eventually Brick's Hyde personality took over, and every date became a groping session that ended with a full blown argument. Each disagreement left her with less and less self-esteem. She felt like she was being backed into a corner. Six months into their relationship, Kady was dealt the final blow. While visiting one of her girlfriends in an off campus dorm, she literally caught Brick with his pants down. The semester was just ending and just like the book he hoped to write, Brick was gone with the wind!

Brick's betrayal and departure left Kady confused, shocked and deeply hurt by the promises he had never meant to keep and had broken. Kady finally realized that all Brick wanted was sex. Her shy personality had made her an easy target. All he really felt for her was lust. Immature lust, not unlike the young boys in high school who would tell the girls anything they wanted to hear, just to get into their pants. All his talk about being engaged, about love and commitment was just a facade to get her into bed. Just another line, by a master manipulator who figured out another way to get what he wanted...sex. When the dust cleared, she felt lucky to have escaped. While all those sweet-talking lies might be enough for some women, Kady would not accept anything less than the real thing! It was a troubling lesson that she would never forget. It also was the first time Kady had dealt with a broken heart, but deep down inside she was glad to be free from Brick's manipulative personality. The relationship had left her feeling mentally and physically drained. From that moment sexy, charming men were definitely *verboten*.

It was difficult for Kady to explain to her family why their courtship had ended. While they had not been privy to the extent of Brick cruelty, neither had they been blind to the changes in Kady's loving personality. Everyone gave Kady the space she needed to heal, and she was grateful for the support of her loving family.

Then one day, her clever sister Rose finally put it all into perspective. She said, "Kady, I'd always known that BJ was a few bricks short of a load and that the affliction was caused by too much testosterone." She'd even dedicated a poem to Brick.

> Brick has got a penis
> With a mind that's all its own.
> And like every man I've ever known
> Too much testosterone.
> He charmed you with his lies;
> He even made you cry.
> Although he hurt your pride,
> Thank God you're not his bride!

Kady laughed so hard she cried over Rose's crazy comforting sense of humor! Her cathartic tears were exactly what she'd needed to put her life back into perspective.

THREE

*D*amn it!" Colin O'Dannaher exclaimed, bumping his knee trying to lower his six-foot-two frame into his hunter green office chair. He desperately needed to elevate his swollen ankle. It was a beautiful, sunny day and he longed to be outdoors, but unfortunately he was recovering from a recent accident. The attending physician who treated his injury in the emergency room had advised him to stay off his feet for a couple of weeks. It was like telling the leaning tower of Pisa to straighten up! Colin gave new meaning to the phrase "man on the go!" He was unaccustomed to having so much down time, and it was difficult for him to control his boundless energy.

His primary job was general partner in O'Dannaher's Construction, a company co-founded and owned by his grandmother Edna. Colin was dedicated to his grandmother's company and worked long hours, but his true love was his second job. He was a psychic medium who dealt in the various aspects of the paranormal. For him, his ability to act as clairsentience (a medium who can communicate with spirits in a room) was more of a passion than a real job.

Colin led a jet set life style which kept him continually on the go. Twice a month he lectured across the country on the various aspects of psychic phenomena. Focusing on his ability to contact the dead, Colin had recently made the rounds promoting his new book, *The Psychic in You*. His Chicago connection became a powerful tool with the initial introduction of his book, when a young producer on the Oprah Winfrey Show got an advanced copy and fell in love with it. Colin's television appearance on Oprah's was both successful and controversial. A group of psychic skeptics called "Defenders of the Living," were present in Oprah's audience. They believed any purported communication with the dead was blasphemy. During the show, the "Defenders" publicly accused Colin of fraud, hoping to discredit him. For the telecast, Oprah had flown in parents, spouses and friends who had experiences with Colin's psychic abilities. Each individual told story after story of Colin's aptitude to accurately describe details and events surrounding the lives of their loved one. He then went on to demonstrate his telepathic skills by contacting several audience members' loved ones who had passed on. He was a bona fide hit. This one appearance on Oprah's show increased the sales of his book tenfold, catapulting it to the top of the *New York Times* best seller list.

Colin was blessed with the irresistible charm of his Irish ancestors. His ink black hair, alluring smile and mesmerizing sea green eyes were a combination that made most females weak in the knees. The success and power of his public persona only added to his mystique. His television appearances and all the fluff pieces in the news made him the latest male hottie in town. A bevy of superficial woman willing to cater to his ego began to appear. Many of them wanted to be seen with him and share in the spotlight of his moment of fame. Their self-centered fantasy led them to presume that this association would make them a celebrity, too. Colin's grandmother Edna cautioned him not to believe in his own press. He assured her that he knew exactly what these women were after and that all he wanted was to have a little fun and enjoy his success while he was still young and single. Edna hoped Colin would not get caught up in his notoriety and miss the chance of finding true love like the one she'd found with his grandfather. She prayed that she'd raised Colin with higher moral values than all those movie stars and rock stars that were constantly in the headlines with their fast interchangeable women of the week. Colin assured her that he wouldn't get caught in a bimbo trap. He told her there was plenty of time to have a serious relationship and that he'd know when the right woman came along.

The past few months of overwhelming media frenzy had left Colin emotionally and physically drained. When his friend Ana DuPré suggested the use of her boss's condominium in the Florida Keys, he jumped at the offer to get away from it all! Ana and Colin had been dating on and off for the past few months. They'd met at his first major book launching event, shortly after his Oprah appearance. Ana was drawn to Colin's fame and charming personality. Linking their names together would make great press and boost both their careers. Ana was getting close to the age when models had to start thinking about an alternate occupation and getting her MRS degree was just what she was looking for.

Colin was all set to have fun in the sun relaxing, skiing, snorkeling and enjoying the water with an attentive woman at his side. During their stay in the Florida Keys, Colin decided he wanted to do some water skiing. Ana's boss owned all sorts of high priced water toys including a top-of-the-line Bayliner. On a good day this boat could surpass sixty-four knots.

Ana hated the water; it messed her hair and make-up. Straight from the shower without her perfect cosmetic mask she looked like a skinny wet poodle. Ana liked attention and made sure she was always packaged well. She wouldn't dream of getting into the water. She preferred to sit on the shore perfecting her beach bunny image.

For the last few days every time Colin had wanted Ana to join him in some water sports, she would bow out with the coquettish batting of her eyes, "Colin honey, you know it's important for me not to be exposed to too much sun." Colin secretly suspected that her fear of the sun was as shallow as the ocean during low tide. Ana liked to be seen, and she made sure everyone noticed her as she paraded around in the altogether on the condo's private beach front.

"Come on, landlubber, you're no fun. I need someone to drive the boat," Colin said after they had been in Florida more than a few days. He scooped her out of the lawn chair. "Oh Colin," she sighed, as she threw her arms around his neck.

Colin grabbed her terry cloth sun suit and carried her to the boat.

"Put on some clothes, Ana," he exclaimed handing her the skimpy outfit. "I need you to drive this thing for me honey. A little direct sunlight will be good for you. It will give your skin a healthy glow," he said, appealing to her vanity.

"Dear, dear Colin, I love when you take care of me. Of course I'll drive the boat so we can have some fun together!" a clinging Ana cooed as she ran her long painted fingernail down his arm, in a proprietary manner.

Taking her time, Ana dressed provocatively right on the deck for all to see, wiggling her fanny as she stepped into her sun suit. Hey, thought Colin, let them all look. Today she's with me.

Colin liked Ana but felt she was a pampered princess. She knew the rules, but lately she had been stepping over the line. Colin began to wonder if this vacation would turn out to be a mistake. Going to the bow he started the boat, cruising out about a mile while Ana finished dressing. When she sauntered over, he plopped a big straw hat on her head, one that had been lying on the passenger seat. He had no desire to be stranded out in the middle of the Gulf with a woman suffering from sunstroke!

"You're such a good sport. What more could a man ask for?"

Ana gave him a model-perfect smile that made up for all the years she'd spent in braces. She simpered and waited until Colin got situated in the water. Finally Colin waved and yelled, "OK honey, let's take off."

Thinking this was a funny game, Ana squealed and suddenly pushed the throttle forward. The boat shot forward like a shell bursting out of a cannon. Colin tried to maintain his balance, but the jolt knocked him completely off keel. Before he could straighten up, the tow rope snagged him by the foot and spun him around, giving his ankle a violent twist.

Colin worked extremely hard at keeping his body in tip-top shape. He prided himself on his rigorous fitness routine.

So after Ana fished him out of the Gulf, he wasn't sure what hurt more, his bruised body or his bruised ego. They spent the rest of the day in the emergency room where it was determined that Colin had incurred a sprained ankle and a hairline fracture of the heel. Colin decided to cut short his stay. He told Ana that he needed to get home and recuperate. He wanted her to stay, have fun and finish her vacation on her own. He was sure she wouldn't lack for company. Conniving Ana could not let that happen; it would spoil all her plans. Hearing that her prize fish was about to cut bait, Ana decided to play nurse. During their plane ride home Ana made an attempt to take care of Colin's needs. But she couldn't keep her usual self-centeredness at bay and quickly tired of the game, sulking the last two hours of the plane ride home.

This accident convinced Colin that his spiritual guides were telling him to slow down. So today Colin was determined to stay home and take it easy. He settled his ankle comfortably on his antique Queen Anne foot stool, turned on his computer and began his research. Scanning the screen, he hacked away, unconsciously taking a sip of his sugar-free decaffeinated ice tea. It was a remnant from his last party, and the only liquid left in the refrigerator that he could take with his pain medication. Colin grimaced as the sour flavor touched his lips. With a sigh, he set down the glass, wishing it was filled with a quick sugar pick-me-up loaded with caffeine instead.

Ryder, his half-breed three-month-old boxer mutt, let out a big yowl as he lay on the floor in his favorite spot in front of a large palladium window. Acting as if he could read Colin's thoughts, Ryder threw a big brown paw over his eyes and continued to make human-like sounds.

"Yeah, you try working with a throbbing foot and no caffeine in your system, and we'll see how agreeable you are!" In response, the dog let out a loud bark that Colin took as understanding.

Colin leaned closer to his computer screen and focused on the latest bit of information he had pulled up from the site at the UCLA library. Only a handful of hackers were able to hone in on this new technology. Carefully he inspected the site on the native Americans of the Chicago land area.

His sudden interest in this topic had begun with his latest project for O'Dannaher construction. The firm had been contracted for renovation of a block of historical homes on a street lined with one hundred-and-fifty-year-old elm trees in Lincoln Park. The original owners had been some of the wealthiest upper middle class families of the 1800s. This was a neighborhood of many self-made men, from bankers to doctors to owners of small businesses. Colin himself had recently purchased a vintage Victorian gray stone at 270 Magnolia Street. He had immediately fallen in love with its decorative carpenter gingerbread trim as well as the perfectly preserved cherry wood kitchen.

One day while restoring the mantle on the fireplace in the master bedroom suite, he discovered that some of the bricks were hollow. Following a hunch, he crawled inside the chimney and found a metal door molded directly behind the hearth. It measured about two feet by two feet and was secured by a large rusted lock. Using a crowbar to pry it open, he found a storage bin, similar to a wall safe. Immediately his psyche was on red alert. The box held a native American peace pipe, a ceremonial war bonnet, and a deed showing the name of the original owner of the house.

From the moment he'd made the discovery, Colin had been itching to do research on the treasures he'd found. The injury to his foot finally afforded him time to search out more information on the artifacts. Staring intently at the computer screen, Colin sipped his ice tea and double clicked on the mouse. "Bingo!" he yelled as he read out loud to Ryder.

"Between the 18th and 19th centuries, Native Americans used the wide open spaces of their homeland near the rich and plentiful Lake Michigan, to supplement their food supplies during the harsh winters in the Midwest. The Waushanee and Winnebago were two of the Native American tribes to use the many trails near the shores of Lake Michigan. These early tribes of hunters and fishermen roamed the marshy lands bordering the western boundaries of the lake. Later, when Chicago's first white settlers arrived, they sensed the commercial possibilities and traded with the Native American tribes for their lands. More often than not, these transactions favored the settlers.

In 1819 Secretary of War John C. Calhoun decided that an Illinois canal was an important transportation project for national defense. The property plundered from the five major tribes including the Waushanee was now in the hands of the state planners. Most of this land was used in the construction of the canal. There was very little left as a reminder of the tranquility of life on the Native American frontier.

In 1836 work began on the canal. A large work force of Irish immigrants, were recruited from the East Coast. Trade and prosperity grew around the mouth of a city that possessed a port that could ship goods as far away as Liverpool. Native Americans continued to lose more and more of their land.

In 1837 civic leaders made sure that some of the property from Fort Dearborn became public land. As they entered the twentieth century, Chicagoans wanted their own seaport. The result was a grand municipal pier. This was built on the same land that Waushanee and Winnebago tribes had occupied for hundreds of years. During the massive construction of the pier it was not uncommon for the Irish immigrants to tell tales of American Indian sightings. After a pint or two of Guinness, the stories grew to epic proportions.

Journalist Finley Peter Dunne caught the mood of the ever changing city in the many newspaper columns created in 1895. Dunne was famous for his cartoon creation of Mr. Dooley, a portly, red-headed Irish Bridgeport saloon keeper who dispensed wisdom, drinks, and Native American folklore in equal measure!

In 1915 several native American artifacts were unearthed during excavation at the municipal pier site, including various pipes, tomahawks, spears and an ancient shield. The shield was a tool used by the Waushanee medicine men to heal the sick.

In 1930 the municipal founders of Navy Pier dedicated a room in the Grand Foyer to the various Native American artifacts discovered in and around the site. During renovations of the Pier in 1939, a theft took place involving many of the priceless objects on display. This coincided with a tragic accident that killed three workmen doing renovations at the Pier site. The artifacts were never recovered."

"Wow, Ryder, that's really something," Colin said, picking up the peace pipe and turning it over in his hand. Colin wasn't sure what any of this meant, but he was certain that the psychic vibrations that he was feeling were real. Suddenly Colin's hands felt clammy, his face flushed. Adrenaline started pumping through his veins as a vision appeared. Streaks of lightning, peals of thunder and a woman's scream momentarily flashed before him.

Lost in thought, he ignored the ringing of the telephone. Only the mention of his grandmother's name jarred him out of his trance. "Love to Edna" was the last thing he heard. Colin decided to play back the message, thinking it might be important to his grandmother. As he listened, he heard Willa Newton confirming his speaking engagement at the Twilight Club.

"Attention! Attention, everyone. Our Twilight meeting is about to begin!"

The small banquet room at Widow Newton's restaurant was filled to capacity with senior citizens from all walks of life. Willa Newton tapped the microphone in her hand with her red-lacquered, manicured nails. "People, please, we're already running a little late. There'll be plenty of time to catch up on all the latest gossip after our meeting!"

It had been a long, exhausting day for Willa, even though she was a well preserved seventy-two year old restaurant entrepreneur. Except for an occasional bout of arthritis and food-induced migraines, Willa could boast of being in relatively good health. She kept herself physically fit with daily walks through the Water Tower mall and self defense classes with her senior citizens' group. Although Willa tried to maintain a healthy diet, she had to admit to a weakness for rich, French-inspired cuisine. She also believed in regular skin care and hair maintenance. Her monthly ritual included treating herself to a day at the Oak Street Spa with a facial, a manicure, and a pedicure.

She'd had numerous male suitors over the years, many of whom had even offered marriage. Always flattered by their attention and sincerity, Willa knew in her heart that no one could replace her beloved Daniel.

"Attention, everyone. Attention. Our meeting is about to start. I would like to introduce you to our guest speaker and a dear young friend of mine, who is a nationally known psychic. He's come tonight to discuss mediumistic development as it applies to the many levels of heaven. I know that his paranormal abilities will astound us and provide us with insight to help reconcile the many emotions we have regarding the passing on of our dear loved ones. Ladies and gentlemen, I would like to introduce—Colin O'Dannaher."

"Thank you, Willa. Good evening. Although I'm acquainted with some of the lovely women in the audience who are friends of my grandmother, there are many faces I don't recognize. So I will begin by explaining who I am and how I began developing my psychic powers. For all of the skeptics in the audience, I would like you to know that there was a time that I, too, considered mediums, psychics and clairvoyants, as magicians who practiced sleight-of-hand."

Suddenly there was a murmur of voices and a shuffling of chairs as Kady made a late entrance into the restaurant. Catching the attention of her Aunt Willa, Kady pointed to a table at the back of the room. Shaking her head negatively, Willa gestured toward an empty chair at her front table. Embarrassed by the commotion she'd caused, Kady complied and quietly sat down next to her aunt.

"I'm glad you could make it, honey. We'll talk later," Willa whispered, patting Kady's hand with affection.

Undisturbed by Kady's arrival, Colin continued. "I have been a student of psychic phenomena for at least twenty years. I have tried to use my gift as a medium to bridge the gap between the physical and spiritual worlds. The more we learn about the supernatural, the more we'll be open to the suggestion of life after death. And yes, even communicate with those who have departed."

As he spoke there was a flicker of recognition in Kady's mind. She rolled her cerulean blue eyes and stared directly at Colin. Seeing her skepticism, Colin grinned at her and gave her a flirtatious wink. Kady was not amused. However, she could not explain the bizarre quivering in the pit of her stomach that had been brought on by his man-on-the-make smile! Boy, she thought, this guy hasn't changed one bit!

Colin continued. "As a clairsentient, I have been blessed with the ability to sense when spirits are in a room. I can actually feel their personality. I am also able to receive messages, sent through the wills of their spirit. On rare occasions I have even experienced the way a person has died. Needless to say, I do not look forward to those occurrences. I'm also a clairsentient who believes in the many levels of heaven. I believe the level of heaven we reach upon our death is determined by our thoughts, words, and deeds here on earth. Like the old saying goes, 'the choices we make determine the life we live.' If we have grown to the same spiritual level as our loved ones, then we will live with them in heaven. What I would like to explore this evening is how to come to terms with the death of a loved one. There may be some here tonight who believe death is finality. I'm here to help you see that it is not. In many of our religions we have been taught to believe in the existence of angels. What are angels but spirits who exist in a heavenly plane and come down to guide us in times of need? These spiritual guides help us through the difficult times in our life. Whether you refer to our helpers as guardian angels or spiritual guides, working with them through prayers and spiritual communication will allow us to open our hearts and minds to loved ones who have passed over. Through acceptance and recognition, contact with these guides can help you to endure your loss with greater peace of mind."

Although raised a Catholic, Colin was considered a rogue medium for his recognition of all deities when using his psychic powers. He accepted all forms of organized religion. He had devoted much of his life to helping others and used himself as a channel for people wanting spiritual communication.

"Let us begin! First, we must clear our minds so we may replenish all our thoughts with positive energy."

Colin always began his meditation with a blessing and invocation. He bowed his head in concentration and began his shamanic journey.

"Holy spirits, powers that be, guide us with your wisdom and bless us with your knowledge. Father Time and Mother Earth, speak to us in this hour of need and help us with our cause. May our thoughts be one. Blessed be!"

"Now I would like you to recall the last time you were with the loved one whose spirit you wish to contact."

"Oh, brother!" Kady mumbled.

"Shh! Shh! Shh!" A small group of interested senior citizens hissed. They were seated at a small corner table in the rear of the hall.

"We appear to have a skeptic in the crowd. Maybe the lovely young lady at the front table would be kind enough to assist us with our first reading?" Colin asked, getting a chuckle from his audience.

"Go ahead, sweetheart. It'll be interesting," Willa prodded.

"Aunt Willa, please. I feel foolish," Kady replied, wishing she had never agreed to come to the meeting.

Colin walked to the edge of the platform, "It's all right, Miss. I don't bite."

Not wanting to look silly, Kady begrudgingly approached the temporary stage set up at the front of the restaurant. As Kady ascended the steps, Colin could hardly believe his eyes. This girl possessed a natural radiance and beauty that Colin found almost overwhelming. Rarely was Colin so taken by members of the opposite sex. In fact, he had a reputation for being cool and always in control around women. There was something different about this girl.

"Hello. I don't believe we've had the pleasure of being introduced." He extended his hand in a gesture of friendliness, unprepared for the sexual current that coursed through his body as they touched. He lost control of his trance state and unintentionally held her hand much longer than customary. The immediate contact between them created a sensation that sparked all of Kady's intuitive capabilities. She instinctively put up a mental block in an attempt to regain her composure. Feeling all eyes on her, she quickly pulled her hand free and said. "Mr. O'Dannaher, perhaps you don't recall, but we have already met!"

"We have?"

"Oh yes, about fifteen years ago. Let's see, I was about twelve and you were maybe seventeen?" A torrent of memories rushed through Kady's mind as she reflected on one humiliating summer at her parent's lake cottage. Aunt Willa had been visiting with her friend Edna and her extremely handsome grandson. She had an enormous crush on Colin. She followed him around like a lost puppy dog begging for his attention. He was the featured attraction in all her girlish fantasies. What a geek, she thought. She'd always wondered if he had suspected.

"I'm sorry, but I know I wouldn't forget meeting someone as beautiful as you." Kady's expression made it clear that she'd heard this kind of blarney before. "If it's true that we have previously met then perhaps we can use our past meeting to our advantage. Why don't you concentrate on connecting with the spirit that will bring us together?"

A spirit will bring us together, he thought. Where the hell did that come from? What made me say that? He wasn't sure why, but the psychic energy levels on the stage were abnormally high. Colin could actually feel the vibrations. He knew that as a true channeler he should be able to turn his intuitive powers on and off at will, but Kady's presence was making it very difficult to refocus his wandering mind.

"I'm having trouble feeling the harmonious energies that we need to begin this exercise. Kady, try to relax, and calm your inner fears. Shall we begin again? Quiet now, everyone take a deep breath. Exhale slowly. That's right... much better now," he said as the soothing tranquility of his voice filled the room. "I feel the presence of a man, a brother... or uncle... yes it's an uncle. He's speaking with an accent... no, a brogue, an Irish brogue. I see he has bright red hair, and a jovial pie-shaped face."

Reaching out to touch Kady's hand again, Colin closed his eyes and continued, "He says this message is for two people in this room. He has sent down a spiritual guide to help them restore honor to their family name." Colin paused as a look of surprise washed over his face. "Why, Kady, he's called you by name! He's telling me that he needs you to trust in your special gifts. He says with your help, all will be revealed when the lark sings."

Kady's insides quivered, hearing almost the exact words spoken by her aunt the night before. No matter how much she loved her aunt, Kady was not prepared to open up her heart and mind to the pain she'd experienced as a young girl! She'd already fought that battle.

Kady heard her aunt gasp, "Oh my God, it's Daniel!" Drawn to the voice in the audience, Colin looked at Willa as tears welled up in her eyes.

"Willa, I believe that the man standing next to me is your husband Daniel."

Willa nodded her head. "He came to me in a dream the other night in the visage of a native American. It just doesn't

41

make much sense to me. Would you ask Daniel what this all means?"

Colin nodded his head slowly, trance-like, as he tried not to analyze what he was hearing. Sometimes words that seemed insignificant to him were meaningful to the grieving loved ones in his audience. Those who relayed these messages from the other side were known as sitters in the world of psychic phenomena.

"Willa, Daniel has asked me to tell you that there are spiritual laws that do not allow him to directly interfere with the karmic progression of another. He's telling me that his messages must be subtle. Follow the signs left by the spiritual guide he has sent you, and everything else will fall into place. Daniel seems very insistent that you never give up. He says to remember that the good book lights the way. Does that make any sense to you?"

"Well, I'm not exactly sure what he means. Perhaps he's referring to our family Bible," said Willa. "Please tell him I will look for it. Can you tell me anything else? Anything," she asked, not wanting to lose contact with her deceased husband.

"Yes, he said to tell you that he is proud of all your accomplishments and that he loves you very much...oh, he also wants you to know that he approves of the new menu."

"Oh my. I just submitted changes to the printer today that included three of Daniel's favorite dishes."

Nodding, Colin continued, "You are not to give up, he says, and remember you are soul-mates who will meet again in a higher life... you will always be beautiful to him."

Willa sat down to ponder all that was said. A portly gentlemen sitting at her table leaned over and put his arm across Willa's shoulder, giving her a slight squeeze for comfort. Willa's big blue eyes looked up at him, quickly closing shut as she tried to control her tears.

"Ladies and gentlemen, as you can see, direct contact with the spiritual world can be enlightening and informative. It also can be tremendously emotional and stressful." Colin turned to Kady, "Thank you very much for your help, Ms. Dailey. I hope this hasn't been too upsetting?" He extended his hand helping her down from the platform. He took a sip of water from the glass offered by a passing waiter, attempting to break the spiritual connection with Daniel.

"Let me continue. I believe there is someone else in the room that has recently lost a loved one. Has someone recently lost their daughter?" Colin asked, touching his ear trying to hear the spiritual voice.

A woman named Connie stood up. She was small and delicate with white hair that had been tinted blue.

"Have you recently lost your child?" Colin questioned.

"Three months ago I lost my daughter. She was forty-seven years old when she passed away."

"Is her name Christine?"

"Yes. Yes it is."

"She says to tell you that she has never been happier now that she is out of pain."

"Oh my. She was in great pain the last few years of her life. We discovered she had Hodgkin's disease when she was fifteen years old. We thought she had beaten the odds. Then three years ago she found a lump. The doctors tried every available chemotherapy treatment," Connie confirmed, dabbing her eyes with a white lace handkerchief.

"Christine wants you to get on with your life. Her children and husband need you to be strong. She says that you all need to help each other through your grief. She wants you to know that you were a good mother and that she loves you."

"Thank you so much," Connie replied as she sat down. Hearing another voice in his head, Colin proceeded, "The voice I'm hearing now is quite faint. I get the feeling that this spirit was a very quiet, soft spoken woman. I feel she died tragically in an accident. I think it was an automobile accident!"

A loud sigh escaped from a man at a table in the rear as he stood up and said, "It's me. I lost my wife to a drunk driver three years ago. Can I speak to her?"

"Yes, she wants to tell you that she has put in a garden with all your favorite flowers—Balsam roses, Cannons and Roses of Sharon. She's even planted a vegetable garden with tomatoes and green beans, and…"

"Is she in pain? Is she happy?" the slight, gray haired gentleman asked.

"She was in pain for a little while—when the car crushed her spine and legs."

"Yes, my Maggie lived for a few agonizing hours after the accident."

"She said to remind you that you always called her your Maggie Mae. She wished she could have seen her firstborn grandchild. Eric, she says, is a good name. She's happy. You were a good, faithful husband and she misses you. But you shall be together again."

With tears streaming down his wrinkled cheeks Elmer stammered, "We just had our first grandson; his name is Eric. Thank you, thank you, son."

At times it was difficult for Colin to conduct these psychic connections when large groups were involved. Emotions typically ran high, and voices from many spirits would flood his consciousness. Only through intense concentration was he able to focus his energies on the call of a single spirit. These sessions were both mentally and physically draining and often left him emotionally exhausted. He had also been standing on his throbbing ankle for over an hour and badly needed to get off his feet. Colin raised a hand to quiet the murmur in the audience and said, "I would like to take a break for few minutes."

Willa stood up and hurried toward the stage.

"Thank you, Colin. Let's give this young man a loud round of applause; he is truly gifted." The audience complied and Willa continued, pointing toward the white cloth-covered tables. "Please feel free to help yourselves to the dessert buffet. Chef Jean Paul has turned out another culinary masterpiece for us, Chantilly Cream Strawberry Soufflé."

Willa suspected that the recently increased membership of the Twilight Club was due to the growing reputation of Widow Newton's chef, Jean Paul Trotiers. Her little club had become quite popular with the dessert connoisseurs. The restaurant's casual elegance was reflected in a warm and inviting Mediterranean decor. With its glass-sheathed view of Lake Michigan, spacious tables, and intimate booths, Newton's provided a chic atmosphere that catered to a wide variety of clientele. The group of senior citizens always appreciated Willa's efforts toward making their meetings delicious as well as informative.

Majestically the sun began to set over the city's skyline and dissolved into a fine mist that faded into the night. The surreal setting magically aided the ethereal atmosphere created by Colin's karmic revelations.

Colin left the makeshift podium at the front of the restaurant and headed toward Kady's table. She was still in shock, trying to make sense of what had just happened. Turbulent thoughts whirled through her mind. "Is this guy for real? Oh, he was good... real good, I'll give him that! But he must have some inside information ...OK, so I'm attracted to him, but I don't want to get involved, even if it means helping Aunt Willa. I don't want my premonitions to return. Darn! Why are the good-looking guys always so sure of themselves? It must be that testosterone overdrive Rose always talks about!" Her head was spinning. Get a hold of your self, girl, she thought.

She felt Colin's presence even before he spoke, as the hairs on her arms stood on end. Looking for a quick escape, Kady recognized the elderly gentleman seated beside her. She turned, hoping to start up a conversation. "Excuse me. Aren't you Martin Williams? My father is Ignatius Dailey, and I'm his daughter Kady. I believe I've seen you at the Knights of Columbus services at our church, Blessed Lady of the Angels?"

"Why, yes, young lady, I sure am. How's your father's health these days, and how's that beautiful mother of yours?" Martin asked.

Her attempt to block Colin from her thoughts ended abruptly as he gently tapped her shoulder. His touch was as light as a caress!

"My parents are doing just fine, thank you. I'll mention you asked about them. Excuse me please, Martin?"

Reluctantly Kady turned her head to acknowledge Colin. She hoped that he could not see the effect his nearness was causing her; she felt so transparent.

"Hi, Kady. I was hoping that since we'd already met, maybe we could get together for dinner and reminisce about our first date?"

"Date?" She chuckled. "I don't think so, Colin. It was hardly a date! The last time I was with you, I fell into a lake!"

"A lake?" Suddenly a long forgotten memory flashed across his mind. "That was you, of course. You're Seth Dailey's little sister. I remember. I fished you out of the water after you fell from a tree. My, haven't you grown up!"

"That was me, all right! I almost drowned, and it was years before my brothers stopped calling me Kady the Karp."

"As I recall, the fishing stunk. You were definitely the catch of the day!"

"Well, it's nice to know that I meet with your approval, but I'll have to say good night. I have an early work day tomorrow. Good night, everyone," Kady said, addressing the guests at the table who had become interested bystanders to their conversation. Kady slid her chair back from the table in an attempt to leave. Colin blocked her path.

"Excuse me, Colin. I need to say goodbye to my aunt," Kady said sidestepping his wide shoulders.

"I'll walk you over there. We still need to discuss our date!" Colin exclaimed as he limped after her.

Kady quickened her step as she approached her aunt who was standing near the buffet tables chatting with some friends. "I've come to say goodbye, Aunt Willa."

"Must you leave so early? Why, you haven't even sampled the dessert trays. You know how irresistible Jean Paul's sweets are. Besides, I had hoped Colin could give us a private reading."

"I'd love to stay longer—maybe another time. You see, there's a large private tour set up for tomorrow, and I have to be at the office quite early. Motioning toward Colin, Kady whispered, "A little spooky, don't you think? Do you believe he was actually communicating with Uncle Danny?"

"I do, but I'm not sure he understands what has transpired just yet. I have a few ideas of my own that I'm going to look into. Perhaps we can pull our thoughts together and come up with some answers." Willa replied.

"Why don't we plan to meet at the end of this week? We'll have more time, and it will be more private," Kady asked.

In an effort to move away from Colin's hovering presence, she accidentally backed up into a passing group of seniors on their way to the desert buffet. Kady was knocked off balance. Wobbling, she fell back into Colin, who grabbed her shoulders to hold her steady. They both started talking at once. "Excuse me," "Excuse me," they stammered in unison.

Not missing a beat, Willa turned her head, first glancing at Colin, then at her niece, who was now being held firmly within the young man's grasp. The pair had dazed expressions on their faces that reminded her of the first time she'd met her beloved Dan.

Kady abruptly pulled out of Colin's arms, leaning over to give her aunt a hug. "Goodbye, Aunt Willa. We'll talk about all this later," Kady said, whispering into her ear.

"OK, honey. I think we should try to arrange a time when the three of us can meet. I'll call you both in a few days," Willa said, giving her niece a wink. She glanced back toward Colin, who couldn't take his eyes off Kady as she hurried out the door.

FOUR

*W*ilhemina Rae Dailey was the eldest of five children born to Seumas and Katherine Dailey, Irish immigrants who came from the small town of Tullamore in central Ireland. When Willa was two years old, her parents bought a balloon-frame cottage and settled in the Chicago south side neighborhood of Bridgeport. It was the summer of 1921. There was a new female addition born to the Dailey family for each of the following three years. Then, four years later, when Katherine had given up all hope of having a son, Ignatius Dailey entered their world weighing ten pounds and two ounces. The proud parents loved all their children, but Ignatius couldn't help being spoiled when his four sisters made him the center of their world.

Opportunity in America greeted the Daileys with open arms. Seumas, an industrious man, had the foresight to transport a small baking oven from their tiny village in Ireland. With very little money he opened a bakery. Turning out some of the finest bread in their neighborhood, the business quickly prospered. In time, he was able to expand and add on a grocery store that catered to the hardworking inhabitants of Bridgeport.

As their family grew, so did their business. More and more of their family members migrated to America to help with their growing enterprise. Working long hours at the store, as with many immigrant families of the time, the children helped in any way they could. Katherine Dailey, however, would not allow the family business to interfere with their schooling. She insisted that all her children finish their education.

Willa was the first Dailey to graduate from high school. As she grew older, blue-eyed, raven-haired Willa had no difficulty in attracting many an Irish lad. When she was sixteen years old, Daniel Newton and his family arrived from Ireland and bought the house next door. From the moment Willa met the kindly young man, she was impressed by his old world manners and chivalrous ways. He had dark, rust red hair that was as thick as his brogue. His wide-eyed, pie-shaped face could never be considered handsome, but he was blessed with a heart that was filled with laughter and a generosity that knew no bounds.

One unseasonably warm March day Willa and her little brother were playing catch in front of the bakery. An errant throw from Willa caused Ignatius to chase the ball blindly into the street. Daniel had just returned home from work when he heard Willa scream. He looked up to see that Ignatius had tripped and fallen onto the streetcar tracks. Daniel dashed from the curb and snatched him out of the path of the Ashland Avenue streetcar. From that moment, Willa was smitten. Daniel courted Willa for the next two years, and they were married soon after her graduation.

Daniel was a boilermaker by trade. He owned a small company. He was an honest and hard working man whose reputation attracted the interest of John Fitzpatrick, the president of the Chicago Federation of Labor. He chose Daniel's company for the renovation and installation of new boilers at Navy Pier. Fitzpatrick's choice of a young Irish immigrant was met with immediate and violent objections from the Chaddack Boiler Company. Heretofore, the Chaddack Boiler Company had been the sole contractor for all repairs and installations of boilers in municipal buildings. William Chaddack, son of Alderman Sedley Chaddack, filed formal complaints with the city's planning board, accusing Fitzpatrick of Celtic cronyism.

On the first day of renovations, ethnic tensions reached their peak. The Chicago Police were called in to disperse a brawl between workers from Chaddack Boiler Company and Newton's Boiler Company. No arrests were made, but a bloodied William Chaddack vowed revenge.

From 1937 through 1939 Daniel and Willa prospered and even gained entrance to the prestigious social club, The Chicago Dynasty. This was a club whose members exerted enormous power and influence in Chicago's business community. It was a place to see and be seen, where major deals were made between the many courses of dinner prepared by the former chef to the King of England, Ian Baldwin.

This group of wealthy citizens, predominately white Anglo-Saxon Protestants, frowned upon immigrants gaining entrance to their elitist club. They especially disliked the Irish, who had a well-deserved reputation for drunken, boorish behavior. The Newtons' wealth and noteworthy acts of charity made it difficult for these affluent socialites to reject their petition for entrance into the socially prominent club. Daniel and Willa never responded to the petty prejudices and bigotry of their fellow members. They were, after all, extremely proud of their success and accomplishments.

When Daniel received the lucrative Navy Pier contract, he was certain his company's future was finally secure. Then, on December 8, 1939, tragedy struck. It had been nearly two months since the initial brouhaha at the Pier. Willa and Daniel had just retired for the evening when the phone rang. A hysterical John O'Leary, Daniel's night foreman, told him of an explosion on the newly replaced main boiler. "My God, it's a living nightmare," said Daniel turning to Willa. "Three of my men have been killed. I don't know when I'll be back." As Willa watched Daniel rush out the door, she was overwhelmed with a sense of dread. It was at that moment she sensed nothing would ever be the same. Little did she know how accurate her feelings would prove to be.

The next day Daniel was accused of hiring cheap unskilled Irish laborers who were rumored to have been intoxicated when the explosion took place. Empty whiskey bottles had been found near the site of the explosion. The police began their investigation into the causes of the blast by enlisting the services of the Chaddack Boiler Company. Chaddack's men determined that simple neglect was the culprit in the disaster. The Irish workmen had been playing cards and drinking instead of minding the critical balancing of pressure with the main boiler.

Three days after the preliminary findings were released; another bomb shell was dropped on the Newtons. Several priceless Native American artifacts which had been on display at Navy Pier were found to be mysteriously missing. Rumors suggested that Newton's men had been stealing the treasures and selling them for profit. Daniel vehemently denied all these outrageous charges, claiming it was impossible for the Chaddack Boiler Company to be impartial in this matter.

It was all to no avail. Although no criminal charges were ever filed, the Newton Boiler Company's reputation had been irreparably damaged. The once proud, joyous Daniel had become a shell of the man Willa had married. She was certain that jealously and a inborn hatred of the Irish were responsible for the calamity. The resentful so-called upper class people wanted to justify their mistrust of the wealthy, *nouveau-riche* Irish immigrants. They went to the newspapers and portrayed Daniel Newton as a man without honor who would cut every corner to make a quick buck! He never recovered from these scandalous accusations.

In the latter years of his life, Willa was able to get him interested in opening a restaurant at Navy Pier to help rebuild its declining popularity. He finally seemed interested in something once again. Side by side they worked long hours together, planning, designing and overseeing its construction.

Then tragically, while working late one night, Daniel suffered a fatal heart attack. The night before the wake, Daniel's spirit came to Willa in a vision and told her to fulfill their dream of building the restaurant. Willa was devastated by the loss of her one true love but vowed at his funeral to let nothing stand in the way of the completion of their dream.

With the support of her family and best friend Edna O'Dannaher, Willa finally opened her restaurant in the spring of 1975. Over the years, Widow Newton's became an enormously successful enterprise that lead to the franchise of two additional establishments in the Chicagoland area.

For the past forty-five years, Willa had lived in the same neoclassical Georgian revival two-story home at 117 North Astor Street that she had shared with Daniel until the end of his life.

Alone with her memories, she gazed into the beveled glass mirror on her dresser. "Oh Daniel, my love, I still miss you so," she murmured. With painful fingers, Willa started her nightly ritual of applying moisturizer to a face lined with the strength of wisdom. She then brushed her silver strands of shoulder length hair fifty times.

Completing her routine, Willa picked up the St. Brigid's gold cross that Daniel had given her on their first wedding anniversary. A smile began to form at the corners of her mouth. She thought about Kady and Colin. She decided that it was time to play matchmaker and invite them both to dinner.

After breakfast the next morning, Willa set her plans in motion. She knew that ever since Kady had broken off her engagement with Brick, she'd had sworn off all men, so she was determined not to let her niece know that Colin was to be her surprise dinner date.

She decided to enlist the help of her good friend and occasional dinner companion, Henry Mueller.

Henry was a portly, balding, sixty-eight year old veterinarian whom Willa had known for many years. Henry was the perfect choice, for he and Kady were old pals who shared a love of animals. During her high school years, Kady had occasionally volunteered her services at his clinic on Saturday afternoons. Picking up the phone, Willa dialed Henry's number.

Willa explained her strategy to Henry, who was more than willing to help with her scheme. She left a message with Patti confirming their plans for the Friday night dinner party, knowing the less conversation with Kady the better. Getting

Collin to agree to dinner was a snap. She told him that she'd found the old family Bible, but had come up empty handed in her search for clues that would tie in the information discovered at their earlier meeting. They both agreed that a séance would be necessary.

Kady decided to stop off at a local florist shop to bring her Aunt Willa a bouquet of flowers to grace her dinner table. A few minutes before closing time she rushed into the store. Her purchase took longer than she had expected. Apparently, she was not the only last-minute shopper.

Not accustomed to arriving late, Kady put her foot to the gas pedal, accelerating as she drove east on Division, and according to Murphy's Law, proceeded to get every red light. The early Rush Street revelers had already crammed the downtown bars and restaurants. Making a left on State Street to avoid the crowds, Kady was cut off by a green Volvo. The driver leaned on his horn while flicking his finger at her in an obscene gesture. Kady was thoroughly ticked off by this childish display and yelled out her window, "Is that your age or your IQ?"

Realizing that this was totally out of character for her, she slowed down and decided that it was better to arrive a little late than not at all. Her luck changed when Kady slid into a rock star parking spot right in front of her aunt's house.

Kady had always loved the simplicity of her aunt's home, with its pitched roof and painted white pillars. A visit to Willa's house always made Kady feel like a princess when she played house with her dolls on its large wraparound porch.

Grabbing the bouquet of flowers and her purse, she flew up the long set of stairs. Kady reached for the brass door knocker, rapping it three times, and lost her grip on her purse. The door opened and Kady watched in dismay as the entire contents of her handbag spilled out.

"Here, let me help you!" a familiar voice said.

She raised her head slowly, glancing up from the top of a pair of white Cortez Nike gym shoes. She could hardly believe her eyes.

"What are you doing here?" Kady asked, blurting the first thing that came to her mind.

"I'm about to help a lady in distress, if she'll let me," Colin grinned with a sexy indulgent smile.

"No, I mean what are you doing here at my aunt's house?"

Kady's astonished look glared out of the most fascinating blue eyes Colin had ever seen. The mental image he had conjured up over the last week did not compare to the reality. He didn't need to be in a shamanic trance to appreciate her ethereal beauty—or her great legs! Even his creative imagination couldn't have envisioned a lovelier sight than the curvaceous Kady Dailey dressed in a knock-out, heather colored, off-the-shoulder sun dress.

"Let's start over," Colin said. "Hello, Kady, you look beautiful. I'm a guest of your Aunt Willa, who was kind enough to invite me to dinner. May I give you a hand?"

Colin bent down as Kady started to stand up. Her head connected with his chin and Kady nearly lost her balance. Colin grabbed her by the shoulders and pulled her toward his hard, muscular chest.

The unexpected contact with Colin's chin had Kady seeing stars. She regained her equilibrium, feeling as though his touch had just disrupted her safe, secure world. She took a deep breath, stilling her senses, and was assaulted by the earthy fragrance of his after-shave and the clean smell of spring scented soap.

Fighting the sexual attraction, Kady said, "Let me go!" Clumsily, she pulled herself out of his embrace.

"Where's my aunt? Aunt Willa!" Kady yelled, standing on her tiptoes trying to peer over his broad, muscular shoulders.

"Oh, no!" Willa thought. "Kady has arrived." She knew her niece was fighting her attraction to the handsome young man and would not have accepted the dinner invitation had she known that Colin O'Dannaher would be there.

Trying to avert a disaster, Willa rushed to rescue Colin from the famous Dailey Irish temper. It was slow to rise, but volcanic when it erupted. "Kady, honey, I'm so glad you could join us," Willa babbled, leading Kady to the den. "Come right in. I've already put Colin to work. He was just about to pour us some wine. Won't you join us?"

Henry Mueller, Willa's friend, was seated comfortably in a green leather recliner chair. He immediately sensed the awkwardness of the situation and rose to greet Kady with a big bear hug.

"Kady, lass, we've all been waiting for you. Your aunt was getting a little nervous. What can I get you to drink?"

"Hello Henry. Sorry I'm so late. I stopped to get these for—" She stopped in midstream turning to her aunt. Kady lifted one eyebrow, gave her aunt a killing glare and handed her the fresh bouquet.

"Thank you, Kady. They're lovely. Let me put these in water. I'll meet you all in the dining room in just a few minutes," Willa exclaimed, quickly exiting the room before her niece could start asking questions.

Colin, an innocent bystander to Willa's match making, realized that Kady had no idea he was to be her dinner companion. That must be why she acted so startled to see me, he thought, salvaging his bruised ego. Colin had accepted Willa's invitation hoping that Kady would be there too!

When Colin had reached out to catch Kady from falling down the stairs, he had felt the silky softness of her skin and felt the wild rhythm of Kady's heartbeat as he drew her close. He couldn't be positive, but he sensed that its reckless pace was because of him. If she was determined to ignore their obvious chemistry, that was fine, but he certainly wasn't about to deny the attraction. He'd never been one to accept defeat easily. Colin decided it was time to display a little of his Irish charm.

Willa set the bouquet of flowers in the center of the table. Looking around the dining room she made a last-minute check to see that everything was in perfect order. Willa had put a lot of thought into the planning of this intimate dinner party. Satisfied with her results, Willa lit the tapered candles on her sterling silver candelabra, noticing how the light reflected in the cut crystal chandelier that hung overhead. She'd convinced her friend and noted Chef Jean Paul Trotier to prepare a romantic dinner. He knew of Kady's fondness for chocolate and promised to prepare a very special dessert! His penchant for creating chocolate masterpieces would tempt the pallet of a saint during Lent. As a special favor to his friend and employer, Parisian born Jean Paul even volunteered to play waiter for the evening.

Willa took out a Tyrone crystal dinner bell from her red lacquered oriental China cabinet and gave it a quick shake. The high pitched sound beckoned her three guests.

"Please be seated, everyone," said Willa. "Jean Paul will begin serving dinner, after we express our thanks to God."

Bowing her head, Willa recited a short prayer. "Bless this food, O Lord, as we give you praise for our bountiful meal, and thank you for bringing my family and friends together. Amen."

On cue Jean Paul served the first course, scallops dripping in a caramelized garlic butter sauce. Delicious aromas escaped the Belleek chafing dish as Willa passed the bowl to Colin.

"Edna tells me you're taking a hiatus from lecturing," said Willa. "I was very grateful you were able to fit our Twilight group into your schedule. Your lecture and readings were instrumental in helping us understand how death is not the end. It is so comforting to know that the deceased can be reached through our memory and come to us in our dreams. So many of our members have had a difficult time coping with the loss of their loved ones, but you've given us the faith not to fear the eternal journey. I hope you'll speak to us again?"

"Thank you, Willa. It was my pleasure. I plan to include the mediumistic readings for your group as part of the research on senior citizens for my next book. I would love a return visit. Getting around has been more difficult because of this darn sprained ankle, but I was thrilled to accept your dinner invitation. What great food, great conversation and a beautiful dinner companion," Colin said, winking at Kady, attempting to draw her attention away from the food she was devouring like it was her last meal.

Colin was not accustomed to women who enjoyed their food. Most of the ones he dated were always on some sort of diet. Why did women think that men would be attracted to someone who was basically skin and bones? Here was a girl who certainly had a healthy appetite, although she didn't appear to have an ounce of fat on her petite frame.

Colin made her nervous, and when she was nervous, she ate. Kady ignored his blatant flattery. She was not about to be tricked into accepting this handsome Casanova as her dinner companion. Listening to him talk, she couldn't help but admit that he had accomplished a great deal in his short life. If he was just another BS, artist he was definitely good at it. The more she listened the more she wondered if her initial assessment might have been too harsh. She wondered how much of what she feeling toward Colin had to do with her relationship with Brick. Been there, done that, didn't like it.

Kady began to sense that beneath his typical male charm there might be a real heart. After all, she had certainly been impressed by the comfort his words gave her aunt's friends. She felt herself weakening, but remained determined not to allow herself to be swayed. Her peace of mind was at stake. She did not want to confront the inner turmoil Colin's psychic power unleashed.

The uncomfortable lull in the conversation caused Willa to answer for her. "Thank you, Colin. Kady was blessed with the Dailey family's good looks, forgiving heart and a good deal of Irish charm, weren't you, honey?"

Kady was unable to ignore her aunt's attempt to apologize. Her soft-hearted nature and respect for Willa compelled her to reply, "Aunt Willa, the food is superb. I don't know when I've enjoyed a finer meal."

"That's an understatement," thought Colin, as he looked over her shapely form and complimented Kady by saying, "You certainly don't look as if you have to watch your weight!"

"I don't and never have!" Kady curtly replied, knowing that her nervous eating had been observed. She knew her abruptness was rude but blamed it on the embarrassment caused by her clumsy accident on the front stairs. Once again, visions of the helpless young girl being fished out of the lake flashed through her mind. She may have had a schoolgirl crush on Colin, but memories of Brick and his deceptions convinced her that she must protect her heart at all cost. Once again she tried to ignore Colin. This was becoming her life's work! She hoped the evening would soon end.

"So, tell us, Henry, just how did my aunt get you involved in this little scheme of hers?" Kady quietly asked.

Stalling, Henry helped himself to another slice of pork loin stuffed with a savory fennel-spiked sausage. "You know your aunt, honey. When she gets an idea in her head, there's no stopping her!" he sheepishly replied. Clearing his throat, Henry changed the subject, "Haven't seen you at the clinic for quite a while. I hope you haven't outgrown your love for animals."

"Oh, no. I still love animals so much I want to bring them all home with me. Unfortunately, my bedroom is barely big enough for me and Midnight. You remember the stray cat that I brought to your clinic a year ago? Well, I kept him. Rose doesn't have much use for animals, but she sort of has this agreement with Midnight. If he stays out of her way, she tolerates his presence in the apartment."

"Knowing your sister, I'm surprised she let you keep even one animal in the house." Henry said.

"Oh, you know Rose. Her bark is worse than her bite," Kady said with a smile.

Willa could not figure out why her niece continued to be hostile toward Colin. He was such a nice young man. They would be perfect together. Why, even in her day he would have been considered quite a catch! Still match making, Willa used another tactic in her diversionary arsenal. She silently gestured for Jean Paul to bring in the dessert, hoping this would sweeten Kady's disposition.

"Doesn't this look scrumptious, Kady? I know you love chocolate, honey, so I had Jean Paul whip this up just for you!" Willa explained as she passed Kady the magnificent soufflé.

Dipping into the hand cut glass dessert bowl, Kady took her time savoring the first spoonful. She closed her eyes, lost for a second in culinary delight. She felt the healing balm of chocolate calm her restless soul.

"This is heavenly, Aunt Willa," Kady said looking over her shoulder with a wink. "Jean Paul, will you marry me?"

"Ma petite, if only I were a few years younger! Perhaps you will settle for the recipe, Cherie?"

"Oh Jean, I'll be your slave for life!" Kady replied as she indulged in another delightful morsel. Unconsciously, she ran the tip of her tongue over the top of her lip and sighed. Colin nearly groaned out loud. He could not take his eyes off of the erotic gesture.

"Colin, the other night you mentioned that you were doing some historical research on the native Americans of Illinois," said Willa. "Kady might be able to give you some help. She teaches American history in the ninth and tenth grades and is very passionate about Chicago's history. You should take a ride on one of her tours. She has a wealth of information stored in that pretty little head, like family heirlooms in an attic, I always say." Willa chuckled as she complimented her niece.

"Actually, I was looking forward to both Kady and Henry joining us in our psychic reading this evening," replied

Colin glancing around the table. "I know we're all aware of Willa's recent dream involving Daniel, so I've been doing a little research on my own, hoping I'd uncover some new information. So far, there's been nothing substantial. I was wondering if you would all be willing to help."

"Sorry, old boy, you'll have to count me out on that psychic mumbo jumbo Willa's always talking about. I'm calling it a night right after I finish this delicious dessert! I have to perform surgery on an old Cocker Spaniel first thing in the morning," Henry said, enjoying the last scoop of Chef Jean Paul's Chocolate Dream Soufflé.

Afraid that all her scheming was about to go up in a puff a smoke, Willa glared at Henry. Her sensitive lower lip trembled as she stammered, "Hen…Henry, remember your promise!"

"Oh, OK. Willa, I suppose I did agree to go along with your shenanigans!"

"Now, Kady honey, what about you? I know you're afraid your premonitions will return, but your uncle specifically mentioned you both at the reading and in my dream."

This information was a new piece to the Kady puzzle that Colin was trying to figure out. He wondered what would turn up next.

"You're right, Aunt Willa. I promised to help you and Uncle Danny, so I guess I'll be staying, too!" Kady reluctantly replied. She prayed that Colin's mediumistic readings would not amplify her intuitive perceptions.

"Well, then," Willa said, satisfied with the results of her subtle scheme, "let's all adjourn to the library where we can be more relaxed and comfortable."

The library had always been Daniel's favorite room. As a young girl Kady had spent a great deal of time in this captivating space. The ten-foot ceiling adorned the hand-carved cove moldings that were lined with books from all over the world. The whole room smelled of old leather. During their marriage Daniel and Willa traveled extensively collecting many original volumes and manuscripts. This room had always held a wealth of information that fueled Kady's fascination with history. She looked around and immediately noticed the odd arrangement of furniture placed in the middle of the room. Four tan leather folding chairs graced a rich mahogany card table. Aunt Willa had obviously counted on everyone's cooperation, thought Kady.

Entering the room last, Willa indicated the order in which she wanted everyone to be seated. Henry was seated to Willa's right. Colin was placed to Willa's left, and Kady was positioned between the two men. As they all sat down, Colin removed his sport jacket and placed it on the back of his chair.

"Well, now, is everyone comfortable?" Willa asked. "Colin, is there anything you need to begin our reading? Oh, I'm so excited!"

"Yes, thank you, Willa. As a matter of fact, since we last spoke I've given this some thought, and I think we need to explore two areas of your past. First, I'll need something personal belonging to Daniel, and second, I was wondering if you had made any progress finding your old family Bible. Last, but not least, I'll need a damp cloth."

"Excuse me, Colin. Does this mean that you also practice psychometry?" Kady had done some research on the history of psychic phenomena in her youth, trying to make sense of her own abilities.

Colin was impressed. Psychometry was not a term well know by those outside the professional psychic mediumistic realm. "Yes, Kady, I do some psychometry." Colin was one of the few mediums that had the ability to feel or sense the history of an object simply by touching it.

"I am fortunate in that I am able to recognize the sensations imprinted on things which connect the living and spiritual. My grandmother claims it is my empathic and receptive nature that wants to help souls in need."

There was that pride of accomplishment in his voice again. Kady was at a loss. She had never received encouragement to explore her psychic powers. In fact, she was embarrassed by them and frightened whenever they appeared. She squirmed uneasily, wishing she were anywhere else.

"Why, Colin, that's wonderful. No wonder Edna is so proud of you. Speaking of our families," Willa said searching the room, "I did find the Bible as I believe Daniel suggested. However after poring over it for hours, I still couldn't find anything that would help us. Now let me think for a moment. Where did I put it?" Tapping her finger on her chin, Willa continued, "it was just here this morning. I'm getting so forgetful. Oh, yes. Now I remember." She walked toward a row of books and stopped at a tier just above her eye level. "Here it is!" She exclaimed waving her prize in the air.

"May I see it?" Colin asked as Willa brought it over to the table. Colin took hold of the book, closing his eyes immediately. He felt its shape, texture and temperature. Images and feelings raced, forming ideas in his conscious mind. Suddenly Colin whispered the words, "M'turas, m'turas." He was quiet for a few moments and laid the book down knowing that he could still feel the images without interrupting the flow of information. "Do those words make any sense to you, Willa?" Colin questioned.

"No, not really, Colin. However, I do believe that you were speaking Gaelic."

"Is there anything in the Bible written in Gaelic?" Colin asked.

"Just a minute," Willa said, taking the Bible from his hands and turning to the first page. Skimming down, Willa pointed her finger, "Here it is—a list of our family heirlooms that were brought over from Ireland. Look, Kady, even Grandfather's watch is listed. You remember, honey, when your mother had it repaired for your dad's fortieth birthday?"

"Oh yes," Kady said. How could she ever forget that particular day, for it had altered her life forever.

Willa continued scanning the list, "Colin, take a look at item number four. It's my great-great-great grandmother's book. I believe that was written in Gaelic."

"Do you still have this book?" Colin asked feeling his extrasensory faculties precipitating an important discovery.

"Yes, I believe I still do," Willa said. She walked back toward the row of books that were next to the Bible and pulled out several large volumes. Willa stuck her hand inside and drew out a very old velvet sack, passing the pouch over to Colin.

He immediately sensed the emotional energy seeping through the cloth. Reverently he placed it down in the middle of the table. "This is perfect, Willa. I'm feeling a spiritual force, and I'm receiving some vivid images."

Willa sat down at the table, removed jewelry from around her neck, and handed it to Colin. "Daniel gave me this Saint Brigid's cross on our first anniversary. His mother gave it to him for his Holy Communion."

Colin gently placed her memento beside the velvet bag. "I think it's time to begin. Willa, may I draw the shades? There's a full moon and sometimes it's easier for me to work in semidarkness." Colin got up, to close the shades and dim the lights. A soft amber glow brought calm warmth to the room. "Now I would like everyone to relax and take three deep breaths. Good. Now let's all join hands as we begin!"

Colin was not prepared for the feelings that stirred inside him at the touch of Kady's fingers. Slowly he rubbed his thumb across the back of her hand, and a myriad of emotions passed through him. These feelings were new to Colin. He had never felt this way before. He was fascinated by the light aglow in Kady's eyes; she was so vibrant and alive. But, at the same time he sensed her incredible need for protection. He knew he must help her find the way toward her spiritual path. Her fear was tangible to him. He searched for a logical explanation for her apprehension but found none.

He refocused his attention on the pouch before him. Never before had he been so distracted. It was an uncomfortable feeling for Colin. As he looked up at Kady, he noticed her face had drained of all its color. He wondered if she had felt the same sensations.

Kady caught herself staring at Colin's powerful hands. She felt his caress, like a lover trying to convey his longing. Glancing up, she noticed his full, sensual lips and wondered what they would feel like pressed against her mouth. Her fantasies allowed her to block out the apprehension she felt about the reawakening of her intuitions. Against her will she swayed toward him and was startled by the sound of his voice!

"Let us begin with a short invocation." Colin fell into a trance as he focused all his energy on connecting with the spirit of Daniel Newton. "Daniel's spirit is not prepared to cross over. He has unresolved issues that we need to help him with. Wait, there's another spirit in the room. This one's telling me that you must all persevere in your beliefs, so that Daniel's honor may be restored. Be true to your heart; life is precious. He also says we need to examine the book carefully; it's very important. Daniel is in agreement and asks that we accept the spiritual guide he has sent us. Do not be afraid, for Kady has seen the river of forgetfulness."

Kady gasped thinking of the native American apparition and knowing that the Greeks referred to this river as the link between the visible and invisible worlds. Unnerved, she tried to pull her hand away, only to have Colin tighten his grip.

"It's OK. No one will hurt you. He wants to give us some more clues."

"Can you ask him what he is looking for or what he wants? Tell him that we feel helpless not knowing his plan," a confused Willa questioned. Colin picked up the cross and held it between his fingers, feeling the vibrations.

"Daniel is now speaking and he's telling me that you need to be patient; his soul's plan is not complete. He says, Willa, that your love bond will never be broken and that one day you will be together again in a place where love never dies."

Hearing a sniffle, Henry let go of Willa's hand and gave her his handkerchief. With the connection interrupted, Colin paused for a second, listening intently to the voices within.

"Kady, Daniel says do not be afraid to take the journey toward the path of love, for you will find your true soul mate. He also has some words for Henry. He thanks you for watching over Willa. Your kindness will not go unrewarded." Colin paused momentarily. "One last thing. He wants us all to remember that when the lark sings, all will be revealed!"

Emotionally drained, Colin reached for the damp cloth to break the psychic connection. Suddenly a cold draft filled the room as he felt the energy of the two spirits departing. Colin knew that you could not summon spirits at will, so he wiped his hands and recited the invocation necessary to end his reading.

"We are thankful for your divination," said Colin. "So Mote It Be! May the spirit of Daniel Newton and our spiritual guide rest in peace!" Taking a deep breath, Colin reached toward the middle of the table. "Now, with your permission, Willa, I'd like to examine this bag." Slowly he untied the knot of the velvet drawstring sack, feeling the vibrations of the past. Then Colin pulled out a tattered, leather-bound book. Gently turning the pages, he noticed the foreign script.

"This appears to be a journal written in Gaelic. I think our first step is to get this book translated. The dates that I can decipher seem to indicate that it was written in 1860. Does this make any sense to you, Willa?"

"I seem to recall my mother mentioning that my great-great-great grandmother returned to Ireland around that time. Colin, do you know someone who can translate this book for us?"

Still flipping through the pages, Colin hesitated as he said, "This looks like it might be some sort of a bookmark. I wonder if this page holds the key to our mystery."

Holding up a pure white feather edged in black he heard Kady cry out, "Oh, no! That looks just like the feather I found on my bus the other day. Remember, Aunt Willa?"

Picking the feather up, she felt the weight of her fears. Her fingers tingled and she tried to remember the native American's face. Was he a figment of her imagination, or was he truly a spiritual guide? Had he been trying to tell her something she'd been too afraid to listen?

"Yes, dear, it surely looks like the one you had when you came to my office."

Colin reached out to comfort her as he felt her unease. He stopped short of touching her, afraid it would disrupt the energy flow of their spiritual quest. Hoping she could confirm the connection, yet wanting to reassure her that she had nothing to fear, Colin spoke tenderly. "We'll work this out together, Kady. I'll make sure we stay centered and that your world does not spin out of control. Fear is just a roadblock that stops us from loving ourselves. I feel this feather is an important clue, and I promise we won't do anything you can't handle."

The soft veil of his voice calmed her inner turmoil. Nodding to Willa, he said, "First, we need to find out what's in this journal, and then Kady and I will do a little research on our own. Is that all right with you?" Colin asked Kady.

With a growing sense of serenity she discovered an inner strength and said, "I'd like to help you, Aunt Willa. I know this is important to you, so I'll give it a chance just as long as we proceed slowly."

"Oh, this was wonderful. I'm so happy we were able to contact my Daniel!" Willa cried. "I actually felt his presence in the room. Thank you everyone, for coming and participating at this meeting."

Henry leaned over, giving Willa's shoulder a squeeze. Suppressing a dainty yawn with her hand, Willa then gestured to Kady and Colin, "I think I've had enough excitement for one night. A woman my age needs her beauty sleep. So, let's plan another reading sometime soon?"

Closing the journal, Colin put it back into the velvet bag. Holding it up, he said, "That's fine with me, but with your permission Willa, I'd like to take this home. I have a colleague who has studied Gaelic. I'll contact him on Monday." Rising up from the table, Colin retrieved his black silk sport coat, tucking the book under his arm. "I'm sure we'll be able to figure all this out, just as soon as we have more information."

Kady sat silently as she attempted to come to grips with Daniel's personal message to her. Colin wanted to speak with her privately and try to lesson her fears, but was unsure if the moment was right. He had yet to come to terms with his own reactions to the spiritual journey that they had just embarked upon. He knew there was a powerful physical and psychic attraction between them that needed to be explored. He wondered what Kady was thinking. Did she feel it, too?

Putting a close to the evening, Colin extended his hand to Henry and Willa. "Thank you for a wonderful dinner and a delightful evening. We'll keep in touch." He turned to Kady and asked, "Kady, can I give you a ride home?"

"No, thanks. I drove myself," Kady explained, as she gave her aunt an affectionate peck on the cheek.

"Well then, let me walk you safely to your car." Colin said.

"Thank you, Colin. I appreciate your concern, but I'm parked right out in front." Kady opened her purse, took out her keys and proceeded down the stairs. Colin followed Kady to her car.

"Here, let me," Colin said, taking the keys from her hand while he helped her get in and gently closed the door. Then he motioned for Kady to roll down the window as he held up her keys.

Kady slowly rolled the window down. "I'll need a few days to get this journal transcribed, and then I'd like to take you to dinner. Would you be free next Saturday?" he asked as Colin leaned into the open window. Mesmerized by his handsome face resting inches away from her, Kady found it hard to refuse.

"Yes, I'd like that, but no more readings till I'm able to handle them. Why don't you call me later in the week and we'll talk details?" She replied haltingly, hoping she didn't sound too anxious.

"OK. I'll call you in a few days and let you know as soon as I make the connection with my colleague. I'm pretty sure he'll be able to help us with Willa's journal. Maybe we can also spend a few hours doing some research?" Colin asked, looking forward to spending more time with her.

Kady nodded, relieved that he could not read her thoughts. She felt her uneasiness began to fade and the bricks of clay encasing her heart started to crack. Colin placed two fingers on his lips, gently touched her face, and whispered, "Sweet dreams, Kady." Then he pressed down on the lock button and withdrew from the window as Kady slowly pulled away from the curb.

FIVE

*C*olin lost no time in contacting his friend and colleague Professor Michael Clearfield, who was currently teaching at the University of Dublin and was proficient in ancient Gaelic. Their paths had crossed five years earlier during an archeological dig on the Causeway Coast in Ireland. It was here that they had become great friends, sharing the same passion for the eerie ruins of Dunluce Castle. Its bizarre basalt columns had been the subject of many mysterious myths, legends, and psychic phenomena. Many Druid artifacts had turned up over the last century, prompting renewed interest in the mysterious Irish coast. The two men shared a mutual love for the past and had remained friends ever since.

After a lengthy conversation about Willa Newton's dreams and her ancient diary, Mike was hooked. He asked Colin to send him a copy immediately.

Soon after, Colin called Kady and arranged a date for Saturday. He promised an afternoon of research at Chicago's Historical Society, followed by dinner.

As the weatherman predicted, the day was hot, with temperatures reaching in the middle eighties. Colin spent the earlier part of the morning cleaning and polishing his pride and joy, a classic 1965 burgundy Mustang convertible. Before noon, he made reservations for an early dinner at Chicago's romantic La Lumiere restaurant.

He then took a quick shower, dressing in a pair of beige tailored linen pants and a black polo. Casual yet elegant, it accented Colin's recent tan and well toned physique.

Still favoring his injured leg with faltered movement, he grabbed a copy of Willa's journal from the stack on his desk, threw his sport coat over his shoulder and headed toward Kady's apartment. Colin parked across the street from her home and arrived on her doorstep five minutes ahead of schedule. He hoped that she was not one of those women who liked to keep a man waiting.

Colin rang the bell and Kady immediately answered, speaking into her intercom. "I'll be right out!" Kady's bedroom was below street level so she hurried up the apartment staircase and hoped to be out the front door before Rose got wind of who it was she was spending the afternoon with.

"Rose, I'll get the door. I'm going out anyway! Don't wait up!" Kady yelled as she passed her sister's bedroom, quickly grabbing her purse and keys. Kady did not want to appear too anxious, so she deliberately slowed her steps and made a last-minute check in the hall mirror. Releasing the deadbolt on the sturdy metal door, she stepped out into the vestibule, greeting Colin.

"Hi, you're early. Rose isn't dressed, so I won't ask you in. We might as well get going!" Kady explained slamming the front door. Then she hitched her handbag over a shoulder and proceeded down the stairs at a breakneck speed.

"Have you heard from your friend about Aunt Willa's diary? Do you have a plan for the research we're doing? Do you think we'll find anything at the Historical Society?"

Caught off balance for a moment, Colin reached for Kady's elbow to slow her down as he said, "Do you want me to answer those questions in any order?"

Stopping in her tracks, Kady looked up into the emerald depths of his eyes. "Sorry. I'm always in a hurry."

"That's OK. Let's start again. Hi, Kady, you look great. I admire a woman who's prompt. Yes, I'm as anxious to get started as you are. I've got a copy of Willa's journal in the car, and I do have a few ideas about where to start our search!"

Colin let his gaze slowly take in the gentle flow of her pale yellow sundress that hinted at the soft feminine curves beneath. He might be considered old fashioned, but he liked seeing women in dresses, especially short dresses that showed off their legs. OK, so maybe he was a bit of a chauvinist too, Colin mused. Turning his head, he caught high-lights from sun dancing around her auburn curls creating the allusion of a fragile buttercup.

When they reached the bottom step, he slightly increased his grip on her arm and escorted her across the heavy traffic on LaSalle Street. Opening the car door, he helped her ease carefully into the front seat. As much as he loved his classic automobile, he was sorry that the interior had bucket seats. Whatever happened to those great old bench seats? he thought.

Colin was a stickler for safety. He fastened his seat belt tightly across his lap, and he glanced over to make sure that Kady's was also secure. Then he reached back and handed Kady a red flower encased in foil, a chocolate rose.

"Colin, this is so sweet of you. How did you know?"

"I'm a psychic, remember?"

Kady blushed. "It's been hard to forget! Thank you so much." Unable to resist, she peeled away the wrapper and broke off a piece. Savoring the small bite she said, "Um, this is so good! Would you like to share?"

"No thanks. I never interfere with a woman and her chocolate."

Kady felt the fire of his gaze creating warmth within her heart. It must be the sun, she thought, or maybe the sugar that was making her light-headed. She berated herself for acting like a silly teenager on her first date, remembering how easily she'd fallen for Brick's irresistible charm.

Knowing most men couldn't resist talking about their cars, Kady tried to begin a normal conversation. "Your car is beautiful, Colin. How long have you had it?"

"Long enough. I started working on this baby during college, and every year I make some improvements."

"You mean you restored this automobile yourself?"

"Hey, don't look so astonished. I'm more than just a pretty face," he said with an infectious grin.

"Well, you did such a great job, you could have fooled me," she teased.

"Be careful with those compliments. I might get a big head," Colin answered, glad that she was loosening up.

They continued the short drive to the Historical Society in a comfortable silence. Colin pulled into the LaSalle Street outdoor parking lot. He got out and walked around to open Kady's door.

"I'll be right back. Just let me pay the attendant," Colin said, helping her out of the car. Then he flipped the black leather seat back to retrieve his notes.

Kady felt butterflies fluttering in her stomach and wondered if they matched the color of her dress. She reached into her handbag, retrieved her sunglasses and placed them on her face, shading the heated emotions hiding in the sapphire depths of her eyes.

Kady watched Colin walk toward the small parking enclosure that held a very sweaty man. Her eyes took in Colin's long-legged stride and the sun-kissed muscles flexing in his forearms as he paid the parking fee. Now she knew what Rose meant when she said there should be a law against men having too much sex appeal. She had to admit, he really was quite good looking. What was it about Colin that caused her to react this way? Even as a young girl she could not resist his animal magnetism. "Get yourself together. Don't be so superficial," Kady argued with herself.

"Ready?" he asked, reaching for her hand as they headed in the direction of the red-pillared Georgian contemporary brick building. There was something about his touch that shattered even the best of her self-imposed intentions.

"I know you've probably been here before, but first I'd like us to take a quick look through the Chicago History Galleries. I think we might be able to pick up a few clues, and then we'll head upstairs to the research center," Colin paid the five-dollar admission fee and led her up the grand staircase. "I think we should look for information dating back to the middle of the 1800s. The first date I can decipher from Willa's journal is 1860, so I guess that's our starting point."

"Sure, follow me," said Kady, leading Colin through the double door opening. "I know this place like the back of my hand. While you spent your college summers restoring your Mustang, I haunted these rooms any time I had a free afternoon. The attendants and I were on a first-name basis."

The eight dimly lit room dioramas held the scent of time standing still, as the echoes of the past filled the air. Kady was in her element!

She ushered Colin past the early editions of Chicago's first newspaper, the *Chicago Democrat*. She knew the oblong glass case filled with Old Chicago's memorabilia would not hold his interest today. They would have to look at the colorful artifacts and posters of native Americans advertising Kirk White Cloud Floating Soap and the first Sears and Roebucks catalogue another time.

Near the end of the room Colin stopped in front of a later edition of the *Chicago Democrat* dated November 26, 1833. There was an article that described the relative advantages of constructing a canal, an interesting map of the first railroad route to Chicago and an 1856 poster advertising the cheapest fares from Boston to Chicago on the Lake Shore and Michigan Railroads.

As they continued walking, Colin sensed that there was some connection. Like an artist facing a blank canvas, he knew that a greater knowledge could be revealed if he were receptive to the spiritual journey he needed to take. However, Colin was not able to fully concentrate on the emotions and feelings he was receiving because he was so keenly aware of Kady's presence.

Lowering her voice, she interrupted his thoughts. "Let's walk just a little further. There's something I want you to see."

"Why are we whispering?" Colin asked, matching her tone of voice.

Smiling, Kady rolled her eyes. "Because I'm afraid we'll wake the dead. Come on, it's just around this corner. Doesn't that look like Aunt Willa's journal?"

Even though she tried to suppress her perceptive powers, Kady felt this book held a key to the past they were trying to unlock.

Colin nodded, reaching into his pocket for his reading
glasses and leaned forward to read the inscribed note card:
"'A Narrative of the Life of Mrs. Mary Jamison,' by James
E. Seaver."

Colin jotted down what little information there was,
knowing he still needed more time to be receptive to the telepathic impressions he was receiving. "Let's head upstairs to
the research center. I think we're onto something."

They left the noiseless room filled with artifacts from
the past and became aware of the flurry of activity in the
grand hallways. Banners were suspended from the ceiling
while employees were hard at work setting up a bar and
tables filled with red and silver decorations for a special
event. On the door of the research center there was sign that
read, "We will be closing early for the Studs Terkle Day Celebration."

Colin glanced at his watch and realized they still had a
couple of hours before the center was to close.

"Come on. We'll have to work fast. I think we should
concentrate on Mary Jamison and her diary. I hope we can
find some mention of your family's surname."

Kady and Colin spent the rest of the afternoon poring
over reference books and old newspaper clippings. Only a
few pages of Mrs. Mary Jamison's journal were available.
They described her life as a twelve-year-old native American
captive and the two native American chiefs to whom she bore
children. The pages also mentioned a Lieutenant Joseph
Delore and his heroic deeds.

Colin felt they were on the right track, but knew he had
to dig further. When the overhead speaker system announced
that the building would be closing in ten minutes, Colin realized he would have to continue his research with the help of
his connections at the Washington Library. He concluded that
this would be a perfect excuse to invite Kady to his home so

he might show off his newly acquired computer hacking skills. Colin knew she could not resist delving into the secrets of the past.

Gathering up their notes, Kady and Colin headed down the stairs toward the entrance. To their surprise, the lobby had been transformed. The bottom of the stairs had been roped off, and women in tuxedos greeted those with personal invitations to the event. They handed each person a black scroll wrapped in a bright red corded tassel. The press waited outside to catch glimpses of the Chicago dignitaries descending from a line of black limousines. The gala atmosphere that filled the air seemed like a delicious fantasy that heightened their desires. Neither Colin nor Kady wanted this special feeling to end.

"It's still a beautiful day. Would you like to take a short walk through the Lincoln Park Gardens?" asked Colin. He knew that they didn't have enough time to walk through the entire thirty-five acre park and zoo, but the newly renovated park's flower beds were in full bloom. Taking Kady's hand, he led her across the street where the floral tribute to summer filled the air with the lavish aroma of romance. Kady was entranced as she took in the beauty of nature.

"God, I love this city—the rich architecture, the lakefront, and people. Tell me, in your travels have you ever come across a better place to live than this?" Kady, trying to encompass the entire city, twirled in a circle.

Colin was mesmerized by her radiant smile. A slight breeze off the lake caressed the hem of Kady's dress, exposing her incredible, slender legs. Colin was caught off guard and his imagination flared into overdrive. He pictured her legs intertwined with his, her arms holding him passionately, their lips joining as his hands caressed each silky auburn curl. She made him feel like an adolescent caught with his father's Playboy magazines. Trying to dampen his ardor, Colin gulped. What was wrong with him? He was feeling like a randy teenager, but damn, she was beautiful!

La Lumiere, one of the most romantic restaurants in town, was located on the top floor of the beautiful Reluire Hotel. Its posh yet comfortable, cozy booths and wonderful cuisine were created to impress even the most reluctant date. The atmosphere of gentility was enhanced by the sounds of a live string quartet. Their music filled the room with melodies created by some of the great composers of the past. Kady and Colin were greeted by the strains of Mozart's "Eine Kleine Nacht Musik" as the Maitre d' escorted them to their table.

Colin had arranged in advance for them to be seated with a view of the lake. Ordering a bottle of *Domaine Gramonte Les Beaumont,* they sat in companionable silence and watched as the fading daylight cast a rose-colored hue over the horizon.

As the natural light faded, a soft glow infused the room from the hand-crafted iron candelabras that flickered on each table. A prim waiter in a black tuxedo, suggested the chef's specials: pan-fried medallions of ostrich for an appetizer followed by spicy red snapper soup and aged *filet mignon* for the entree.

Raising her fluted wine glass to her lips, Kady looked up, making eye contact with Colin. She felt the sensual magic of his gaze down to the depths of her being and was suddenly afraid. Was she being overly sensitive?

She knew anything could knock a hole in her self defensive wall and trigger a premonition. Would her attraction to a psychic make matters worse? She hoped not! A tiny voice inside her heart encouraged her to take a chance.

"Colin, this restaurant is wonderful. Even Aunt Willa would be impressed. I've never had fried ostrich before."

"The few times I've been here they've always had an impressive menu," remarked Colin. "Dining here is definitely an adventure even for the experienced palate, and I'll admit I wanted to impress you."

Reaching for the vintage bottle of Les Beaumont, he replenished their goblets and continued. "Your brother Seth used to keep me informed on the major happenings in your family, but for the last few years we've been out of touch. Tell me about yourself. I'd like to get to know the real Kady Dailey. What have you been up to the past few years? Have you always been interested in teaching history?"

"I lead a pretty normal existence. I graduated from the University of Illinois with a Masters degree in Education and a minor in History. It was then I decided I wanted to teach. I guess I've always been interested in how the past shaped the world we live in today. My parents fueled that curiosity by planning family outings that taught us about nature and how things evolved. I also love children and take great pride in teaching them, even though it isn't the most lucrative profession. During the summer months I supplement my income by working at the family business. How about you? I've read quite a bit about you in the newspaper lately. I understand that you and your grandmother recently donated some valuable artifacts to the Historical Society."

The solemn waiter handed them dessert menus, as the last remnants of their meal were removed.

"I guess you got your information from Willa. The announcement won't be official until next week, but we have made quite a find. We were reinforcing some structural beams in an old factory loft space across from Goose Island when we came across a series of letters written by Abraham Lincoln. Can you imagine? We're just waiting for verification of authenticity from the Smithsonian so we can announce the find. For me the greatest joy in restoring old buildings is discovering the links between the past and the present. I was taught that history is valuable to the educated mind because it broadens our horizon and allows us to see the world from a different perspective. It sounds like we have a lot in common."

Picking up his dessert menu, Colin continued, "Kady, this place is famous for their Chocolate Frangelico tortes. Shall we share one?"

"No, thank you, Colin. I couldn't eat another bite, but promise not to tell my family I turned down dessert. I have an image to keep up!"

He loved the fact that she finally felt comfortable enough around him to tease. "Your secret's safe with me! How about a carriage ride? I can point out all the buildings our company's restored and you can tell me about their history?'

"You're on!"

It was a beautiful night. The stars twinkled overhead as Kady and Colin rode in an open air carriage through the Streeterville and Gold Coast neighborhoods. Colin put his arm across the seat as he and Kady got comfortable. The air was filled with the sweet smell of summer lilacs and the fresh scent of innocence that was Kady's alone.

Kady and Colin found that they had so much in common. They both loved old John Wayne and Maureen O'Hara movies, Chicago's Vienna hot dogs, Pizzeria Uno's deep dish pizza, the Chicago White Sox and the Bulls. Basking in the glow of shared interests, they traded stories as a lover's moon smiled down upon them.

"Did you know this area was named after a genuine rogue?" Kady asked.

Colin shook his head no.

"Oh yes. He was George 'Cap' Streeter, and he called himself ruler of the District of Lake Michigan. He ran his steamboat onto a sandbar east of Michigan Avenue in 1886. He and his wife used the debris from the wreck to build up the sandbar. They sold beer on Sundays in their saloon, created a makeshift chapel inside and claimed to perform legal marriages. They suckered in a boat load of unsuspecting citizens. No pun intended."

Colin looked at her in disbelief. "Cross my heart, I'm not making this up!" Kady said making the childlike gesture.

"OK, OK. I believe you, but my memories are more recent," said Colin. "A good friend of mine built a recording studio out of an old warehouse and named it Streeterville

Sound. The rock group Styx even recorded some tracks there. The owner is a friend of mine, and I listened in on one of their sessions."

Their conversation led to a lively discussion about rock groups and favorite songs. They were both surprised to learn that they shared similar musical tastes. They both loved the Beatles and were shocked to learn that one of their favorite songs was "The Best of Times." "That was our prom song," Kady announced.

They also agreed that the best musical of all time was Andrew Lloyd Weber's *Jesus Christ Super Star.* "I had that brown album in my collection until about three years ago when it was destroyed in a basement flood," Colin added.

The hansom carriage turned west on Grand Avenue and headed back toward the Magnificent Mile. The close contact of Kady's body nestled in the crook of Colin's arm played havoc with his senses. With every intoxicating glance he felt he was being swept into the vortex of this amazing woman. The half-hour ride ended much too quickly.

In silence they rode home with the top down on Colin's convertible as the wind blew gently in their faces. It was a delight, Colin thought, to be with a woman who did not constantly complain about the wind messing her hair!

They arrived at Kady's house and walked hand in hand up the stairs to her front door. Taking the keys from her fingers, Colin turned her gently toward him.

"May I kiss you good night?"

Mesmerized by the brief flicker of something Kady could not define, she looked up into the depths of Colin's emerald eyes and acquiesced. He began with a light touch tenderly exploring the contour of her soft lips. He deepened the kiss as sparks whispered down Kady's spine like delectable little fingers about to ignite a prairie fire! The bodice of her sun dress stretched tightly, and the heaviness in her breasts caused her nipples to swell. The fiery season of summer cast a spell as the air between them sizzled, increasing their pleasure.

Stunned by the natural power of their passion, Colin carefully drew away. He knew that he had better move slowly because Kady was not the kind of woman to be rushed.

Like so many first dates, there was the awkward moment of silence when one has to say good night.

"I've had a wonderful day," Colin finally said. "Would it be all right if I called you during the week? Maybe we can take in a baseball game?"

Dazed, Kady nodded as he opened her door. Enchanted, Colin was not able to resist one last kiss!

Six

*K*ady's week began with the normal flurry of activity that accompanied her busy summer schedule. Daily tours ran at full capacity during this active season. Kady's days were occupied with buses loaded with happy, inquisitive tourists hoping to make the most of every moment of their vacation. The humid, sultry nights were filled with memories of Colin and their first kiss. On a scale from one to ten, it broke the meter. She could only hope for an instant replay.

On Thursday, when Kady was almost certain that she had been put on the back burner, Colin called and invited her out Saturday night. He explained that for the last four days he had been trying to meet the deadline on his latest book. Now that it was finally completed, he was ready to celebrate. He wanted to relax and enjoy America's favorite pastime: a night at the ballpark.

The last time Kady had been to a baseball game was on September 30, 1990. It was the final game in old Comiskey Park when the Chicago White Sox defeated the Seattle Mariners 2-1. That game would be remembered for its historical significance by all diehard Sox fans. It brought to a close the eighty-year-old stadium's record of 3,024 wins to 2,927 losses.

Long-standing fans, Kady and her family attended the last game in the south side Irish neighborhood of Bridgeport. They were there to pay tribute to a Chicago landmark and their special home team. Adding to Kady's pleasure was the fact that her favorite rock group Styx sang the seventh inning anthem, "Take Me out to the Ball Game."

Kady had not had the opportunity to visit to the new, blue, oval cookie cutter shaped stadium because the team was having a record attendance season and tickets were hard to come by. It seemed like every time someone in her family had tickets to a game, she was the last to know about it. So when Colin called boasting of seats in the third row behind the White Sox dugout, Kady was thrilled. He even had preferred parking passes, compliments of Ed Farmer, an old friend. Ed was a former White Sox All Star pitcher and currently a sports broadcaster for WMAQ Radio.

As Kady gazed around, she was in awe of the numerous concession stands filled with a wide selection of food that circled a large portion of the stadium. She never would have thought that they could have replaced the old Polish sausage and hot dog vendors. The venders had been as much a part of the park as the venerable wooden green chairs that were now collector's items and a reminder of the stadium's illustrious past. In their place were contoured sky blue plastic seats, smaller than the old ones.

Kady and Colin filled their arms with bratwurst and sauerkraut, smothered in mustard and wedged in between a crusty French roll. Knowing beer vendors would regularly case the stands, they waited to buy their drinks and followed the uniformed Andy Frain usher to their seats. They had arrived just in time for batting practice to begin. Taking advantage of the empty seat next to her, Kady plunked a large handbag down.

"I'm so excited to be here," Kady said. "I can't wait to tell my brothers. They're gonna be green with envy. Now tell me in detail how you managed to get such great seats."

"The truth is my grandmother was a friend of one of the previous team owners, Bill Veeck," said Colin." "For years, we had season tickets. When I was younger, I wanted to be a major league pitcher. It was great fun to go into the locker rooms and meet the players. In my teens I discovered that one of the youngest players in major league baseball was none other than Ed Farmer. Ed was an all-star pitcher for my high school *alma mater,* St. Rita. He was a few years older than me. He would often return to St. Rita's to give motivational seminars. We met after one of his speeches and began a

A LOVE FORETOLD

friendship that continues today. The rest, as they say, is history."

"Well, I was a bat girl one year," interrupted Kady.

"You're kidding! How did that happen?'

"I entered a contest where I had to guess the number of home runs the White Sox would hit that season and I won! Boy, were Seth and Malachi jealous! I had the greatest time, even though I was never allowed past the dugout. I've been a devoted fan ever since."

"Beer! Get your ice cold beer right here!" A young man with cases of beer in a large box strapped across his back, sang out. "Beer! Get your ice cold beer right here!" Colin passed a ten dollar bill down the line of patrons to the vendor, a practiced ritual that all good sports fans know. And, as always, the loudmouth fat guy with a cigar pretended to palm the change. Right on cue, everyone chuckled as two cold beers and a bag of salted peanuts were handed to Colin and Kady.

"How did you know the only time I drink beer is with peanuts?" Kady asked.

"I'd like to say I'm psychic, but I'm afraid I'll end up with your beer all over my lap. How'd you figure out the number of home runs the Sox were going to hit?"

Kady quickly turned a revealing shade of red.

"Don't tell me you had a premonition? Oh, Kady, you are psychic! I'll tell you what. Let's make a bet on who will win this game, and we'll see just how good you are at predicting." Colin realized this was the perfect opportunity to prove to Kady that she had nothing to fear in admitting her psychic abilities.

"Well, I don't know if being paranormal had anything to do with it. I think it was just a lucky guess."

The spirit of fun and anticipation was in the air as Kady continued, "Let's up the ante on this bet and see if we can guess the winner *and* the final score."

"You're on. Winner gets to choose his prize!" Colin exclaimed, hoping to collect more that just a good night kiss.

83

"Or *her* prize. Don't go spending your prize money yet, because it ain't over till the fat boy swings!"

"I'm guessing the Cleveland Indians will take and hold the lead in the bottom of the seventh inning and win 5 to 3."

Kady turned to watch the first pitch of the game after the public address system announced, "Let's play ball!"

Licking the mustard off her fingers, Kady placed her bratwurst down on the seat beside her and reached into her large handbag. Taking note of its size, Colin commented, "Boy, is that ever a huge purse. It's bigger than my first apartment."

Kady pulled out a well-worn catcher's mitt, placing it on her left hand as Colin continued. "Wow, I didn't know that you were planning to join the guys on the field."

Kady chuckled, "I've come prepared for the foul ball that I'm gonna catch during the sixth inning."

"Is that a wish or a premonition?" Colin asked.

"Both," she said, "and don't tell me you never caught a baseball at old Comiskey Park."

Colin raised an eyebrow. "And you did?"

"Yup," a confident Kady replied.

"OK, OK. So you're one up on me, but it wasn't for the lack of trying."

Placing a few well-chosen punches into her mitt for effect, Kady chanted, "Hey batter, batter, batter." She turned to Colin. "The truth is I was just in the right place at the right time, but really it's been one of the joys of my life to lord it over my brothers."

An amused Colin thought to himself, This girl is really something!

Sox starter Jack McDowell pitched shutout baseball as the Sox and the Indians remained scoreless after five innings. In the bottom of the sixth inning, Cleveland Indians pitcher Charles Nagy struck out the side. In the top of the seventh, White Sox pitcher Jack McDowell retired the first two batters in order when Cleveland's left fielder Albert Bell stepped up to the plate. On the first pitch, Bell hit a towering pop-up into the seats, just behind the third base dugout.

"I've got it! I've got the ball!" Kady screamed as she raised her mitt above her head. Suddenly, three men behind her leaped high in the air in an attempt to catch the ball. They crashed into each other, parting like the Red Sea, leaving just enough space for the ball to squirt through and clunk Kady on the top of her head, knocking her to her knees.

As her world spun out of control, Kady had an out-of-body experience. She felt her eyes searching for something toward center field. Standing just behind second base was Mr. Tonto! He was waving four wiggling fingers in Kady's direction with one hand and pointing toward the scoreboard with the other.

"Kady!" Colin yelled over the screaming crowd. "Kady, speak to me. Kady, can you hear me?" Colin gathered Kady into his arms to prevent her from falling further. The woman seated next to him doused a couple of napkins with her bottle of water and handed them to Colin. The cool rags on her face helped Kady wake up.

With a low moan, Kady said, "Holy Cow, the Sox are gonna win four to nothing...Did I get the ball?"

"Here, little lady, you deserve the ball," the fat guy with the cigar said handing over his coveted prize.

As Kady became more alert, she was aware of her embarrassing position. She was half in and half out of a seat with her derriere snuggled between Colin's legs. Shielding her eyes from the direct sunlight, Kady reached for her sunglasses and realized that somewhere along the line they must have fallen off. Gingerly she touched the top of her head and discovered a throbbing golf ball size bump.

"Kady, are you OK? Can you get up?" Colin asked as he took her face in between his hands and slowly examined her for more bruises.

Suddenly out of nowhere, a loud booming voice yelled, "Kady...Kady, honey, are you all right, are you hurt?"

Kady looked up to see the concerned faces of her father and brothers hovering overhead. Trailing behind them was a burly uniformed security officer and a paramedic.

"Dad, what are you doing here?"

"At the last minute your brother Seth called to say he had a few extra seats for the game tonight. There we were, quietly sipping our beers, watching the game, when we see this foul ball fly into the seats. I look up, and to my everlasting surprise, there was the face of my little angel on the center field Jumbotron getting smacked on the head by a ball. Next thing I know your brothers jump out of their seats yelling, 'Kady! It's our Kady and she's hurt!' Are you hurt? Should we get a doctor? And who's this young man you're with?"

Not waiting for an introduction, a security man and the paramedic stepped in front of Kady.

"Excuse us, sir. We need to speak to the young lady," the security man said, nudging Kady's dad out of the way. "Miss, can we take you downstairs to see the doctor?"

Never a man to be overlooked, Ignatius Daily blustered, "What do you mean, young man? This is my daughter and I'll—"

"—Dad, Dad it's OK. It's just a little bump on the head. Officer, could you please get me an ice pack, to keep the swelling down?"

Still sitting on Colin's lap, Kady looked up with a twinkle in her eye and continued, "I've just decided that the Sox are gonna win four to nothing and I'd like to stay till the end of the game."

Colin shook his head and chuckled. "You're certain you want to stay?"

"Oh, yes. Absolutely."

Huffing and puffing from the exertion of carrying his large first-aid kit down a flight of fifty steep stairs to reach the injured party, the overweight paramedic dug into his bag and handed Kady an ice pack. "Hold this on your head, miss, while I check your pupils for a concussion."

Getting an affirmative nod from his partner, the police officer waved his burly arms and said, "OK, folks, let's clear the area and give this woman some breathing space. Sir, you and your boys will have to return to your seats. Don't worry. We'll take good care of your daughter."

Seeing his father's red-faced anger build, Malachi, known as the peacemaker in the family, stepped in. "Dad, the three men in the next row offered to exchange seats with us. We can sit right behind Kady and make sure she's OK."

Kady gave a grateful smile to her brother as she reclaimed her seat, holding the ice pack on her head in one hand and her prized baseball in the other.

Seth anticipated further trouble from their father and also interjected, "Dad, you remember Colin O'Dannaher, don't you? He used to come to the house with Aunt Willa and his grandmother Edna O'Dannaher."

"Oh sure, sure I do. Good to see you, young man."

"How's that beautiful grandmother of yours?"

"She's fine, Mr. Dailey, and I think Kady will be OK, too."

Colin settled back to enjoy the game, keeping a watchful eye on Kady. He wouldn't admit it to anyone, but the few seconds that it took to knock Kady down and out had scared him to death.

He flashed back to a Little League game he had played in as a young boy. He recalled his teammate and best friend Jimmy Yates screaming the same words, "I've got it, I've got the ball!" Then that horrible thud as the ball smashed into Jimmy's face, shattering his cheekbone and breaking his nose. At the last moment, Jimmy had lost the ball in the sun. The screams of pain and blood that Colin remembered were responsible for his immediate concern for Kady.

Detecting his unease, Kady smiled and put her coveted prize in her purse. She then laid a hand on his arm and whispered, "Its OK, Colin. I'm just a little sore, but really I'm all right."

Malachi leaned in, "She's got a hard head, that sister of mine. Don't you worry; she's gonna be just fine."

Slipping her hand through Colin's arm, Kady snuggled closer, feeling comfortably safe with the dawning awareness of her new emotions for this kind, caring man. Lost in her thoughts, she continued to watch the game.

It was still scoreless in the bottom of the ninth inning when Colin leaned forward, blocking Kady's vision of the field. "Hey, Kady, I thought you said the White Sox would win four to nothing," he teased. "Doesn't seem very likely now, does it?"

Kady took her time to answer, taking a long look at the players on the field. She slowly sat back, giving Colin a wink. "Your bet's already blown," she said, "but not mine. Patience, Mr. O'Dannaher. Patience."

No sooner had Kady uttered those words when Cleveland starter Charles Nagy walked the first two batters. Then manager Mike Hargrove brought in relief pitcher Jose Mesa. Mesa, in a like fashion, walked the bases loaded, bringing little Ozzie Guillen, the spray hitting shortstop for the Sox to the plate.

Colin looked over at Kady smugly. "Well, old girl, looks like the best you can hope for is a one-run win for your White Sox."

On the first pitch from Mesa, Ozzie hit a low inside fast ball down the right field line for an unbelievable game winning grand slam home run. As the crowd leaped to its feet, a stunned Colin looked up at the scoreboard that read Sox win 4-0 and shook his head. "You're unbelievable, Kady. You truly have a gift. When are we leaving for Las Vegas?"

SEVEN

*E*very morning before work, Kady and Rose stopped for a cup of coffee and a quick breakfast at Mama Caws Café, so named for the incessant sound of seagulls hovering around Navy Pier. Since neither were morning people, by mutual agreement they did not speak until they had their first cup of java.

"I don't know how I'd make it through the day if this place closed down," Kady sighed, biting into her chocolate caramel croissant.

"I know what you mean," said Rose, licking a drop of cream from her lips. This café latte is the only fat extravagance I allow myself all day."

"Do you know anything about the tour that's planned for today?" Kady asked.

"Yeah. We're picking up those executives from the electronics show. It's their annual convention. Remember? We took a similar group around last year."

"Oh no. Not that bunch of ogling men that kept flirting and quizzing us on Chicago's night life!"

"They're the ones. I have a feeling it's going to be a very long day!" Rose moaned, tipping her cup to catch the last drop of caffeine.

"Come on, our chariot waits," Kady said, linking an arm as she dragged her sister from the breakfast bar.

Even though this particular group of tourists was not one of their favorites, both Kady and Rose were professionals and always gave one hundred percent. After the strange, wonderful weekend Kady had spent with Colin, she was more than happy to keep herself immersed with activity.

Colin had called every night. Even though he'd completed his latest book, he still had last-minute details that kept him busy during the week. Colin had creative control over all aspects of his work, which included designing the book's cover as well as working out a marketing campaign. Even though their conversations were short, Kady felt a special relationship building during those few intimate moments. She looked forward to their next date.

Most of the shops at the Pier were just opening and readying themselves for the onslaught of tourist that kept them in business. As Kady and Rose entered the parking garage they could smell fumes coming from the busses. The powerful diesel vehicles were checked and then started by the mechanics first thing in the morning, to insure that they were in perfect working order. The sisters climbed aboard and were ready to begin another day.

Heading toward their destination, they arrived at the Hilton Towers a little before nine a.m. Kady stayed on the bus as Rose went to greet their passengers. Fifteen men and five women were gathered in the luxurious hotel lobby awaiting their arrival.

"Welcome, ladies and gentlemen, to Dailey City Tours. My name is Rose Dailey and I'll be your tour guide for the day. Before we board our bus, I would like to give you a brief history of the Hilton Towers. When it first opened it was called the Steven's Hotel. Their promotional staff billed it as the largest hotel in the United States, boasting three thousand rooms and a rooftop miniature golf course of real grass. It was the first of its kind anywhere. There are twenty-five stories, and a four-story tower. It has two lower level basements that are used as storage space for the myriad of functions hosted at this beautiful hotel. The portico entrance where our bus is parked and adjacent garage can accommodate up to five hundred and ten cars. The west wing has been billed as the largest single level exhibition space of any hotel in the world. I believe that's where your convention was held for the past several days, so I'm sure you all can attest to the enormity of its size. OK, everyone, let's get on board!" Rose exclaimed as she ushered her passengers on the bus.

"How soon do we stop for coffee?" a young woman questioned with a loud yawn. She was dressed in a bright red sundress, and matching three inch high sandals.

Oh boy, thought Rose. I'll bet she had a late night with all these men buzzing around her like bees to a honey pot!

"We have some refreshments on the bus, and we stop for lunch at twelve noon at the Palmer House," answered Rose. After making sure everyone was comfortably seated, Rose picked up her microphone.

"My sister Kady is driving our tour bus." Kady raised her hand in acknowledgement and caught her sister's smirk in the rear view mirror. "She teaches American History at the Latin School during the school year. Please feel free to ask either of us any questions you may have about our city."

"Our first stop is Buckingham Memorial Fountain. It is modeled after one of the Fountains of Versailles. However, Chicago's fountain is about twice the size of the original in France. It has one hundred thirty-three jets of water, some of which shoot about two hundred feet in the air. Every evening from nine to ten p.m. during tourist season, the fountain displays a colorful light show. Built in 1926 as a memorial to the wealthy socialite Kate Buckingham's late brother Clarence, it had the most advanced technical lighting system of its time. In the evening it becomes a playground for families and romantic lovers, who watch in awe the majestic symphony of the changing lights."

Listening to the drone of her sister's voice, Kady suddenly felt she needed to make a sharp left turn on to Michigan Avenue. Immediately, Rose sensed that something was wrong; this wasn't their normal route.

Not wanting to alarm her passengers, Rose made her way casually toward the front of the bus and leaned over to Kady whispering, "Hey, Sis, what's up?"

"There's a traffic jam on Wabash. One of the El trains came off its track."

"How do you know?" Rose asked as Kady's CB began to crackle to life and function.

"Kady, this is home base. Can you hear me?" Her sister Patti questioned over the air waves.

"Yes, Patti. You're coming through loud and clear!"

"There's been an accident on Wabash. An El train has derailed. Try to avoid it if you can! Did you get that, Kady?"

"Yes, I heard you, and I've already made a detour on to Michigan Avenue. Call cousin Matthew. Rita was on the last car and they've taken her to Northwestern Hospital."

"How'd you find all this out?" Patti asked.

"I'll tell you later, over and out!" Kady responded, shaken by her psychic perceptions.

"Wait!" Rose said, thinking about their passengers. "Radio back and tell Patti to inform the Palmer House that our tour bus will be arriving in less than thirty minutes for lunch!"

Giving her sister a suspicious look, Rose said, "We'll talk later." She then proceeded to her seat at the rear of the bus wondering about her twin's very peculiar behavior.

Kady was not looking forward to a confrontation with Rose. She suspected this latest premonition was brought on by her date with Colin O'Dannaher. Rose would demand a full explanation, leaving no stone unturned until Kady revealed all. How could she explain her feelings to her sister when she could barely figure them out for herself?

With a decisive plop, Rose returned to her seat and sat down. She did not want to alarm anyone, and she quickly ran a few explanations around in her head. Rose continued with a slight diversion to her previously rehearsed speech.

"We're taking a slight detour, folks. There's some heavy traffic in the State Street area, so for all you hungry campers, we're going to stop for an early lunch. By then the traffic should have cleared. We've also arranged for you to lunch at the famous Trader Vic's, located in the beautiful Palmer House."

Some of the men in the group mumbled about its being too early to eat lunch, but the lady in red flashed Rose a crooked smile with lips that were a little too thick to be real!

"That's great, honey. I can't tell you how in need I am of food, and a strong cool cocktail."

Rose tapped her mike and continued. "Looking to your right and then left you will see the designs of sculptor Ivan Mestrovic. These are two native American horsemen with their bows drawn. They were created to form a grand entrance to Buckingham Fountain. Further down, you can see Grant Park, with its gardens that were loosely patterned after the Palace of Versailles. Daniel Burnham was the grand master of what was known as the Chicago Plan of 1909. His visions for the lake front are considered far ahead of their time. Now look again to your right. You will see the statue of Abraham Lincoln sitting in his office chair. It was the last work of the famous sculptor Augustus St. Gaudens."

Heading East on Monroe, they finally reached the Palmer House. Awnings that held twenty feet of theatrical lighting graced the black marble of the entry way. Footmen dressed in black and green tails escorted the passengers off the bus and past the enormous brass knobs on the doors.

"Don't forget, folks. Reservations for lunch have been made for you at Trader Vic's," said Rose. "You'll have about two hours to take in the sights of this glorious hotel."

Not wasting any time, Rose made her way to the front of the bus like a concerned mother hen. "OK, sis, fess up. Is this about Mr. Tonto? Are you getting those premonitions again? C'mon now. Tell me what brought all this on."

"I'm starving! Why don't we get off this bus and grab a bite to eat? I'm always in a better mood to talk after I've eaten."

"You're on. Let's get out of here, but don't think I'm letting you off the hook! Would you like to eat at the Coffee House on the lower level? They make a mean Julienne salad, and you love their greasy hamburgers and fries."

Stepping through the marble-faced doorway, they entered the lobby of the hotel. The rush of cool air was a welcome relief from the hot, muggy, early afternoon temperatures. Chicago, known for its sultry humid summers, was just starting to feel the onslaught of the heat.

Kady proceeded through the crowded lobby and suddenly felt a tingle of awareness down the base of her spine. She stopped and turned to look around. Her gaze fell upon a group of people standing at the bank of elevators down the hall. There was a blonde with thick glossy hair swirling over her shoulder, dressed in a skin-tight red leather pantsuit that was hanging onto the arm of Colin O'Dannaher.

Remembering how secure it felt being held in those very same arms, Kady stopped and watched as the two of them walked straight toward them. Before she had a chance to make a detour, Colin and his clinging vine stepped directly in front of them.

"Kady, what a surprise! I didn't expect to see you here today," a stunned Colin said.

"Hey, don't I know you?" Rose blurted out. "Yeah, I saw you on Oprah about a month ago. You're that psychic guy, right? The one who talks to dead people."

Kady was thankful that Rose had given her a moment to collect her thoughts. Just last night she'd accepted another date with Colin on Friday. She hadn't planned on seeing him so soon, and certainly not with another woman who was obviously giving her the once over. Damn Seth and these hideous uniforms, she thought.

Colin felt awkward and mustered up a weak smile. "Psychic guy, that's me. And you must be Kady's twin sister Rose."

Colin attempted to untangle Ana's vice-like grip on his forearm. It reminded him once again that she was too skinny for his taste. Momentarily free, he focused his attention on Kady and was immediately entranced by her beautiful makeup-free complexion. Colin had noticed her air of fragility before, but today she seemed even more vulnerable. Looking into her eyes he saw a flash of uncertainty. Suddenly he felt a pinch in his biceps. Ana's long fingernails were a deadly reminder that he had not made an introduction.

"I'd like you both to meet a friend of mine, Ana DuPré. Ana, this is Kady and Rose Dailey."

Smiling like a queen before her paltry servants, Ana said, "Nice to meet you both." Ana then swept her fake dark-lashed blue eyes over Kady's and Rose's matching uniforms. She puckered her too thin lips, then lifted a perfectly arched penciled eyebrow and asked in a superior fashion, "I take it you both work here?"

Meow, thought Rose, who was not about to be one-upped by this cellophane bimbo. She replied in an equally haughty tone, "No, as a matter of fact, we're here on business." Wondering if her sister had turned to stone, Rose elbowed her twin. "Right, Kady?"

Kady kept thinking, Don't stare. Do not even flinch when he looks your way! Once again Kady was caught off guard by Colin's powerful presence. She abruptly shifted her attention with a nervous laugh.

"Oh yes, we're here five days a week on business, our own company business!"

Put that in your pipe and smoke it, Ms. Sushi Breath, thought Kady, who realized that Miss High-and-Mighty was giving the hands-off-he's-mine signal to both of them. "Well, she can have him, the big flirt." To think she almost fell for this guy's phony caring sincerity. Not again, she vowed. Life was full of choices and never again would she make the choice to fall for charm over substance.

Grabbing her sister's arm, Kady decided to have the last word. "Well, nice seeing you both, but we've got a company to run! 'Bye!"

Walking away with her head held high, Kady pretended like nothing had passed between them. She didn't give Colin a second glance.

Colin felt like an innocent bystander to the fireworks that were flying between these women. He did not understand what had been going on. He looked over at Ana and noticed her smug smile. Women, he thought. Who can figure them out?

He was certainly glad that he had called Kady last night and arranged a date on Friday. Just seeing Kady again made him anxious for the weekend.

As soon as they were out of earshot, Kady turned to Rose, "Did you get a load of that muffin?"

"I hate to tell you sis, but that was more than just a muffin. I've seen her photo once or twice in a lingerie magazine. Also her name's been mentioned a few times in the *Chicago Tribune's* Inc. column. You know the type, constantly trying to been seen with the latest celebrity who comes to town. I wonder how Colin got mixed up with the likes of her?"

"Ana DuPré!" Kady groaned. She suddenly felt quite inadequate. Hell, she thought. I'm nothing like her. I never even stood a chance!

"Big deal. Humph! Welcome to the wonderful world of plastic, skinny arms, tiny waist, fake boobs, yeah right!" Rose continued thinking out loud, "You know, I thought I read somewhere where she was dating some author of psychic books, but I never put the two together."

Suddenly, Rose stopped and grabbed her sister by the elbow before they proceeded into the restaurant. "Oh my God! He's the reason for your premonitions isn't he? I knew something was up! Have you dated him? That's it, isn't it? No wonder you looked so shocked to see him." Glancing at Kady, she saw her bewildered expression and sensed her sister's disappointment. "Come on, Kady, let's get some lunch."

Dragging her twin forward, she greeted the hostess. "Hi. We'd like to be in the non-smoking section, please."

She seated them at a small booth in the back, handing them a list of daily lunch specials. Slowly Kady picked up her menu, calming herself as she tried to explain.

"Look, Rose, it's nothing. We ran into each other a couple of times at Aunt Willa's. She's been having those dreams again...you know, and she's asked Colin to help since he's written that book on all that psychic stuff. That's it, nothing more."

"Riiiight. Then why did you look like someone who had been punched in the gut when that bimbo started staking her claim? Huh, sis? You can't fool me. There's more to this."

A young waitress with purple hair and black fingernails quickly diverted Rose's attention by asking for their order. Glad for the reprieve, Kady hoped her sister was mistaken and that her feelings could not be so easily read!

With a decisive inward nod, Kady decided that she was not going to have anything more to do with the likes of Colin O'Dannaher! She had no intention of becoming his next flavor of the month!

What a day, thought Kady as she reached the sanctuary of her street-level bedroom. She threw herself down on the soft yellow hand-crocheted bedspread, not stopping to remove her clothing. Her mind raced with a myriad of thoughts, all involving the perplexing question of how to get out of her date Friday night.

She was confused. Throughout the day her mind replayed the encounter in the hotel lobby. Every time she did, she became even more upset. Still, she was unable to discount the peculiar attraction she'd felt for Colin.

Without warning, Midnight suddenly jumped into Kady's arms. Taking out a few minutes to scratch between Midnight's ears, Kady said a quick prayer to her patron saint for inspiration and dialed the phone.

After four rings and a click, Kady listened to Colin's answering machine. Great, no one is home. Thank you, St. Katherine! Feeling more confident, Kady decided to keep the conversation short and to the point.

"Hello, Colin, this is Kady Dailey. Sorry to cancel our date. I'm working late on Friday, but thanks for the invitation." Feeling honesty was the best policy, Kady decided to make sure she took over Rose's paperwork that night so she wouldn't be telling a lie.

She gave herself a mental shake and headed toward the kitchen and the Hershey chocolate bowl, hoping to distract herself from all thoughts of Colin O'Dannaher. She intended to cook up a storm and eat everything sweet in sight, then curl up with the likes of Lord Byron Winston, the hero in the latest novel she was reading.

She pulled out her old recipe box and thumbed through the food-stained index cards. Kady peeled off the foil covering a chocolate kiss and popped it into her mouth, immediately feeling it sooth her bruised ego.

"Um, let's see...something healthy yet sweet!" she said out loud, picking one of her favorite desserts, fruit fondue. Rose, who had gone out on a dinner date, couldn't complain about her unhealthy eating habits. This was a treat they both could enjoy. The dip was filled with a gazillion sugar calories, but Kady could claim that the fruit was good for you.

Checking the cupboards for supplies, Kady realized she would have to go out to the local grocery store. Good. An excuse to be out of the house when Colin calls...Correction, if he calls, Kady thought.

After his disastrous lunch date with Ana, Colin returned to his office. He immersed himself in the partially completed transcript and letter that his old friend Professor Clearfield had sent him. He read the message with dismay as it dawned on him that trying to decipher Willa Newton's old family journal would take longer than he expected. Michael Clearfield's letter went on to explain that he was readying himself for a summer archeological dig in South America. He would only be able to send him the translation a few pages at a time.

Thinking positive, Colin hoped for a small tropical storm, knowing that the excavation would be delayed and perhaps Mike might be able to get the translation to him a little faster. On the other hand, this delay would give Colin a good reason to see Kady before Friday. Maybe he would just stop over tomorrow night with the papers as an excuse for his visit. Colin decided to call Kady that night.

Ryder greeted him with a hungry half bark and moan. "Sorry, old boy. I forgot Gilly's on vacation," he said, referring to his housekeeper who usually fed Ryder before she went home for the day.

It was then he realized that he hadn't had much to eat that day himself. He had barely picked at his meal with Ana, knowing that breaking off with her was not going to be pleasant. She was one of those clinging women whose attraction wore thin when she asserted her bold personality. Colin had seen glimpses of the real Ana throughout the time they dated but he ignored them. He hoped they could just have a good time together.

Colin was aware of the fact that Ana wanted to take their relationship to the next level, but in good conscience he couldn't do it. Colin didn't want to hurt her, but he no longer wanted to continue seeing her. She knew how to package herself well, but there was no depth or substance to her personality. Truth be told, there was really only one reason why he really wanted to break it off, and it was a simple four-letter word—"Kady." She had made him feel different from the way any woman he'd ever been with before had made him feel.

When Colin broke the news to Ana over lunch, she wasn't very happy. After all, what man in his right mind would ever break up with Ana DuPré? Seconds before she stormed out, Ana turned to Colin and asked, "Tell me the truth, psychic boy. This is about that little bus driver, isn't it? Well, I hope you and Miss Uniform Girl are very happy together. When you're through slumming you'll know where to find me, between the pages of a Victoria's Secret's catalogue." She handed him a photograph of herself. With that Colin was more convinced he'd made the right choice. As soon as she was out of sight, he tore her photo into small pieces, dropping it into an empty ashtray.

Wow. Lucky escape, Colin thought.

Colin walked into his pantry and took out a can of dog food for Ryder and a can of chicken soup for himself. His grandmother always claimed that chicken soup was good for what ails you.

Colin's recently renovated kitchen gleamed with antique copper pots and pans that hung in the center of the room. He had just refinished the original cherry wood cabinetry and was anxious to show it off to Kady.

The light on his answering machine blinked on and off reminding him that he still had to play back the unanswered messages. Colin hoped that Ana would not call demanding a postmortem on their relationship.

The first message was from his grandmother, reminding him of tomorrow's business meeting. The second was from Willa Newton, asking if he had anything to report on the journal. Next, Kady's voice rang out as he placed a pan on the top burner of his stove, preparing to pour in his can of soup. He was filled with a sense of dismay as he listened to her message canceling their date.

"Damn, damn, double damn!" Colin said, glancing down and realizing that it was Ryder's dog food heating up on the stove instead of his chicken soup! Taking the pan off the burner, Colin sat down at his kitchen table and immediately dialed Kady's number. He cursed the invention of the impersonal answering machine as he left a message.

Throughout the remainder of the evening Colin continued to call. Remembering the uncomfortable look on Kady's face during their inopportune meeting, he realized it wouldn't take a psychic to know why she would not be returning his calls. Thinking back on their extraordinarily potent kiss, he came to the conclusion that he would have to take drastic steps to convince Kady that he was serious about their relationship!

Colin sat down and decided that he needed a foolproof strategy to win Kady's affection. Before going to bed, he called the information hot line at Dailey City Tours. Colin listened to the scheduled time and location for the next day's events. He started to formulate his plans.

Colin had set his alarm for a six a.m. wakeup. After a quick shower and shave, he decided to forgo his usual routine of coffee, hot oatmeal and the daily newspaper. Colin needed the extra time to pick up a few things.

EIGHT

*C*olin lived in a neighborhood buzzing with early morning activity as people left home for their jobs. Impatient for the day to begin, Colin hardly noticed the early morning dew that had settled on his lush green lawn. He was a man on a mission, ignoring the beauty of his gem stone patch of paradise as he drove toward his goal.

Putting in a Styx tape, Colin listened as the Grand Illusion blared from his speakers. Bobbing his head in time with the beat of the next song, he sang, "The best of times are when I'm alone with you..." Before he knew it he'd arrived at the Hilton Tower thirty minutes before the scheduled bus tour. Armed with his secret ammunition, Colin decided that he had better check the lay of the land before setting his plan into action. He questioned the young attendant at the front desk and proceeded to the side entrance of the hotel.

Taking a leisurely stance, Colin surveyed his travel companions for the day. The group consisted of twelve well-dressed women and a handful of men. Good-natured teasing indicated that they all knew each other. It looked like the bus would be nearly full.

Colin wished he was a magician creating his own grand illusion as he wondered how he was going to get on the bus unnoticed. Spotting an attractive middle-aged woman, Colin flashed her an engaging smile and walked towards her to enlist her help. Before he could formulate his actions, he was greeted by a delightful English accent.

"Excuse me. Aren't you that psychic I saw on Oprah a few weeks ago? Your name is O'Dannaher, Colin O'Dannaher, isn't it?"

"Yes, it is, and you are—" Colin questioned.

"—Beatrice Cartright, but you can call me Bea." She said holding out her bejeweled hand.

"You wouldn't happen to be Beatrice Cartright the world renowned romance writer, would you?" Colin asked, kissing her outstretched hand.

"Guilty!" she said. "So tell me, young man, what brings you to a bus stop so early this fine morning?"

Beatrice Cartright listened intently as Colin told his story. She was intrigued by the romantic possibilities of his plight. After all, she had spent the last thirty years of her life searching out and writing about love's trials and tribulations. Plus, Bea could never pass up an opportunity to help a gentleman in distress, especially when it came in such a handsome package and with such superb manners. She might be a little older these days, and moving just a tad slower, but she wasn't dead!

"Just give me a few seconds to think this through, young man." She placed her index finger on her chin and began tapping. Without a second thought, Bea's mind began to spin and she came up with a plan.

Then, with a flick of her gold-laden wrist, she explained, "Colin, this is your lucky day! Plotting romance is my specialty. Just follow me!" A determined Bea turned and approached her friends.

"Talley ho, girls and boys. We have to help this young man. This is our chance not only to write about a budding romance, but to actually live it! Come close now and listen carefully!"

As the tour bus drove up, Rose gracefully exited and walked toward the first group of passengers. "Good morning, ladies and gentlemen. I'm Rose Dailey, your tour guide today." Looking around she continued, "I recognize a few passengers from last year's National Romance Writers Convention. You'll be happy to hear that Dailey Tours has planned a special diversion from our regular scheduled sights. We hope you'll all enjoy the day's events!"

Like the director in a Hollywood film, Bea announced under her breath, "Action, people. Let's get this romance on a roll!"

Two women quickly entered the bus and engaged Rose in conversation. Another heavy-set woman stood directly in front of Kady, blocking her view of the oncoming passengers as Bea smuggled Colin on board.

Unaware of the secrecy that surrounded them, Rose gave Kady the signal as the automatic bus doors closed with a loud whoosh. As they began their journey, Rose did a final check to make sure that all her passengers were accounted for.

Her list did not compute. There was one passenger too many. Her eyes traveled toward the back of the bus to do a recount. Seated in the last row next to Bea Cartright, Rose caught sight of Colin O'Dannaher. What the heck was he doing there? She knew he was not on her list. There was something strange going on.

Setting her clipboard down, Rose got up and headed toward the rear. Colin jumped up, stopping Rose in her tracks. He held up an armful of roses and a box of chocolates. He placed his index finger to his lips in a silent message and pointed to Kady. Well, thought Rose, something is definitely in the air. Sitting back down, she realized that the bus was unusually quiet, so she picked up her microphone and began to speak.

"Welcome, everyone. As I mentioned earlier, we have a surprise in store for the passengers who have taken this tour before. Um...apparently you've planned a surprise, too!" she said, eliciting a chuckle from the crowd. "We know some of you write historical love stories, so with the help of my sister Kady, who is our resident history buff, we have devised an exciting day with romance in mind." Rose paused to clear her throat. "Err, you all remember Kady, our bus driver, don't you?"

"We sure do, honey. She's one gorgeous bus driver. Quite an improvement over Ralph Kramden," one of the men exclaimed.

At the mention of her name, Kady glanced back into her rear-view mirror and located the speaker in the second row. He was a middle-aged man with thinning salt and pepper gray hair combed straight across the top of his head in an effort to conceal his loss. An unlit cigar was stuck between his teeth.

Kady shifted gears and concentrated on the traffic. This was not their normal route, and she needed to keep her mind alert. Her heart was heavy, and she consciously tried to avoid thinking about Colin.

Rose continued her conversation with the passengers as she cleverly revealed their destination. "We're going to start with a little history lesson, folks. Our travels today will take us on a trip that was once considered a must for all tourists visiting our city in the late 1800s. In 1871, the editor of the *New York Chronicle* sent one of the few published female writers of that time, Caroline Kirkland, to write about our city. Her article explained that while our Chicago streets were picturesque and friendly, she hadn't seen a single female traveling on her own. Every woman was accompanied by a male escort! This was so distressing to her that she convinced her editor to let her devote an entire page to the forlorn aspect of our streets being devoid of all single women.

"I think, somewhere along the way a very insightful gentleman named Palmer Potter read Ms. Kirkland's article. Soon after that, he began to formulate his now famous State Street project. He took many visits abroad to the cosmopolitan capitals of Europe. While on these trips Mr. Potter was once again reminded of the necessity of attracting female shoppers. He had plans for a world class development in downtown Chicago, and he was convinced that women shoppers would hold the key to success."

Feeling she was losing her audience's attention, Rose asked a question that she was sure would get a boisterous response.

"Hey, any of you ladies like to shop?" An affirmative answer echoed throughout the bus.

"Then, old Palmer Potter created the most fashionable commercial boulevard west of Broadway, on this very street that appealed strictly to woman shoppers!"

"All right, lead us on, McDuff!" A woman shouted from her seat.

Rose loved the crowd participation and continued. "Palmer devised and created all kinds of attractions that catered to the female shopper. Did you know he introduced the first customer-service policy? He guaranteed his customers a full cash refund if they were not fully satisfied with their merchandise! Palmer's store had a refined environment. The windows were brightly decorated and stocked with expensive and exotic merchandise. He even remembered the names of their beloved pets that accompanied them. He strived to enforce the customer-is-always right policy!"

"What a guy," Rose sighed, as her audience nodded their heads in approval.

As much as Bea loved to shop, she sensed it was time to put her plan into action before they stopped for lunch.

Half listening to Rose's history lesson, Kady mechanically drove toward State Street, that great street. It was a clear day, and the sun shone through a sky colored in a magnificent blue. Kady ignored the beauty of her beloved city as she tried to make sense of all that had happened in the last week.

Colin was finding it very difficult to contain his impatience. Even though the bus was air-conditioned, he was feeling the heat and was having an even harder time sitting still. While he appreciated the history lesson, his mind was elsewhere. He was nervously awaiting the opportunity to make his presence known. He wasn't sure how to approach Kady, but Colin was not about to give up.

Bea Cartright sensed his patience wearing thin. Quietly she reached over, patted his knee and whispered, "Don't worry. The hero always gets the girl of his dreams."

Bea called to Rose, "That's fascinating, my dear. We all love to shop, but you know we romance writers are more interested in the amorous allure of your beautiful city. For instance, where would we go for an intimate dinner for two?"

Before Rose could answer, an attractive brunette seated across from Colin chimed in, "Yes, Rose. Where could one find a quiet little spot if, say, I was planning a big seduction scene. You see, I'm writing about this hero who's in love with a woman who won't return his calls. Got any ideas?"

A woman near the exit aisle chirruped, "How about a romantic dinner? You know, let him wine and dine her?"

"Yes, that's very good, but let's thicken the plot a little," Bea said discreetly pointing at Kady. "How do I get her there? Let's suppose she saw him with an old flame and now she won't have anything to do with him. Any ideas on how he can get her attention?"

"He could send her roses, you know, to soften her up," suggested the gentleman with the cigar.

"Offer to take her to a musical and pretend to enjoy it! That shows real commitment," a man shouted from back row."

"Yes, but how would she know he was serious?" The lady in the front row questioned.

"How about flying a banner from a blimp announcing his love for her to the world?" a gentleman expressed light-heartedly.

Rose finally understood where all this was leading. Now she knew why Kady had seemed so out of sorts and uncommunicative this morning.

Approaching the Palmer House, their designated stop for lunch, Rose felt the powerful pull of the breaks as the bus began to slow down. Knowing that she would have her sister's undivided attention, Rose decided it was time to have a little fun with her serious twin.

She leaned over the front of her seat with the microphone still in her hand and asked, "Kady, where would you like to go to be wined and dined by your special man?"

"What?" Kady exclaimed.

"Flowers, Kady, do you like flowers?" Rose repeated.

"Yes. All women like flowers."

"But, can they soothe a woman's wounded heart?" Rose questioned.

"Sure, I guess so," Kady said as she pulled into the designated parking area at the hotel.

"Is there anything else?" Rose questioned?

"Huh?

"Aren't you listening, Kady? These writers want to know if there is anything a guy can do to win your affection."

Thinking they were still on the history of Palmer Potter, Kady said, "I'll bet no one ever had to tell Mr. Palmer how to understand woman. Did you know he included a large sum of money in his will for his successor—you know, just in case he died first and his wife Bertha ever remarried? He's quoted as saying 'He'll need the money.'" The women on the bus thought that was hilarious.

Bea appreciated the humor of the situation, but she felt the momentum slipping away again and quickly asked, "How about yourself, dear? What could a gentleman do to make your heart go pitter-patter?"

"Oh, I'm easy. Just give me a box of chocolates and I'm his for life!" Kady said as she shut off the engine and turned to the group. She was finally getting into the spirit of things.

Knowing this was his moment, Colin sprang to the front of the bus with his gifts in hand. Playing to the crowd, he swiftly pulled Kady from her seat and gathered her into his arms whispering, "Let's give them something to write about!"

On her way out Rose scrawled the words "Mia Sofia's for lunch" on her clipboard and placed it within Colin's line of sight. She knew that it was her sister's favorite restaurant.

"Kady, will you give me a chance to explain, please?" Colin asked.

Stunned, embarrassed and amazed by the state of witless wonder she seemed to be in whenever she was in Colin's arms, Kady nodded yes.

Maybe I'm going mad because what I really want to do is kill him, knock him over the head and leave him in some dark alley for some other unsuspecting female to find, she thought. Yes, she was definitely losing her mind, and she was just as certain he was trying to steal her heart!

Colin ushered her out the door and hailed a Yellow cab.

"Where to, sir?" the driver asked as Colin helped Kady into the back seat.

He hesitated a moment. "How long is your break, Kady? Will you have lunch with me?"

Colin didn't give Kady time to answer, quickly instructing the cabbie, "Mia Sofia's, 1204 North Wells."

"You mean I really have a choice?" Kady asked.

"Of course. We could go somewhere else, but I have it on good authority that it's one of your favorite restaurants."

"Rose again, huh? I never thought she was the meddlesome type," Kady said with a smile that took the sting out of her words.

"Look, Kady. Just give me time to explain, OK?"

The taxi came to a sudden stop as the automated meter droned, "Your fare is five-twenty-five. Please check the seat and make sure you take all your belongings when exiting the cab."

The trendy restaurant was crowded, but the Maitre d' recognized Colin and escorted them to a quiet table with a picturesque view. A waiter appeared with a bottle of olive oil and cheese, taking their drink order. After the waiter left, Colin said, "I guess I should apologize for the underhanded method I used to get you here?"

"An apology would be a nice start."

"OK. I'm not very good at this. I haven't had much practice, but damn it, Kady, I'm crazy about you. I wanted to see you, and Ana is just an old friend."

Kady raised her eyebrow, questioning his old-friend routine, as the waiter returned to take their order.

Colin grabbed a piece of Italian bread, ripped it in two and dipped it into the small saucer of spice-flavored oil as he continued. "Well, maybe not an old friend, but she's history. I invited her to lunch to break off our relationship. The truth is there was never much of a relationship. Whatever we had was over before I even met you. We had an agreement, neither of us was ready to get serious, and suddenly she changed. She became very high maintenance, and I could see she wanted more. I've been trying to let her down easily, but she kept inventing excuses for us to be together. The other day I told her that I had met someone that I wanted to explore a serious relationship with, but she doesn't let go easily. I'm sorry if Ana upset you."

Reaching out for Kady's hand, Colin said, "You're special, Kady. I'd like you to give us another chance."

Taking a deep breath before she spoke, Kady wondered where all her intuitive power went when she really needed it!

"All right, Colin, but first there are a few things I'd like you to understand. Life's not a game to me. I don't know how to play. No, that's not true. Once before I tried to play and got shut out. I'm not sure I'm ready for a second round. There are a lot of other things that are going on that you don't understand." Kady paused and took a deep breath, trying to calm herself, knowing this was going to be hard to put into words.

"You're right, I don't understand. So why don't you explain?" Colin quietly encouraged, lining up the salt and pepper shakers in strategic order like soldiers preparing for battle.

"By now you've figured out that I have some psychic ability, right?"

"Yes, but I don't see how that can be a problem. If anything, I'd assume that we have a lot in common."

Their waiter interrupted to hand Kady a cordless phone. "Excuse me, sir, but the lady has a call," he said. Kady placed the phone to her ear as a familiar voice boomed. "Sis! Kady. Is that you?"

"Yes. Hello!" Kady answered, abruptly pulling the screeching phone away from her ear.

"This is your lucky day. Seth sent us another driver to fill in for you. Take the rest of the day off. See you later— much later." Rose rang off before Kady could get in another word. Once again she was annoyed by Rose's take-charge-of-her-life attitude.

"I guess you heard?" said Kady.

"Don't be upset. Now we have the entire afternoon to ourselves."

"I suppose, but don't feel that you're obligated to spend the day with me."

"Kady, I'd like to spend night and day with you. But first I'd like us to spend time together, get to know each other better. So now explain, what exactly is the problem with your psychic abilities?"

"I don't have a problem with my psychic ability. I choose to ignore it. You, on the other hand, exploit yours!"

"Kady, I don't understand. I've always felt blessed that I was able to use my understanding of the spiritual realm to help others."

"Let me explain. When I'm around you it seems like my extrasensory perception goes into overdrive, and for years I have tried to block it! Because of my premonitions, I grew up thinking I was a freak. First my family teased me, and then my friends got wind, and I never heard the end of it. I don't think I can handle those negative feelings again."

Colin took her hand as he looked into the depths of her beautiful, troubled eyes and slowly kissed her fingertips. "Kady, hasn't anyone ever explained to you about the marvelous powers of the mind and how we grow spiritually as we tap into them? The evolutionary journey can be a wonderful experience. My grandmother was the first to notice my extrasensory perception powers. She thinks they first began to manifest in my dreams, shortly after the death of my parents. When she realized that I possessed the power to actually speak to my parents and hear their thoughts, she encouraged me. She told me that this was a form of grieving, and it was OK because it brought me peace. She was right. It did! Then she began telling me stories of wise holy men, prophets who were revered in ancient history because they could speak to the dead and foretell the future. As I became more comfortable with these occurrences, I discovered that I could somehow converse with others who had passed on. My grandmother supported me. She made me feel special."

"Colin, you don't understand!" Kady said, withdrawing her hands and placing them in her lap for control. "These experiences have never been positive for me! My parents tell me I was around five years old when they began to noticed my 'odd behavior,' as they called it. That summer we were all set to go on a camping trip when I stubbornly told them that we couldn't leave because of the rain. With no rain in sight, my parents refused to listen. I threw such a tantrum that I broke out in hives and we had to postpone the trip!"

"So, kids do things like that all the time!"

"You're right, they do. However, later that day when my father was checking on the weather conditions, he found out that the road to our old campground had been washed away by a flash flood and several families were left stranded. My premonitions continued throughout my childhood and even became much stronger. Sometimes I knew things that I didn't want to tell my parents because I was frightened, frightened by what I knew and frightened to hear my parents' response. Once, when one of my premonitions was right on the money, my mom got real upset. She didn't understand how I could know about things before they happened. She took me to our priest and they prayed over me. They never understood, and I never stopped feeling different. And my siblings, well, let's just say that they wouldn't let me forget that I was the odd one!"

"Kady, I'd like to help you understand that your abilities are just a part of what makes you so special. The telling of the future is a gift. But let's not get confused with the real issue here. I'm attracted to you, and I want to see you again. I won't push you any further than you're willing to go. When you're ready to accept the fact that we can work together as a spiritual team, I'll be there, every step of the way, to help you face your fears. Remember though, we both made a promise to help your Aunt Willa. I think in your heart you're willing to help discover why Daniel's spirit has remained earthbound. Now we just have to convince your mind to open up to the spiritual world and let love grow within. Together we can help Daniel cross over and find everlasting peace. Will you put your trust not only in me, but in us?"

Kady paused sensing the importance of her decision. "OK. You're right; I did promise to help Aunt Willa, knowing full well I might be opening a Pandora's box, but I feel I must protect myself against emotional harm, so please don't push me, Colin. As far as our relationship is concerned, you know there's an attraction here, but I don't think I'm ready for a serious commitment. We can go forward but we're going to do this my way...slowly."

Dusk gathered along the beautiful Chicago skyline as Kady and Colin left the restaurant and made plans to spend the rest of the evening together. Taxiing back to the Hilton Tower Hotel, Colin said, "After we pick up my car, how about if I drop you off to change, run home and be back before the street lights turn on. Then we can find a place to dance the night away. Are you game?"

"Sure, but remember I'm a working girl and on the weekdays I need to be home at a reasonable hour."

"Don't worry. I'll make sure you're home in time to get plenty of beauty sleep...not that you need any."

"Flattery will get you anything!" Kady said with a chuckle.

Kady stood in front of her open closet. While trying to decide what to wear, she thought about Colin. Kady had spent most of the afternoon listening to Colin trying to persuade her to give their relationship a chance. For the time being she'd made up her mind to worry about the effects of her psychic abilities later. Maybe she wouldn't have to worry about them at all; Colin seemed genuinely concerned about helping her work through her fears.

Kady dressed in a shimmering oyster colored spaghetti-strapped dress with a matching bolero jacket that fitted snugly under her full breasts. She dressed quickly. The soft creamy material swished lightly across her legs as she ran up the stairs to answer the door. "Hi. I'm ready with minutes to spare."

"I like prompt women, especially beautiful, prompt women," Colin countered as he took in Kady's appearance. He was amazed to find she had gone from uniformed efficient business attire to a beautiful, sexy and alluring appearance in less than one hour.

"I know we had a late lunch, so I thought we'd spend the evening at Pops for Champagne," said Colin. "That way we could order a few appetizers, dance and listen to great music all night."

"That sounds wonderful. Their outdoor garden is open in the summer, and I love looking up at the open sky."

Kady and Colin danced to the spirited sounds of Buddy Bix Roe and his band. They played a joyous rendition of "It Don't Mean a Thing If It Ain't Got That Swing." When they returned to their seats, the light lake breeze cooled their heated bodies.

The spotlight shifted center stage to Sweet Dixie Parker. Dixie, a long time local favorite sang a heartfelt rendition of Bessie Smith's "Crazy Blues." Colin and Kady became lost in the shared moment of her passionate voice. They sat, hands linked together, neither wanting the moment to end. The waiter interrupted with their order and re-filled their glasses with champagne.

Colin reached for a chocolate-covered strawberry, offering it to Kady. His fingers hovered over her soft lips as they slowly opened. He ran the tip of the berry over them as they parted, teasing her with the sensuous, sweet taste. Kady's tongue darted out, licking and savoring the flavor as she sucked in the delicious appetizer. Colin lips replaced the ripe fruit as they kissed in a chocolate candied haze.

It became an exquisite game, feeding each other the delicacies while each romantic bite further enhanced their sexual appetite. While sucking and licking the sweet confection from each other's fingertips, they became lost, oblivious to the passage of time. Again and again they sampled the addictive morsels while tenderly kissing each other's lips.

Colin brought their last kiss to an end holding Kady within his arms.

"As much as I'm enjoying every delicious moment, I think we better stop before they throw us out," said Colin.

Kady leisurely caressed her tongue one last time around her lips feeling bereft over their loss, slowly regaining her composure. She looked around noticing the empty tables.

"Gosh, Colin, you're right. It looks like we're closing the place."

Kady glanced down to check her antique Gruen watch. "I didn't realize it was this late. We'd better be going…I have an early morning."

Colin took out his wallet, placed a generous tip on the table and said to the hovering waiter, "Sorry, old man; hope we didn't keep the staff up all night. I'm sure you're eager to go home."

Checking the bills in his hands, the server grinned. "Any time sir, any time. We're here till closing."

Kady and Colin rode home in silence, neither wishing to break the enchanted spell that had been cast over them.

Colin parked his car in front of Kady's apartment and walked her to the door. She hesitated as she took out her house keys.

"Colin, would you like to come in for a few minutes?

"Kady, there is nothing in the world that I would like more. But if I continue where we left off, I'm afraid you'll think I'm rushing you. I care about you, Kady. Promise you'll think about us?"

Not waiting for a reply, Colin drew Kady once more into his arms, blending their bodies, letting her feel the hardness of his arousal. Searing her with a simmering wet kiss that neither of them could forget, Colin took a deep breath and ushered Kady inside.

"I'll be in touch." Colin shut the door and left a bewildered Kady standing in the middle of her entrance way.

She stood there for a second looking into the hallway mirror. Kady was glad there was no one home to see her blush as she remembered the way she'd responded to Colin—in public no less!

Kady climbed into bed with Midnight curled into a ball at the base of her spine. Normally the tiny body's warmth lulled her to sleep. Instead, as Kady closed her eyes, sleep evaded her. She tried counting sheep, but the lyrics and melody to a song by the Four Seasons reverberated over and over, "I think I'm going out of my head. Yes, I'm getting in way over my head, over you...over youoo."

She brought her fingertips up to her swollen lips, still hot from Colin's touch, and wondered if she was ready for the next step. She questioned her sanity, amazed how easily her inhibitions vanished with his kiss. I must be going crazy, she thought. I can't possibly be thinking of taking that next step! It's too soon. I'm not ready for this. It's all happening to quickly." These were her last conscious thoughts as she tossed and turned throughout the night.

Nine

When Colin returned home later that evening, he found a note from his housekeeper Gilly telling him that the volunteers from the Lakeview Nursing Home had called to remind him about Saturday. She also mentioned an express package that had arrived that morning.

The bulky package bore a South American return address. He opened the parcel and found a large envelope and more transcribed sheets of Willa's diary encased in bubble wrap. There was also a brief note from his friend Michael Clearfield explaining how an unexpected tropical storm delayed his expedition, allowing him to send more pages. He went on to say that he found the diary fascinating and hoped the information discovered would be helpful in connecting the dots between Willa's dreams and the diary.

Excited, Colin began to read.

M'duan

November 7, 1835

As I find time to put paper to pen, I realize that I am on the final leg of my journey that began over two years ago. I have survived much and I wish you to know how it all began. I believe we were in God's plan; I believe it was our destiny.

My two brothers and I left our homeland in Ireland with an adventurous spirit and such great hope for our future. The endless months of our crossing on the ship blur into my memory but shall never be completely forgotten. We suffered great hardships and witnessed seasickness, fever and even death. Yet, we were ever hopeful that these misfortunes would someday lead us to a better life. Those of us who survived eagerly awaited our arrival in this new land filled with promise.

Upon landing in New York City, the harshness of immigrant life shattered the dreams we had held so dear. The myth that was America as the land of plenty ended as we confronted the reality. We lived in a filthy, cramped tenement that housed over twenty families. My brothers, Ian and Mikeal, worked sixteen hours a day in a textile sweatshop, barely earning enough to pay our rent. I tried to hire out to do housework for respectable families and found that jobs were sparse.

It was after our first harsh New York winter that we decided to journey westward with a group of Irish settlers also wishing to better their lives. We had heard that they were building a canal in Chicago and that those not afraid of hard work could earn a decent wage. Once again we set out with the spirit of optimism, and the desire for an improved life.

However our hopes and dreams of building a new life together here in America were forever changed the night a band of renegade Indians raided our small campsite and took me captive. I have not seen my brothers since that fateful night. I pray that they are still alive.

January 1836

So much has happened. I am no longer the wide-eyed Irish lass who left home full of fanciful notions. The hunger and poverty in this land are no different than the barren farmlands that stretched across my Irish shores. I discovered this as my captors plundered and raided wagon trains and white settlers' campsites as we journeyed toward the Land of the Five Tribes. My captors took only women as slaves to be bartered. The other people were left for dead.

After weeks of traveling in bondage, I was traded to the Waushanee tribe. Once there, my nursing skills attracted the notice of their young medicine man. He was a fair man who treated me with human kindness. He learned of our ways and to speak English, through the missionaries who traded with his tribe. His natural curiosity led him to discover the virtues of Christianity. He was fascinated by the idea of Jesus Christ as lord and savior. Though he never fully accepted our religion, he believed in the power of forgiveness. He was the son of a medicine man who possessed the knowledge of many ancient healing herbs. He also conversed with past spirits, often resorting to divination by passing his ancient healing shield over the bodies of the sick.

I saw this act of healing work time after time. Once when one of his sister's children had come down with the great black fever, he allowed me inside their tent to watch. He treated the boy with a special poultice of herbs from the bark of the mighty oak and the stems of mushrooms. Then he laid his mystic healing shield over the boy's body, saying healing words and calling out to the spirit of the great prophet Denganawodah. After placing the shield in the ground beside the sick child, he chanted all night. By morning, the fever had broken, and the boy was well on his way to recovery. When I asked Napayshni what purpose the shield held, he told me that it was his strongest medicine against the illnesses that the white man had given to his people.

After that night I was allowed to witness countless times the miracles of his healing shield. I also enlisted the help of my God and said many prayers, in case his gods were not listening. He suggested that my rosary beads were similar to his ancient healing shield and served a similar purpose. He was generous with his encouraging words and never belittled my beliefs. I began to feel alive again and welcomed the dawn of each new day. Our conversations became more intimate.

After living and working side by side for many months, we realized that we had fallen in love and could no longer hide our feelings for each other. We were discreet, although during the days that followed our declaration of love, I could feel the elders of the tribe keeping watch on our activities. I felt as though they knew our secret. I also worried about his half brother Inteus, whose eyes seemed to follow me wherever I'd go.

At night Napayshni and I would meet alone in a teepee hidden deep in the forest amongst the towering oaks. It was during this time that I once again had the dreams.

As a child in Ireland I experienced visions of things that came to pass. Sometimes joyful, sometimes tragic, but without exception, my ability to foretell the future was considered a gift by my mother and father. I confided in Napayshni a vision of horrible brutality.

An Indian warrior dressed in red and black would surprise Napayshni as he slept. I warned him that this vision could become a reality. Napayshni reassured me that he was a man of peace and that no one would wish harm to the Keeper of the Mystic Healing Shield.

I wish Napayshni had heeded my warnings. Oh, how I long for those too few moments we shared together.

Colin set down the unfinished translations. He was tired. Checking his watch, he realized it was late. A little voice in his head told him that he needed to contact Willa; she would be so excited to read the first pages of the diary. However, he was also anxious to share this with Kady. His heart won out over his head, and he decided to call her first thing in the morning.

The following morning was a busy one. Colin had to confirm his meeting at the Lakeview Nursing Home in Rogers Park, a visit he was looking forward to. He also had last-minute details to complete on his latest book. The artwork for the jacket cover needed to be finalized, and he had yet to complete his always-expanding list of credits. This was one job he really enjoyed doing, even though there were so many people to thank. He often wished he'd hired a secretary to take care of the typing and arrangement of his schedule so he could concentrate on the creative end of writing.

Then there was his work at O'Dannaher construction. Colin had been on hiatus long enough. Even though he had hired a competent staff to help him while he was off on his book tour, he knew that his grandmother relied on him to make the final decisions on all new business.

Finally, there was still the task of checking flight schedules for an upcoming metaphysical conference on the East Coast. Colin hoped to convince Kady to join him the following week and share in the experience of helping others with their psychic abilities. Work was piling up, but more than anything, Colin wanted to make time for his relationship with Kady.

Reaching Kady the next day proved to be quite a task. He knew she left for work before eight in the morning, so he tried calling her early only to be thwarted by her damn answering machine again.

He then called her office and left a detailed message with some ditsy dame that answered the phone. She asked so many questions he felt like he was filling out an employment application with the FBI.

Finally, he got her to agree to radio Kady during her lunch break and give her a message with the phone number where he could be reached. Even though his work schedule was exceptionally busy for the next few days, he was determined to spend time with Kady.

Whenever Colin had a moment to spare his thoughts were about Kady. He knew he wanted her and couldn't wait to invite her to his home. He fantasized about her lying in his bed, arms entwined, feeding their mutual hunger. Every time he remembered their date, he yearned for the time they'd share the ultimate gift of their bodies.

He knew that this kind of thinking would only get him trouble, for he had promised not to rush her. He was beginning to wonder how he could keep such a promise.

At three-thirty Colin returned to his office and checked in with his secretary. There was still no message from Kady. He knew she was stalling. He also knew the time would come when she would have to face her anxieties about her psychic abilities. He'd made a pledge to help her work through her apprehensions.

Colin wondered if Kady was dealing with the same emotions that had plagued him throughout the day. He hoped she'd recognized just how special last night had been. Not everyone was capable of such passion with just a few kisses. He wanted more, he needed more, and suspected that Kady shared that same need.

It was time to call in the reinforcements. His floral shop thought his monumental order a bit crazy, but they loved the business. Willa as always was delighted to hear from Colin.

"Willa? Hello, this is Colin."

"Hi, honey. How's your grandmother?"

"She's fine, Willa. I've got good news. I've just received some translations of your great-great-great grandmother's book. Turns out I was right; it appears to be a journal of her trip to America. I'm not sure what relevance any of this has, but it's certainly makes for fascinating reading."

"Are there any clues at all?" Willa inquired, sounding uncharacteristically weary.

"I think we'll be better served to wait before making any predictions. What I believe we need is another séance, to see if there is any connection between your reoccurring dreams and the journal."

"My dreams are coming more frequently. Do you think we're close to a discovery?" Willa asked.

"I hope so, but I really can't be sure."

"I understand," she said. "Would you be a dear and stop by the office today with what you have? I'm dying to read it."

"Of course, Willa. I'll come by during the lunch hour." Colin explained. "The journal will certainly be a help in unraveling this mystery, but I firmly believe that Kady's psychic abilities are the key."

"Colin, by now I'm sure you realize Kady's reluctance to confront her psychic powers. She's had a rough time dealing with Rose and her family. So you and I must take special care in helping her through the reawakening of her intuitive abilities. I have an idea. Let's plan a barbecue and then hold a séance afterward."

"That's a great idea, Willa. This time we'll use my place. You pick the guests and I'll do the rest."

Willa happily agreed. After checking their schedules, they realized that the earliest time their very busy lives would allow was still a few weeks away. Before hanging up Colin assured Willa that he would see her in a couple of hours with a copy of the journal in hand.

Just before noon Colin entered the offices of Widow Newton's. Her bubbly redheaded secretary Rita mentioned that Willa was anxiously awaiting his visit. Colin was shown in and was shocked to see Willa looking distraught.

It was a rare occurrence, but today Willa was showing her age. She had not been sleeping well since the night of the first séance. The after effects of her migraine medication were clearly evident. Her normally clear blue eyes were rimmed with fatigue; her ageless complexion seemed pasty.

Willa was troubled by the spiritual message that Daniel had been truly unhappy during the last years of his life. This added stress contributed to her disturbed sleep. She desperately wanted to clear Daniel's name, and, in turn, free his spirit.

"Colin, I'm so glad that you could make it today." Willa exclaimed, rising from her chair to give him a hug.

"Yes, of course, Willa. I know how important this is to you. I wish I'd had the time to get back to you sooner. As I mentioned, I've only read a few paragraphs, but, if I may, I suggest you read this at home. It will be easier to assimilate all the facts in a familiar environment."

"I feel we're getting close, so very close." Willa shifted in her chair uneasily. "Daniel came to me again last night. He must have known that I've been going through a rough time. Even though I felt he was trying to comfort me, I could sense his frustrations. All these years I never completely understood why Daniel's spirit seemed so restless and tormented. When he first came to me I couldn't tell anyone, not even Edna, for I felt I must be going crazy. I could not stop grieving, knowing that death had robbed me of my one true love. It wasn't till years later that I announced to the family that I had been visited by my beloved. My brothers, sisters and most of my friends attributed my eccentricities to grief. But I knew Daniel's visitations were real. And now, my dear friend, you've given me proof positive that a world does exist beyond the grave."

"Thank you, Willa, for the vote of confidence, but I want you to be sure that this is not too much for you to handle emotionally."

"No, I'll be fine. I'll admit that I was nervous during our first experience, but I was relieved that it was you who helped me bridge the physical with the spiritual world. I know that we are so close to allowing Daniel to find eternal peace. I'm not going to waste the precious time I have left on earth regretting that I didn't help. The way you use your gift, sharing it so freely, is nothing short of miraculous."

Tears welled in her eyes as Willa grabbed a tissue from the box on her desk.

"I promise you we won't stop until Daniel's spirit has been freed," Colin said, placing his arm around Willa to comfort her.

Hearing the buzz, Willa dried her eyes as she reached for the intercom. "Rita?"

"Yes, Willa. Benny has just arrived with lunch, and it smells delicious. I'll send him right in."

Colin checked his watch as Benny brought in two Italian beef sandwiches from Widow Newton's. "Willa, I wish I could stay, but I'm afraid I have another appointment I really can't miss. O'Dannaher construction calls, and I must answer."

"Of course, of course," Willa responded. "I'll call you after I've read the journal, and we'll firm up our plans."

Unable to resist the temptation, Willa opened the package and began to read as Colin walked out of the room.

Kady awakened abruptly from a restless night. She'd lost track of the time and was running late. There had not been time for their usual leisurely breakfast and Rose had been pouting.

After a rushed morning, the bus full of inquisitive passengers kept Kady and Rose completely occupied. Just before noon their sister Patti radioed something about a message from Colin. Kady could barely hear what Patti had said.

Kady's day continued spiraling downward as her emotions spun out of control. One minute she was fantasizing about Colin and the way he made her feel, and the next she was worrying about where it was all leading. Yes I think I'm going out of my head…yes I…damn that song, she thought.

Kady was very confused, never having felt such a powerful sexual attraction. Even her experiences with Brick had not prepared her for such overwhelming emotional desire. Given the heightened state of her feelings, Kady also feared another premonition.

Kady barely touched her lunch. During the entire meal Rose bombarded her with personal questions about her date.

Never content with just the previews, Rose wanted the whole damn movie. She demanded details. Kady put her off by pleading a nagging headache, which happened to be the truth. All this soul searching had given her an ache that started in the back of her neck and traveled down to the tips of her toes. After putting something in her stomach, Kady immediately popped an extra strength Excedrin.

Kady left the cafeteria having artfully dodged the majority of her sister's inquisition and was relieved to get back to driving her bus.

Things were relatively calm for a while. Then all of a sudden she saw Mr. Tonto sitting at the back of the bus. Was he truly a spiritual guide sent to help her, or was he just a figment of her overactive imagination?

Oh my God. Please, not again, she thought.

Kady spent the remainder of the afternoon hoping that someone else would notice him. She periodically checked her rear-view mirror, and sure enough, as mysteriously as he appeared, he vanished.

On the drive home she was relieved to let Rose do all the talking. Thankfully, she was caught up in describing the handsome Chicago Mercantile trader who had given her a few good stock tips! Kady was happy to sit back in the passenger seat and tune Rose out!

"Knock, knock. Can I come in?" Rose said as she let herself into their one and only bathroom. Good thing that lock never worked, she thought.

Kady had been avoiding her all day, hoping to steer clear of any conversation whatsoever concerning the new man in her life. Rose sat down on the toilet lid and fanned the steam filling the small room away from her face.

"Oh, it's a lovely temperature in here, Kady. What are you using to keep the tsetse flies away?"

Getting no reaction, Rose tried again. "Isn't it humid enough outside, or were you planning on growing fern plants in here?" Once more, Rose received no immediate response from her droopy sister.

Kady sat up in the bathtub and took a sip of her glass of Chardonnay and popped a chocolate into her mouth, hoping that Rose would get bored by the silence and go away. She was tired and wanted to wind down from a very long, stressful day.

"Earth to Kady, is anyone home? I'm not going to disappear, so you might as well talk!" Rose quipped as she put her feet up on the ledge of their claw footed tub. "You know, Kady Marie, you're not fooling me with this silent treatment. Besides, you have all the signs—"

Kady's head snapped to attention as she sent her sister a sizzling look and broke her silence.

"—Signs, what signs?

"Oh you know. You look like you're suffering from the S. D. syndrome."

Kady raised an inquisitive eyebrow and said, "OK, I'll bite. What is the S. D. syndrome?"

"You, my moody sister, are suffering from Sexual Deprivation."

With that, Kady threw a wet sponge in the direction of her sister's head.

Slowly Rose wiped the excess moisture from her face. Turning her back on Kady, she grabbed the wet hand towel, swiftly wrapping a small bar of face soap within its folds. Then, with deliberate ease, Rose raised her left arm and threw a perfect pitch that would have made Chicago White Sox fans go wild. It struck the water like a mini cannonball, sending a spray of water all over Kady's hair and face.

Stunned, Kady raised her hands in surrender. "You win, you've got my attention. Now what?" she said with an exaggerated sigh.

"Well, Ms. Drama Queen, why the long puss all day? What did you and that gorgeous hunk of a guy do after you left work yesterday…and why on earth are you sitting in this bathroom brooding, when you could be out with him on a hot date? What's up?"

Kady turned to face her sister, "How do you know he wants to go out with me again?"

"You need to erase any message not for public consumption from our answering machine, kiddo," Rose countered.

"Speaking of answering, don't you think you better see who's calling?" Kady asked as the phone began to ring.

"Don't think this conversation is over!" Rose yelled as she raced to the telephone.

Kady waited, hoping the call would be for her sister. The water in the tub had cooled. She reached across and began to refill the tub with the hottest water she could tolerate. Grabbing a box of her favorite peach fragranced sea salt, she poured the aromatic brew into the swirling waters. That's better, she thought, sliding lower into the tub. I'll become a peach stew.

With a loud sigh, she lay back against the cool porcelain of the high back, Victorian tub and enjoyed the peace and quiet. Her eyes slowly closed as the rhythmic dripping of the faucet and the warm steam lulled her to sleep. She could feel her tired body drifting, floating through clouds, blending with the two worlds. She saw herself sitting in the tree that hung over the lake at her parents' cottage. Watching, she listened to the childish voices below. She recognized the laughter of her brother Seth and Colin.

Suddenly there was a loud crack, and her movement was paralyzed. Then she felt freezing temperatures as her body spiraled into downward turbulence. Her face became wet with tears. She came up for air, only to tumble further into the dark recesses of her mind.

"Air," she screamed. "Please, I need air!"

All at once she was pulled upward toward the light. Reaching out she grabbed onto soft, wet, fringed buckskin. She looked up into the eyes of her Mr. Tonto as he held her in his secure hands.

Her rescuer's thoughts penetrated her mind: "The telling of the future is a gift; fear not. Put your trust in the flame of love and it shall not burn out. Becoming one with your beloved allows the center of your love to expand. Share with him the inner light of your body and soul. Be true to your heart, life is precious and can be so very short."

His hands then lifted and carried her. Her body was protected, shielded within their grasp. Kady turned her head to pull away, but he reassured her: "Do not be afraid. I am here to protect you and shield you from all harm." The man's words slowly dissolved, transforming into the tender sounds of a familiar voice.

Drifting further, she was now in Colin's arms. His gentle lips began caressing her body, drowning her in their liquid warmth. The surge of erotic tension tightened in her loins as his lips sought to give her sexual release. "Oh, Colin," Kady said, slowly coming out of her dream-like trance.

Kady opened her eyes. Disappointment engulfed her as Kady realized that she was alone.

"Kady, Kady. Did you hear me?" Rose yelled. "Hey sis, you better hurry and get out of that tub. You snooze, you lose. Guess who's going to have company in less than one hour?"

As her head began to clear, Kady moaned, "Don't tell me you're having a party?"

Rose peeked around the corner and poked her head into the doorway. "No, silly. You are. That was Colin on the phone. If you were truly psychic you would have known that he's coming over tonight. Now, instead of sitting there with your mouth open, don't you think you better get dressed? Come to think of it, stay in your birthday suit, and we'll have a birthday party."

"Rose, what are you talking about? I didn't invite anyone over. Hand me a towel, please," Kady said, dragging herself out of the tub.

Rose opened the linen closet and threw out a towel. "Oh, did I forget to mention that I invited Colin over for you?"

"You what? Whoaaa!" Kady yelled, slipping on the wet tub. "Rose, someday I'll get you for this!" She jumped out of the water, knowing there wasn't any time to waste on retaliation.

As she hurried from the bathroom, her mind kept replaying the words in the dream: "The telling of the future is a gift." Where had she heard those words before?

Kady wrapped the towel around her body, ran down the stairs to her bedroom, and rummaged through her closet for something to wear. Nothing seemed right. Exasperated, she knew that time was running out. She sat down for a moment on her bed.

"Ouch," Kady exclaimed jumping up as something sharp poked at her bottom. She turned her head, looking down at the prickly mattress, and found Rose's latest shop-till-you-drop purchase: a sleeveless powder blue jumpsuit, with a daringly low sweetheart shaped neckline, just the thing for an intimate evening at home. Pinned on to the bodice was a note. "I'll be gone for hours. Feel free to do everything I'd do!"

Colin couldn't believe his luck! He had finally gotten hold of Kady. Well, not exactly Kady, but Rose, who informed him that Kady would be home alone all evening and was dying for some company.

Colin hoped that Kady would be equally as excited in sharing the revelations he'd discovered in Willa's journal. He'd been too tired to read the entire diary last night, and hadn't had much time that morning, what with a crisis at O'Dannaher's new building site. He'd been literally knee deep in mud most of the day.

While Colin had been working with his grandmother's company and trying to finish his second book, there wasn't much time for serious relationships. However, Colin was now relatively free of his book obligations until it hit the shelves. He vowed to devote himself to Kady and what he hoped would be a serious romance.

Kady greeted Colin at the door looking lovelier than he remembered. The slight flush of her cheeks made him wonder if she was just as anxious as he was to spend the evening together. He certainly hoped so.

"Wow, Kady, you look great." Colin held up a brightly covered square box and a bottle of Merlot. "I hope you like wine with dessert."

"Fannie May chocolate covered turtles, my favorite. Thank you so much. Come on in and have a seat while I put this on ice. Can I get you something to drink while I refrigerate this, or do you prefer your wine at room temperature?"

"Room temperature is fine with me. Here, let me help you," Colin said as he followed her into the kitchen.

Conscious of his nearness in her tiny kitchen, Kady became embarrassingly aware of just how much her outfit revealed. Hoping her nervousness did not show, she quickly grabbed two delicately stemmed wine glasses.

"I'll open that if you direct me to your cork screw," Colin said.

"It's in the second drawer on the right. Would you care for a snack with your wine or will the chocolates do?"

"A turtle will be great," Colin said.

Carrying their drinks into the living room, Colin chose to sit on the sofa next to Kady. He placed the bottle of wine and napkins on the table. Their knees met as he reached over to pick up the manuscript. The touch sent a quick electric shock through both their bodies, making them both aware of the intimate moment.

"I did a quick read-through last night and finished the remaining pages just before I left."

As she fingered the sheets, she appeared more than a little apprehensive.

"Kady, are you OK? Have you had a premonition? We don't have to do this tonight. I was just anxious to share it with you! But we can wait, if you like, until we're with your Aunt Willa. Will that make you more comfortable?"

"No, it's all right, Colin. Lately there have been a few incidents that have made me a bit apprehensive.

"Incidents? What exactly do you mean?" Colin questioned.

"Now promise not to laugh, because what I'm about to tell you may sound crazy. At least four times in the past few weeks I've been visited by what appears to be a living, breathing native American, circa nineteenth century. He never speaks, although most recently he came to me in a dream and conveyed his thoughts telepathically. All I know is I don't like it, and I wish he'd leave me alone."

"Wow, I can hardly believe what you just said. Kady, we are definitely onto something, and remember I won't let anything hurt you. You must trust me. Now please, read this," said Colin, handing the book to Kady.

Suddenly she recalled the words in her dream, "The telling of the future is a gift, fear not. Put your trust in the flame of love and it shall not burn out." Slowly Kady opened the book and became immersed in the story.

Minutes later, Kady set the pages down and exclaimed. "Colin, I didn't realize that this journal was about my great-great-great-great grandmother's life. It's so personal. I feel that we're prying. Do you think it's all right?"

"Kady, I know this is unfamiliar territory for you, but many times I have been asked to reveal messages from the past. Sometimes those who grieve the hardest can't let go of the littlest item in their life. That's when they come to me for help. They need to resolve all the issues that they haven't reconciled with their loved ones who've passed over. I think Daniel and Willa both had some unresolved issues, and for some reason need our assistance."

"You're right, Colin. I know my aunt hasn't ever gotten beyond the grief of Uncle Daniel's death. Colin leaned over and placed his hand on Kady's shoulder. "Keep reading. This next section should knock your socks off!"

February 1836

The voyage home has been wrought with turbulent seas, and I have been sick for the last few weeks. I've made many friends during this trying time and I shall miss them, but I long for this journey to be over. I must continue and not veer from the telling of my story.

I was captured along with seven other white women. We became friends and united through our trials. We were all terrified of the Indians and feared being separated. Soon after our enslavement, I and one other white woman were traded to the Waushanee tribe. I do not know what happened to the others, but I pray they are still alive.

I learned that my new companion was an Italian immigrant named Marietta Asunda Delore who had been abducted while gathering wild strawberries not far from her home. Her husband Joseph had warned her of the danger of wandering unprotected outside the walls of Fort Dearborn.

Marietta was in the early stages of her first pregnancy, and was afraid for her unborn child's life. She spoke broken English, so it was often difficult to understand her. Many times she would rant and scream at our captors, condemning them to hell for leading her to this awful fate. As her condition became more obvious, the natives feared a reprisal from their gods. The child was not of their tribe and it was considered bad luck to bring the pregnant woman into their village.

The Waushanees could not understand Marieeta's violent anger. I expect they had no experience with white women who did not fear them. They finally decided she was possessed by evil spirits. They avoided her completely, making it easier for Napayshni and me to help her through this difficult time.

She despaired that she would never see her beloved husband again. Napayshni tried his best to reassure Marietta that when the spring rains ceased, he would return her to her family before the child was born. He had not been involved in the raids and frowned upon the idea of keeping us captive. We both prayed for a time of peace, when men of all colors could live together and equally share the fruits of this vast land. My Ireland seemed but a small speck of dirt next to this place called America.

It was only after Napayshni and I fell in love that I came to accept my captivity. I began to believe that it had been God's plan to unite us, so that someday our bond could be a shining example of the healing power of love. During our stolen nights together, we talked of uniting our people. In our ignorance we believed that love could conquer all.

I felt safe within my lover's arms, but when he was not by my side, I feared for my life.

His half-brother Inteus constantly followed me wherever I went. He spat out my name, "Larken O'Hare," telling me that I should have been named "Vulture" after the ruthless bird, who, like the white man, had preyed on his people. He claimed that the white devils had stolen their land and destroyed the Indian's way of life.

Inteus was consumed with jealousy for his half brother Napayshni, who was a direct descendant of the great seer Denganawodah and rightful heir to the Mystic Healing Shield. Inteus coveted not only the shield, but Napayshni's place within the tribe.

After Napayshni's mother died, his father Chief Ohitekah took Sapata as his second wife. Inteus was born into a family where Napayshni's birthright had already been established. Inteus never accepted his lesser standing within the tribe. He cursed me and my beloved, spreading evil in our path.

I prayed every night that through the power of the Holy Spirit, our love for each other would someday be accepted by the elders of the tribe. I prayed that we would be able to live out our lives in peace, healing the sick in the praise and honor of God's holy name. I prayed that God's will would be done and that the people of the tribe would not listen to Inteus' vile words. Why, I asked God, must there be so much hatred?

I must close now for I am feeling very sleepy. For nearly a month I have had difficulty in sleeping and have experienced a strange sickness that keeps my stomach in a constant state of upheaval."

"Oh my God!" Kady exclaimed. She glanced around the room then back to the journal and finally to Colin's sympathetic eyes. "Colin, do you think…is it possible…no, it can't be. It just can't be. In a million years I would never have suspected that my family could have ever had any connection with native Americans."

"It's hard to imagine that it's coincidence, Kady. I'm almost certain there's a correlation." Colin said as he sipped his wine.

"You mean you think there's a correlation between Napayshni and my apparition?" Kady asked.

"If there isn't, it would be an unbelievable coincidence."

Kady picked up the journal and held it to her heart. "That poor woman. What she must have endured. This is all so very weird. I don't like it. I feel like something strange has been happening to me and maybe just maybe the missing link is my great-great-great-great grandmother and this Napayshni."

"Look, honey, we can surmise all night, but there is no sense in getting upset about all this until we've received a complete translation."

"Think about it, Colin. If this is all true, what unspeakable atrocities she must have faced," Kady said, pointing to the pages of the journal. "Life in those days was so very hard on women. It's a wonder she survived, and then to have found love... I wonder why my grandmother Katherine never told us about any of this."

"Remember, Kady, this was all written in Gaelic."

"Did my aunt give any indication that she knew what was in the journal?"

"No. I was with her this afternoon, and I'm positive she knows nothing about this."

"Colin, what does this title mean, M'duan?'" Kady asked.

"It means 'my song,' Kady."

"My song..." Kady whispered wistfully. "I'll bet she was like me, a hopeless romantic. Just the fact that an native American healer and an Irish lass met and were able to heal themselves as well as others...I think it's all pretty amazing that these two people who came from such vastly different cultures were able to fall in love. Don't you?"

Colin nodded.

"If it weren't for jealousy and superstitions, theirs would have been a wonderful love story. Wait till I tell Rose. My family has always been known for producing strong women."

"Kady, you did pick up on the fact that your great-great-great-great-grandmother was predisposed to having premonitions, didn't you? It all sounds awfully familiar if you ask me."

"I suppose," Kady hesitantly admitted.

"It also didn't seem like she feared her special powers, but rather believed they were a gift. She even felt blessed that they were able to do so much good."

"Yes, OK. So what's your point, Colin?" Kady asked, suddenly feeling pressured.

Colin loved to get a rise out of Kady. When she was fervent about a subject her eyes glowed with intense passion and her cheeks flushed, becoming a lovely shade of pink.

"Nothing really, I was just trying to help you feel comfortable with your abilities. I do think however that the story is a perfect example of how two people who love each other can overcome all adversities. Seems to me our problems are small compared to theirs, don't you think?"

"What I think is that they were both two very special people who braved an entire culture to love and be loved. I wonder if anything like that exists today," Kady said with a sigh.

"I'd like to think it does. I believe in love everlasting. The woman I choose to spend the rest of my life with will be the only one I will love till death do us part. I also know that my parents and grandparents and your parents and Aunt Willa and Daniel believed in that kind of love. Do you think you'll ever be capable of that sort of commitment?"

"Absolutely. That's the kind of love I was brought up to believe in," said Kady as a sad smile washed over her face. "But it's hard in today's world of expendable this and expendable that not to worry about your love being disposable. I guess I'm old fashioned, but I believe in the fantasy that a white knight will come charging into my life and love me, and only me, forever. It's a bit too much for most men to handle."

Colin smiled. "Not for me. You apparently have never seen the suit of armor I store in the trunk of my car for just such an occasion."

Handing Kady her glass, he picked up the bottle of wine and poured the deep crimson liquid. Colin looked into her lovely eyes and whispered, "Let's drink a toast to all young lovers and to the notion of happily ever after."

"What a lovely idea, Colin," Kady said, slowly raising her glass to her lips, her eyes never leaving Colin's face.

"Oh my goodness," Kady said with an uncomfortable laugh, spilling half her glass of wine on the bodice of her jumpsuit.

"Here, let me," Colin said as he grabbed a napkin from the coffee table and proceeded to help. Dabbing at the stain, Colin accidentally brushed up against Kady's breasts and her nipples immediately hardened, their protruding pout visible through the wet silky material.

Embarrassed, Kady looked down. "Oh, I'm so clumsy! Excuse me just a moment while I change out of these wet clothes."

As Kady jumped up from the sofa, she realized that her wine-stained outfit revealed much more that just a little extra cleavage.

"If you need help with any unbuttoning or unfastening, I'm your man," Colin yelled after Kady's retreating figure. Damn, he thought. Aren't we the subtle one? Open mouth and insert foot.

Kady hurried down to her bedroom, turned on the cold water and threw her stained jumpsuit into the tub. She took out the first thing she could get her hands on from her walk-in closet.

What an awkward situation, thought Kady as she unhooked the front clasp of her lacy blue bra and threw it on the bed. She pulled on her old denim cutoff shorts and slipped them over her matching blue lace thong panties. This is what I should have put on in the first place, she thought. Who was I trying to impress, and how am I going to go back upstairs and act as if nothing happened?

Kady's ranting continued as she pulled a white t-shirt over her head, forsaking her bra altogether. She'd wasted as much time as she could in front of the mirror. She knew it was now time to face Colin, but oh, how she dreaded it! She was mortified by her body's immediate response to his touch. After all, Colin was just trying to be helpful…wasn't he?

Taking a deep breath, Kady closed her eyes for a second, threw her head back and prepared to face her fate.

"Sorry it took so long, but I wanted to make sure I got the stain out. Do you know how difficult a red wine spot is to remove? I put on the first old thing I could find," Kady babbled, feeling self-conscious.

"You look beautiful in anything you wear," Colin said, feeling equally awkward about the sexual comment he had made. He tried with all his might not to stare at her luscious breasts as they strained against her white tee shirt. "Maybe I'd better go," Colin said as he gathered up the journal and headed toward the door.

He opened the door and looked out on to the slick wet pavement as the rain came pouring in. Quickly shutting it, Colin knew he had to make amends before he left. He turned around and looked up into the depths of Kady's beautiful, uncertain, blue eyes.

"Look, I'm sorry about my comment. It was uncalled for. I only came over tonight so we could spend some time together. I don't want you to think I'm the kinda guy who's always on the make. I swear, I didn't mean to make you uncomfortable," Colin said earnestly.

He reached for the doorknob and turned it one last time. "I'll call you tomorrow."

The sincerity of his voice and the undisguised forthrightness of his words reflected in the depths of his emerald eyes. Could she believe him? Was this the man she'd dreamed about? After all, she had waited and guarded her greatest gift for so long that she wanted the memories of her first time to be special.

Listening to the call of her heart, Kady reached up, placed her arms around his neck and kissed him for all she was worth. It was a very long time before either of them showed signs of life. The rain and thunder of the dark summer night pounded. Kady and Colin were oblivious to all sounds, hearing only the beating of their own hearts.

"I'd like you to stay," Kady whispered. That was all Colin needed to hear to spur him into action. Uniting them again with a searing kiss, he scooped Kady into his arms and carried her over to the sofa, never allowing either of them to come up for air.

"Will your sister be home soon?" Colin whispered, his breath sending shivers up and down her spine. "Can we find somewhere more private?"

Kady was hesitant in her response. Making love on the living room sofa was not where she'd dreamed it would happened. "Let's go downstairs to my bedroom. It's more comfortable."

Colin lifted her into his arms as prickles of anticipated pleasure made him hurry.

"Colin, I'm too heavy." Kady was immediately silenced by a searing kiss. He carried her down the stairs and into her bedroom. Colin placed her gently down upon the bed and joined her in the rhythm of their dizzying dance of mutual desire.

In the dark, with only the glow of moonlight, he reached under the thin white material of her t-shirt, cupping her ample breasts and gently swept his palms and fingertips around them.

He had wanted to touch her, feel her and devour her from the moment they first met. She was so shy, so unsure of herself, and so beautiful.

His hands continued their search, sending waves of pleasure and currents of desire through every pore of their heated loins. As their ecstasy increased, Colin tenderly brushed the ends of Kady's nipples with his thumb, gently touching their tender tips. Kady moaned as his lips took the swelling areola into his mouth.

He licked, he pulled, he sucked, he teased seemingly unaware of the electric effect he was having on Kady. Without missing a beat, he removed their clothing and ran his fingers lovingly through her wild auburn curls.

Although she was still a virgin, Kady had experienced her share of sexual encounters. None of them could compare to this. The feeling of total loss of control would have normally frightened her, but somehow tonight with Colin, it did not.

He suddenly stopped, raised himself up on his elbows and brought his lips within inches of hers. Kady, lost in reverie, slowly opened her eyes.

"Honey, if we don't stop soon, this may take us further than you're willing to go."

Colin's concern and thoughtfulness convinced her that he truly cared about her feelings. At that moment she was certain he was the man she could trust. Kady gazed into the undisguised sincerity of his eyes, knowing that this was unfamiliar territory for her, yet feeling that somehow, it was right. Breathless with the enormity of her decision, Kady answered, "Don't worry. It's all right."

He smiled and gently ran his hot moist tongue across her lips. Kiss upon kiss upon kiss, ever harder, ever deeper, returned them to the heights of passion.

From the moisture of her mouth he lubricated his fingers and placed them upon the sensitive head of her clitoris. Colin stroked, massaged and teased, caressing up and down its shaft, increasing Kady's pleasure, as he prepared her for his entry.

Once again he took her breast into his mouth, flicking his tongue over and over the gleaming, hardened nipple.

Kady softly moaned, "Oh God," letting herself go.

Kady gave in to all the wonderful sensations, no longer feeling like she was the one who had to please. She was being pleasured in the time-honored manner that began with Adam and Eve. Kady felt cherished, beautiful and loved.

I love him, Kady thought, closing her eyes and feeling safe and warm. My God, I love him.

Colin continued to tantalize, arouse and stimulate until he felt her moist and ready. Taking his fingers out, he searched for protection. Without his hand inside her she felt empty and ached with a hunger to be filled again.

"Are you sure, Kady?" Colin questioned, giving her one last time to change her mind.

"Yes, oh yes, Colin. I'm sure."

He couldn't believe the raw emotion of passion reflected in Kady's eyes. He inhaled her womanly scent and was captivated once again by the myriad of textures and tastes that were uniquely hers. Colin waited for Kady to take the next step.

Kady answered, gathering him into her arms and taking him inside her world. As their bodies joined, her pain blurred with the sensuality of the moment.

Colin allowed her body to adjust to his sizable proportions with each rhythmic thrust. He moved patiently in and out, each time returning to deepen their desire as they flew across a landscape of love.

Pleasuring them both, he continued caressing each throbbing pressure point. The deeper he drove, the more lovingly he bound them as they soared toward the sky. Just when she was positive they could go no higher, his hands lifted her hips and they reached unimaginable heights.

Kady was delirious with pleasure, filled with his thick erection, and Colin was ready to burst. He spurted his liquid warmth into her as together they landed with an explosion somewhere between the clouds and the heavens above.

"Oh, Colin," she sighed as they completely surrendered to mutual bliss.

Slowly they came down from their wave of pleasure, awakening to the loud sound of a door slamming.

"Kady? Kady, are you home? You'll never guess what I dragged in?" Rose yelled. Ugh! I never met an animal I could like, she thought as she released a mewing, soggy Midnight.

Awkward in the aftermath of their passion, both Kady and Colin scrambled into their clothes as a wet cat bound into the bedroom.

Oh my God. I've never handled a morning-after conversation, thought Kady. How the heck am I gonna handle a five-seconds-after? Kady threw on her shorts, glanced back at the harried figure of Colin hopping on one foot trying to get into his jeans and raced up the stairs.

She could hear Colin following right behind her and prayed he was fully dressed.

TEN

*A*voiding one's sister when you worked and lived with her was difficult at best, but avoiding one's weepy, confused, guilt-ridden sister was next to impossible. After all, it had happened over a week ago. Still Rose had not talked with Kady about the night she had unexpectedly come home to discover Colin O'Dannaher dashing up the bedroom stairs. Rose had planned to stay out later that night, but the torrential rain had kept her from driving to her destination.

Rose tred lightly, for she knew the importance Kady had placed on her virginity. Never before had her sister let her guard down long enough to allow a man into her bedroom.

Kady was in love. Rose recognized the signs; after all, she'd been bitten by the bug once herself. But Kady had never truly been in love. Rose knew her sister had come close to it a few years before with that immature testosterone disaster, Brick, but this was different. Rose knew that Kady had to work this out for herself before she would be ready for some sisterly advice.

Every morning Rose made sure to take her time by dawdling, making the delay just long enough so that they had to eat breakfast on the run. There was little or no time for chit chat, let alone a serious discussion.

Still Kady's loud, drawn-out, sorrowful sighs managed to chip away at Rose's soul. She loved her sister, but Rose knew that Kady had to fight her own demons before she could reconcile what was in her heart.

To keep her sister extra busy throughout the business day, Rose always made sure that the most inquisitive passengers engaged Kady in lengthy conversations. That way the sisters had little time to talk to each other. It took a little ingenuity on Rose's part, but with her sister's vast knowledge of history, the customers were always enthralled listening to

Kady lecture about Chicago. It was also very good for customer relations because Kady was able to reveal information that could never be found in the simple guide books and pamphlets found in the local magazine stands or book stores.

Rose also had to invent ways to avoid her sister during their lunch break. Three times that week Rose planned appointments on Monday, Tuesday and Wednesday with her doctor, dentist and hair stylist. She informed Kady that all were necessary because she would soon be starting night classes at Northwestern. After all, this was the only week open in her very busy schedule.

On Thursday Rose just happened to have a reunion luncheon with the girls from her old sorority, Phi Kappa Phi.

Friday was the hardest day to pretend to be busy for lunch because Rose had run out of excuses.

Quite by accident, their brother Seth came to the rescue when he invited all three Dailey sisters to lunch to celebrate the Dailey City Tours' very successful summer. With Patti there to carry on the conversation, neither the twins nor Seth could get a word in edgewise.

By Friday night Rose knew that Kady was weakening and would soon be ready for a heart-to-heart chat.

Kady was behaving badly and she knew it. She had avoided Colin's phone calls all week and was beginning to think she'd made a terrible mistake. Giving in to her sexual urges was something that was completely new to her. Kady alternated between feeling euphoric and guilty.

On one hand it was obvious why Kady had given in. Colin had been an adolescent fantasy of hers, and damn it, he had to go and turn out to be just as wonderful in reality. But there was no doubt she was going through "a little period of adjustment."

The way their love making ended was just so damned awkward. She was truly embarrassed to face Colin.

144

For the first few days after their encounter, Kady's emotions were more volatile than Saddam Hussein on steroids. Fortunately, by the end of the week, she began to settle down.

Bright and early Saturday morning, Rose woke, determined to broach the subject she had so cleverly avoided. Unfortunately, it was catch-up day, the only time both girls had to do all the things they had put off during the week. The housework, grocery shopping and bill paying had yet to be done.

This was Kady's week to clean the apartment and Rose's turn to buy and cook the food. It was not something Rose liked to do. Kady, the chef in the family, enjoyed every moment she spent in the kitchen. Rose hated standing over a hot stove and would just as soon get by on salads, yogurt and carry-out.

Saturday night was usually Rose's date night with Kevin, but she had decided to cancel their standing engagement. Rose had a plan for the evening that was sure to soften Kady up. Kevin was understanding and wished her luck.

Rose knew that Kady couldn't resist a full frontal food attack. So Rose armed herself at the local grocery store with all the trimmings for a very fattening, greasy evening. And to sweeten the pot, she grabbed a bottle of very dry champagne to complement Kady's favorite dessert.

Juggling two overflowing bags and a set of house keys, Rose pushed her way through the front door. "I'm home, Kady. Kady, are you here?"

Silence was her only answer as she made her way toward the kitchen table, plunking down her groceries. Rose glanced around at the spotless room, and knew that Kady must have finished her chores early. She spotted a note taped to the half empty bowl of Hershey Chocolate Kisses: "Forgot. Promised to visit my Little Grandmas at the nursing home. Be back before dinner."

Great timing, thought Rose, as she planned a girl's night at home.

ELEVEN

$\mathcal{L}$akeview Nursing Home was located on the east side of Sheridan Road facing Lake Michigan. Its majestic view and palatial grounds had been donated by the late Hortense S. Broadsworth, wife of philanthropist and famous Michigan Avenue heart surgeon Dr. Wallace Abbot Broadsworth who had died after a prolonged illness. Hortense had taken on the role of nurse and caretaker during his final months. After his death she immersed herself in doing charitable work for the poor and needy. She soon realized that many of the elderly citizens of Chicago could not afford a doctor or a decent place to live. They were penniless, and the families that they had devoted their lives to no longer wanted them when they could not contribute a steady income.

Realizing something must be done, Hortense decided to put her money and energy into building a nursing home. People from all walks of life were welcomed. Those who had fallen on hard times were able to live out the later years of their lives in its gracious atmosphere.

The only prerequisite for residency was to have succumbed to a poverty income. Hortense established several trust funds in the spring of 1951 that would provide most of the money needed to keep the home solvent. She solicited volunteers in and around the city to give freely of their time and help make Lakeview one of the most sought after nursing homes in the Chicago land area. She created incentives in the form of scholarships for young doctors who would provide *pro bono* services at the nursing home. Many paid back her generosity by continuing to help at the home long after they had met the terms of their scholarship agreement. Hortense continued to endow the facility with money throughout her entire life, leaving the bulk of her estate to the foundation.

The Dailey family not only volunteered their time at Lakeview, but also participated in many of their charitable events. Cousin Rita's husband Matt, a surgeon and general practitioner, proffered his services religiously every Saturday and expected the rest of the family to follow suit.

Kady loved going to the nursing home and had become a surrogate granddaughter to many of the patients at the center. Since her night with Colin, she had been so preoccupied with her own emotions that she'd nearly forgotten she had scheduled a visit. Only a phone call from Rita asking to bum a ride reminded Kady of her commitment.

Kady pulled up to the curb and honked three times. Rita finally came out, waved goodbye to the baby-sitter and her two-year-old twins and jumped in the car.

"Gosh, I'm sure glad I reached you before you left," said Rita. "My damn car is in the shop a?gain. Luckily, Matt mentioned that this was your week to visit the home. I hope I didn't take you too much out of your way."

"Hey, no problem. You're my favorite cousin, and I like having company while driving. I always try to visit Lakeview on the last Saturday of every month. It's a lot easier for my Little Grandmas to remember me. If I set a time and date, they can mark it on their calendars. You know, they don't get callers on a regular basis and they look forward to our visits. I'm so glad that you phoned. This was such a busy week that I'd almost forgotten, and I would have hated to disappoint them. They're so lonely, and they appreciate every minute we spend with them."

Rita's nose began to twitch and sniff, and she looked around the car for the source of the pungent odor. "What have you got in the back seat, Kady? This car smells like a funeral parlor. What did you do, buy out the entire florist?"

Grimacing at Rita's poor choice of words, Kady responded quickly. "I thought my Little Grandmas would appreciate all the lovely colors to brighten up their rooms. By the way, how are my favorite little guys?"

Rita looked up, rolled her eyes and let out an exasperated sigh. "You know what they say. Double your pleasure, double your fun, and double the work."

Kady and her cousin Rita spent most of their ride laughing as Rita described her boys' latest antics. Kady recalled similar mischievous twin moments, assuring Rita that she would indeed survive their terrible twos and live to tell about it!

Kady let Rita out at the front entrance after passing the sign indicating the parking lot was full. As she toured the block for a second time, she got lucky and found parking as a gentleman pulled out right in front of the visitor's entrance.

Kady gathered the boxes of chocolates and as many of the five dozen flowers that she could carry. Kady raced into the building, taking the elevator up to the third floor.

The corridors were clean and brightly lit with a hint of antiseptic in the air. Kady knocked at Room 401, aware that privacy was a valued commodity in shared living.

A slight woman in a navy blue polka-dot dress sat in a wheelchair near the window. "Come in. Oh, my dear, I'm so glad to see you," she said.

"Hi, Little Grandma B. How are you this fine afternoon?"

"I'm fine, dear, and happy you've come. Now put down all those things that are hiding your beautiful face and come give me a kiss," Little Grandma B demanded with a smile.

"Just as bossy as ever, I see," Kady said, placing her bounty on the bed. Kady leaned over the powdery, lined face, inhaling her Lily of the Valley cologne. She reached back and placed a large box in Grandma B's frail, veined hands.

Like a child at Christmas, Little Grandma Barkus shook the box, brought it up to her nose, sniffed and laughed with innocent delight.

"Kady, are you trying to fatten me up so I won't fit into my chair? Really, child, you are too good to me. I can't wait to share this with the rest of the girls.

"Speaking of girls, where is everyone?" Kady asked, glancing around the empty room.

"Oh, we're having a guest speaker today, and I told them to go ahead."

Each room housed three occupants who shared the facilities. Some of the women were more mobile and needed the occasional helping hand. Others like Little Grandma B needed an aide to get around. Although Mrs. Maybelle Barkus was one of the oldest residents in the nursing home, her happy-go-lucky nature gave her a youthful air. She was one of Kady's favorite surrogate grandmothers.

"You're such a lovely young woman, Kady. I don't know why some smart young man hasn't snatched you up." Glancing over at her bed, she exclaimed, "Oh my, aren't these flowers beautiful? Are you holding out on me, Kady? Is there a special young man in your life?"

"Let me put these in water and we'll be off," Kady said, going into the bathroom and finding a large vase under the sink.

"That looks beautiful, Kady. All those colors make this drab room look quite cheery. Now tell me again, where did all these lovely flowers come from?"

Grabbing another box of chocolates, Kady quickly plopped them into her adopted grandmother's lap and released the brake on the wheelchair. "Come on, let's go find everyone else. You're starting to sound like the Spanish Inquisition."

Maybelle loved going fast in her wheelchair and Kady obliged her by whizzing her to the elevators. She giggled, telling Kady again how much she enjoyed each visit.

They stopped on the second floor and met up with Rita who was wheeling an elderly gentleman in the same direction.

"Out for a ride, Mrs. B?" asked Mr. James.

"We're on our way to see the new guest speaker. I hear his messages are inspirational. They say he can tell us about our spiritual future and then help us talk to our departed loved ones."

"Oh, that's all well and good," Grandma Barkus replied, "but with my luck I'll end up in a conversation with all the people I never wanted to speak to again. Besides I'm more interested in the life I still have here on earth and living every day to the fullest until I hear the Almighty call. I'll have an eternity to talk to all those dead people."

Rita and Mr. James chuckled at the feisty Little Grandma. Kady tuned out their voices as she started to wonder about Colin. "Spiritual future? Was Colin the guest speaker? He would have mentioned coming here, wouldn't he? But then again how could he when I haven't even spoken to him all week?"

A shiver of apprehension ran up Kady's spine as the floor dropped, and the large doors whooshed open into the spacious room. For a moment Kady hesitated. She did not want to leave the enclosed quarters of the lift.

The cafeteria was a large open space that was used as an occasional auditorium for the home's special events. It was bursting with activity as patients, nurses, volunteers and guests crowded into the area. Leaving her apprehension behind, Kady smiled and nodded as she and Rita parted, trying to reunite their passengers with friends.

"Look over there," instructed Grandma B. "Ralphaline's with Mrs. St. Jude. We very seldom see her at our events. You know Mrs. St. Jude has been here longer than anyone else. The girls think she was married to a European count or something. The rumor mill also claims that she was some sort of entertainer in her day. Of course, no one knows for sure. After all, how can we check? Anyone who would know is probably dead. Maybe we should ask this hocus pocus guy, see if he knows the truth," Grandma Barkus exclaimed.

"Oh, Little Grandma B, you shouldn't speak so irreverently of the deceased," Kady whispered. "They could be listening,"

"Well, if they can hear us, I sure hope they don't call me too soon. I've got places to go, things to do. Why, I plan to live long enough to see you married and settled down with a few children hanging on your knee. Come on, Kady, let's go and sit with the others."

"Yoo-hoo, Ruffly. Look who I hopped a ride with. Come see all the delicious treats she brought us. We'll have to increase our workout this week. It looks like we'll have to spend another two hours on the Stairmaster."

"Maybelle, you're such a jokester. We can barely leave our chairs," Ralphaline said with a weak smile. Ruffly's pain and confinement left her with little to be happy about. "Oh, Kady, Maybelle knew you were coming today and insisted on waiting. She was very sure you wouldn't disappoint us."

Kady leaned over, giving Ralphaline a hug. "You know I could never forget my Little Grandmas."

"Kady, I'd like you to meet Mrs. St. Jude," Ralphaline said.

"Ladies and gentlemen, may I please have your attention?" Sister Agatha announced as she motioned for those standing to take their seats. "Our guest speaker is a gentleman who has donated his knowledge and services many times throughout the past several years. Today we are fortunate to have this famous medium with us again bringing his inspirational messages. His topic today will center on helping us understand how spiritual love endures beyond the grave. Then he will try to communicate with some of our deceased family members spirits. Please welcome Colin O'Dannaher!"

Colin stepped up to the microphone.

Oh no, thought Kady, it was a nightmare, her worst nightmare and she was reliving it again! There was nowhere she could hide. Sooner or later Colin would see her.

Sitting down in the gray aluminum chairs wearing her bright green sun dress, Kady felt like she stuck out like a sore thumb. Her brain went numb. She was not ready for this! She could hear Colin's voice but had trouble deciphering the words.

"...be true to yourself, listen to your inner voice and you will find happiness. Learn to live for yourselves, appreciate what you have accomplished and the love you have to offer. When you reach the higher life, you will have fulfilled all your earthly expectations and should have no regrets when you pass over. Because you are now entering the twilight of your lives does not mean you are worthless and should give up. How you have conducted your lives, your beliefs and attitudes will influence the quality of your life in the astral world. Do not let emotional blocks stunt your spiritual growth. Ladies and gentlemen, I would like to help you communicate with your loved ones that have passed on and perhaps come to terms with your spiritual future." Colin paused a moment to recite a quick prayer, opening himself up to the spirits, and the session began.

"I'm feeling a great deal of sadness in this room. I think that there are some spirits trying to communicate with us today who regret that they did not live their life to the fullest and have returned to ask our forgiveness. Remember, forgiveness frees the heart. I feel a chill in the room and sense someone in darkness, a soul who's crying out. The woman I see has light brown hair and very deep blue eyes, the color of the sea on a stormy night. She's very sad and unhappy, and in pain but it's not physical: it's emotional. I get the impression of something…cold, like metal, yes, like a gun. Her name is Becca."

A stooped-over gentleman sitting between two crutches spoke out. "It's my wife. Her name was Rebecca and she took her own life…with a gun," he cried out, attempting to stand up.

"She asks that you forgive her for not loving and living her life to the fullest. She's with Timothy and Terrence now. She missed them so much," Colin told the older gentleman.

"Those were my sons. They were ten years old when they died," said the old man, grabbing the back of his chair for support. "She never stopped blaming herself for their death."

"She says to tell you that she's sorry she left you to raise Laura alone, and wished she could have met Bradley and Aaron. Does that make any sense to you?" Colin asked.

"Yes, Laura's my daughter, our only remaining child, and her husband's name is Bradley. Laura gave birth to a son she named Aaron, just two weeks ago. Will you ask Becca if she's finally happy?"

"She says that she finally is. The boys are with her. They live with Rebecca's mama and papa on a farm in Michigan."

"That's right. Her family owned an apple orchard. That's where I met her, picking apples on her daddy's land. She always said she was happiest there."

"Rebecca regrets not sharing her grief with you, but her depression was so deep that she could not love herself. She's learned to like herself now and is rooming with Pepper till you come. Don't rush, she says. Laura and her family need you."

"Oh, my God. Pepper was our little black and white cat who used to sleep at the foot of our bed. He ran off shortly after my Becca took her life. We never saw him again. I can't thank you enough, son. My heart feels so much lighter. Your words have given me great comfort." Shaking, the older gentleman could no longer stay upright without help. Colin motioned to a nurse who had been standing nearby to lower him back into his chair.

"I feel another soul crying out for help and forgiveness," Colin said, taking out a handkerchief and wiping the sweat from his brow. "Could someone please get me a glass of water?" he asked as he removed his beige linen sport coat, revealing a short-sleeved blue knit shirt.

Colin continued, wrapping himself in a trance-like state. "There's a man standing next to me called Willy. Is that name familiar to anyone?"

Mrs. St. Jude, who had been sitting quietly next to the Little Grandmas, suddenly let out a soft cry.

"Willy tells me that the wound on the top of his head has healed, although it left a small scar," said Colin. "Does that make any sense to anyone?"

Mrs. St. Jude spoke out. "No, it can't be. The last time I saw him I—I swear I didn't know who he was. Oh why, why does he come to me now?" she whispered, fear lacing the edges of her voice.

"Willy was a man from my past that I thought I loved," Mrs. St. Jude mumbled, looking horrified as she gripped the sides of her wheelchair.

She suddenly turned, attempting to release the brake on her chair, knocking her oxygen tank over. Her nurse stooped down, picked the canister up and set it back between the brackets.

Sister Agatha, who had been sitting behind her, leaned over to offer comfort. Loosening the old woman's grip, she took the wrinkled hand in her own and whispered, "It's all right, Mrs. St. Jude. No one can hurt you. Colin is a good man. He's only trying to help you and Willy." Sister Agatha's words soothed and calmed the elegant woman who was trying to bring her emotions under control.

"Mrs. St. Jude, if you prefer, we can stop at any moment," Colin said, knowing that the spirit trying to communicate with her was very restless. Colin knew from experience that forcing people to continue under extreme duress was never advisable. After a few minutes she regained her composure.

"I'm sorry, young man. I'm all right now. Please continue!"

"Mrs. St. Jude, I see that Willy has a cigar in his hand. He knows it bothered you and he's sorry for the second-hand smoke, but he says he wasn't aware then of the damage it could do."

"I never smoked, but my emphysema is bad...Tell Willy it's OK; no one knew in those days the damage smoking could cause."

"He's glad that you are no longer hidden away and that they found the medicine to cure you."

"Do you know what he is referring to?" Colin asked.

"Oh my, yes. You see, I was in a sanitarium for nearly three years. At that time tuberculosis was a very dangerous and feared disease, but I was completely cured. It wasn't until years later that I was sent here."

"He says to tell his little songbird that her prayers have been heard and he is very grateful. He has opened up his heart for guidance so that he can enter a higher spiritual realm and no long be tormented by his hurtful actions of the past"

With tears pouring down her proud, lined face she said, "He used to call me his little songbird and tell me that we would fly to the heavens."

Colin stepped down from the makeshift stage, walked over to Mrs. St. Jude and gave her a comforting hug. He then scanned the crowd, doing a double take as his eyes focused upon Kady.

What's she doing here? he thought. Did I conjure her up from my dreams? My God, she looks so beautiful. His heart started to pound, and his stomach began to quiver with anticipation. For a moment he became slightly disoriented. The sudden shift from the audience's emotions to Colin's own had been quite a jolt.

"Concentrate, Colin, concentrate. You're a professional, don't lose your grip." Slowly he tore his eyes away. Turning around, he put one foot in front of the other and returned to the stage.

Once again, Kady was reminded of Colin's amazing compassion for strangers, and it turned her heart to mush. She lowered her head from his gaze, fidgeting with her fingers. Kady felt the familiar racing of her heart. She remembered the feel of his deeply tanned, muscular arms. Although they were powerful and hard, there was a softness and tenderness to their touch. This was the kind of man she had been waiting for. He was her knight in shining armor. Kady was now convinced Colin was a man who loved deeply, and who knew when to place the needs of others before his own. It was time to admit the obvious. Something that she had known, but fought from the moment she had first looked into his eyes. I love him, she thought. What's wrong with me? I love him. No sense in pretending, no reason for hiding any longer.

She exhaled and allowed all her fear and guilt to rush from her body. Taking the first step, she smiled and let all the feelings she had held within her heart shine through her eyes. She then focused her gaze in Colin's direction.

Attempting to recapture his composure, Colin slowly poured himself a glass of ice water that Sister Agatha had placed on the table. Going through simple mundane motions helped him refocus. He regained his concentration and turned back toward Mrs. St. Jude.

"Willy would like you to know that spirits from the past, along with your prayers, have helped him realize the error of his ways. Forgive him, he says. He does not want you to suffer the endless dance of restlessness throughout eternity for his sins. He says, 'Free yourself, my little Jewel. The time has come for us to clean our slate. I wish to hear your voice sing again beyond the range of sound. With the truth you can free my spiritual soul from ignorance and eternal damnation. Go to our hidey hole, reveal my sins, right my wrong.'"

"Jewel...Jewel is my name...tell him that I will try to help," she shouted.

"Do you understand what he means?" Colin asked.

"Yes. Yes I do. I didn't want to believe it. I knew his soul was tormented; that's why I have prayed so hard. Please tell Willy there's nothing to forgive. I forgave him years ago. Now he must realize what he did wrong on earth. God forgives all his children when they repent. Tell him he has to ask God to forgive him for his selfish choices. Will you do that for me, young man?"

Colin nodded and looked into the old woman's hopeful face. "Willy's spirit needs to be at peace so it can begin the cycle of rebirth. He has released his terrible burden of regret for the events that he caused while here on earth. He has carried this incredible weight on his spiritual journey. Your forgiveness will help to free his soul."

As several nursing home residents gathered around her for support, Mrs. St. Jude called out, "Thank you, son. I feel the healing has already begun."

Sensing the need, Sister Agatha spoke, "If it's all right, I think we should take a break for a few minutes." She took Colin by the hand and led him toward the refreshment table.

"You don't know how much your words mean to those who are aggrieved. Do you remember Mrs. Granetti from your last visit?"

"Yes, of course I do. I went to her room for a personal reading. She was the woman who was the lone survivor of that horrible automobile accident on the Dan Ryan."

"Yes, Colin, that was Aurora Granettti. She was completely overwhelmed when you informed her that her entire family was present in the room and that they were happy that at least one of them had survived."

"She was bedridden from the collision and suffering from a tremendous amount of anger and survivor's guilt. She was afraid to die but angry because she'd been left alone to suffer on earth."

Fingering her rosary beads, Sister Agatha continued, "Shortly after your visit, she passed on quietly, but before she died, she asked me to thank you for your comforting words. You helped ease her terrible burden. Colin, I know there's a special place for you in heaven. You'll always be in my prayers."

The Lakeview sessions were always the most difficult for Colin. Many of the elderly residents were all alone in a modern world that seemed foreign and unfamiliar to them. Their closest relatives were either dead or too busy with their own lives to visit on any regular basis. He knew that death and the concept of the spiritual world were ever present in their minds. He firmly believed that he could help them by contacting their departed friends and family. He believed that this connection would lead them to a fuller understanding of life after death. At the very least he hoped he could bring some comfort and reassurance to them in the twilight of their lives.

"Thank you so much, sister. One can never have enough prayers. Now if you'll please excuse me, I believe I recognized someone in the audience. I'd like to say hello." Colin turned and walked toward Kady. Unsure of himself, he decided to grab an extra cup of coffee and a couple of chocolate chip cookies.

Sitting with her legs crossed, Kady's sun dress had ridden up to mid thigh. Colin admired her trim ankles, letting his gaze travel upward. Oh, how he remembered the feel and texture of her smooth satin like skin. Kady had her back to him, but her shoulders stiffened as he approached.

"Hello, Kady." Slowly she turned around and glanced up.

"Hello, Colin."

"I didn't know…" They both said in unison.

"Ladies first," Colin said as he sat down in the vacant chair beside her, close enough to inhale the scent of her intoxicating perfume. He wondered if it was called "arousal."

"I never expected to see you here today," said Kady. "You didn't tell me you volunteered here at Lakeview."

"I didn't expect to see you here today either. As a matter of fact, when you didn't return my calls, I thought maybe you'd left town."

Kady squirmed in her seat. "I'm always here on the third Sunday of every month," she said with her eyes cast down.

"Yes, she is, young man. I can count on Kady's visits just like clockwork. Why, look at this!" Maybelle Barkus exclaimed holding up the large box of unopened chocolates. "She remembered my sweet tooth, and, oh my, all the flowers she brought—why, they'd brighten up any room."

"Oh, I imagine Kady was quite generous this week. Here, honey, I thought you might like to wash some of the

chocolate down with a little bit of crow—I mean coffee,"
Colin said sarcastically.

"Why, Kady, do you know this young man?"

"Yes, Little Grandma B. Please let me introduce you to
Colin; he's an old friend of the family."

Sitting in front of Kady, she released the hand brake
and rolled herself around to get a closer look. "Old friend,
ha. Why, if I were I few years younger I'd make sure you
were more than just a friend," Maybelle exclaimed taking
off her glasses as she peered toward Colin. "What's wrong
with you, young lady, are you blind? This young man is one
of the finest specimens of manhood that I've seen in a very
long time!"

"Put your glasses on, Maybelle, and stop drooling, or
I'll have to call the nurse," Ralphaline interjected. "Don't you
see you're embarrassing these two young people? It looks to
me like they'd like to be left alone. Excuse us, children." Ral-
pholine summoned two volunteers who wheeled them both
down the hall and out of harm's way.

"Colin, I'd like to apologize for not answering your
calls and um…for not thanking you properly for all the
lovely gifts." Taking the proverbial bull by the horn, she
leaned over and kissed Colin smack dab in the middle of his
shapely, full lips.

"Apology accepted," Colin stammered, shocked by her
public display of affection. "Look, Kady, I know that this
might be difficult for you to understand, but I had thought
we'd reached a point in our relationship where we decided to
talk through our problems, not run from them."

"You're right, Colin. As I'm sure you know, the other
night was a new experience for me… and when you were
forced to leave in such a rush, well I—"

"—If I remember correctly, you were the one rushing
me out the door."

Kady halted as a pink flush stained her cheeks.

Ever the gentleman, Colin leaned over and gathered her
hands into his own. "Listen, sweetheart, it's neither the time

nor the place for this kind of a discussion," Colin said, punctuating his words with a kiss to the palm of each of her hands. "Why don't I pick you up tonight and take you to my place for dinner? I'm a pretty fair cook."

Kady smiled warmly. "Colin, we definitely need to talk, but not tonight."

"Well then, how about Sunday? Your Aunt Willa and I spoke earlier this week about getting together for another séance. She suggested a barbecue as well, and I volunteered my place. She's read some of the journal and is anxious to contact your Uncle Daniel again. I'd like you to…I mean… would you like to join us?"

Kady had never seen Colin so unsure of himself. She suddenly felt courageous. Pulling her fingers from his grasp, Kady stood up and saw Sister Agatha approach the temporary stage.

"Colin, I think I'd better get back to my Little Grandmas. It looks like they want you to resume your readings. Oh, and as far as the barbecue is concerned, I can't think of anywhere in the world I'd rather be."

Once again Kady leaned over and gave him a passionate kiss square on the mouth. "See you Sunday, and I'll bring dessert."

Shaking his head at the abrupt change, Colin watched Kady walk over to a group of male volunteers. They all greeted her enthusiastically, each taking a turn to give her a big hug.

Colin felt a nerve in the side of his neck twitch. Had Kady ever dated any of those overgrown boy scouts? Could one of those guys be her ex? Why was jealously rearing its ugly head? It was not an emotion that Colin had much experience with, and he did not like the feeling at all.

TWELVE

*A*fter unpacking and putting away the food, Rose took out her utensils and grimaced as she plopped some lard and a stick of butter into the fry pan. Her stomach churned at the sight, thinking of all the fat cells that would make their way to her thighs. She had always believed that cooking wouldn't be so bad if it all came in a little powdered, no-mess packet. Rose always joked that the thing she was best at making was reservations.

She placed a baggy over her hand, dropping the ground meat into a pan. The feel of raw hamburger had always been like fingernails on a chalk board to her. She added the ready-made spices, hoping Kady would be impressed. She was careful to hide the box at the bottom of their garbage can. Just then, Rose became distracted by the ringing of the telephone. She ran into her bedroom to take the call, forgetting about the sizzling in the pan.

"This darn door is stuck again," Kady said out loud as she turned and twisted her key into the lock. Bracing her hip on the door, Kady jiggled the opener and the knob again, pushing with all her might. Nothing moved except her hip, which was sure to have a bruise. Next she tried shoving her knee into the frame and braced herself. Then she rammed the key into the hole once more and wham, with a powerful thrust, the door opened and Kady flew in.

"Ooow," Kady gasped as she righted herself, feeling her nose twitch and sniff at the offending air. Then her eyes started to tear, and Kady realized that she could barely see through the heavy smoke that filled the room. Oh my God, she thought, and ran helter-skelter screaming her sister's name.

"Rose! Rose, where are you?"

Suddenly the fire alarm went off. Midnight came running up the stairs like the hounds from hell were after him. Rose came running out of the kitchen with a smoking pan in one hand and a singed towel in the other.

Seeing her sister, Rose yelled, "The fire's almost out! It's only in the pan!" Then she dashed out the open front door and threw the offending dish into the street. Kady followed.

"Rose, are you all right? What the heck is going on?"

Never one to mince words Rose said, "The good news is that the house is still standing; the bad news is that I'm afraid we'll have to eat out. I've burned the sloppy Joes, and the kitchen will never be the same again!"

The wail of sirens interrupted Kady's response. A large red fire truck from Station Number Two pulled up. Men in black, oversized raincoats and boots seemed to jump down from all directions. A big hulk of a man ran toward them, dragging the front end of a large hose. Three other men in similar clothing brought up the rear. He ran toward the apartment.

Thinking she should follow him into their house, Kady tried to catch up and screamed back, "The fire's out! It was in the pan!" She pointed to its charred remains.

"OK," he shouted. "Everyone stay out. We still have to check the premises."

Kady stopped and glanced over her shoulder. Had the situation not been so devastating, the look on her sister's face would have been priceless. Ever-perfect Rose had a smudged streak of black soot on her cheek, and her hair was standing on end. She was dabbing her face with the edge of the scorched kitchen towel.

Fifteen minutes later, three men exited the apartment building, dragging the heavy hose behind them.

"Everything seems to be under control, miss. You can come back into the house. We're setting up fans, and we've opened up windows to start clearing the air. It looks like there is some smoke damage, but you were very lucky."

Kady ran down the stairs and gave her sister a hug. "Come on; the captain says we can go back in."

The air was still heavy with smoke, but everything else was intact. Standing in the kitchen, the fire chief had removed his hat while surveying the room, "Most of the damage has been confined to this room...and it's superficial at that; it should clean up with a little soap and water. You'll be able to sleep here tonight." Kady and Rose both looked at him dumbfounded, never dreaming that they would have had to make new sleeping arrangements. As her brain finally began to function, ridding itself of fright, Rose suddenly perked up.

"Hey, don't I know you?" she said as she peered into his deep set chocolate brown eyes.

"Yeah, I was wondering when the haze was gonna clear," he said.

"St. Rita's, Class of '85, star quarterback, right?" Rose quipped.

"St. Mary's cheer leading squad, short plaid skirts, in the back of Eddy Humphrey's Ford Fairlane," the fireman shot back.

"Hey," Kady interrupted, "if you guys are gonna have a reunion let's wait till we get this mess cleaned up."

"Sorry, Brent. This is my sister Kady, and she acts this way when she gets hungry. It looks like we'll be doing carry-out tonight." Kady stomach grumbled on cue.

"That's OK. I'd better get going, I'm sure the crew is wondering what's been keeping me so long."

"Hey, captain! Better fill out our paperwork and get this show on the road!" a voice yelled from outside.

Taking the form, Brent replied, "Sorry, Rose, but all this new paperwork is thanks to his honor the Mayor. If you and your sister could just answer a few questions, we'll be out of your hair."

"Sure. Pull up a chair. Kady wasn't even here when I burnt tonight's dinner, so I'll have to answer all the questions myself."

Two hours and one Chinese takeout later, Rose sat in the middle of her sister's bed, not sure where to begin. They had cleaned up as best they could, knowing that the smell of smoke would linger for a few days. The apartment wasn't perfect, but it was livable.

Rose explained to Kady how she'd been attempting to duplicate their mom's sloppy Joes recipe when she was distracted by a phone call. While on the phone, she smelled something burning. She hurried into the kitchen and was horrified by the sight of a foot long flame shooting straight up out of the frying pan. Rose grabbed a kitchen towel and wrapped it around the handle, trying to carry it to the sink. Just when it seemed the crisis was under control, the towel caught fire, causing Rose to jump back in shock.

After a second she regained her composure and quickly grabbed the sink sprayer, turning on the water to extinguish the flames. Unfortunately, a huge puff of black smoke filled the kitchen setting off the fire alarm. After hearing Rose's story, Kady was just glad that no real damage had been done.

That night they decided to sleep in Kady's lower level bedroom since the smoke had not traveled down the stairs. Rose turned back the yellow crochet bedspread and lay down, closing her eyes. Two seconds later she jumped up, remembering dessert. "Wait a minute. There's one thing I didn't burn."

Rose returned with her arms full, proud that she had salvaged something. "This was part of my surprise," she said setting down a carton of strawberries, a container of melted chocolate and a bottle of champagne. Rose waved her hand over her gifts, "Welcome to Smoky Rose's Café. What do you think? Is this great or what?"

"Oh Rose…" Kady responded with a large, heartfelt sob as the dam broke loose.

Rose hadn't expected a reaction like this to her dessert, but she guessed that the sweet confections definitely had something to do with Mr. O'Dannaher. Gathering her sister into her arms, she cooed, "It's all right, honey. Let it out, let it all out. I get emotional thinking about all that chocolate hitting my thighs, too. And after the day we've just had, I think I'm gonna shed a few tears myself."

Suddenly they were both laughing and crying at the same time. Finally, when it seemed like there were no tears left, Rose put her hands on her sister's shoulders, holding her firmly. "OK, sis, I think we're dry. It's about time for some serious girl talk."

Confusion and guilt, coupled with the annoying sense that her sister had been walking on egg shells around her, had kept Kady in a state of uncertainty. And to top it all off, her usually nosy, meddlesome, sister had avoided her all week. Not once had Rose even mentioned Colin's hasty departure from her bedroom. And no matter how many phone calls, boxes of candy, or flowers she'd ignored during the week, Rose never questioned why. After a while Kady began to suspect that either her sister didn't care or that she was disappointed in her.

Yet, deep down in her heart, Kady knew that couldn't be true. After all, hadn't she been the one wiping her sister's tears when Rose had confessed to losing her virginity in the back seat of Sammy Van Hagen's mini-van?

Did Rose really understand what she'd been going through this week? Had her sister been giving her the time and space she needed to work this out for herself?

"It's time for some champagne and honesty," Rose quipped, twisting the corkscrew one last time as it popped out of the bottle.

Kady held out her glass. "I guess I've let this little life's challenge paralyze me, huh? I'd been going back and forth all week, wondering if I've made a mistake by making love to Colin."

"Well, you know what Tallulah Bankhead said, don't you?" Rose lowered her voice attempting a fake accent, "'Darling, if I had to live my life again, I'd make the same mistakes, only sooner!' You can't get any clearer than that, can you?"

Rose poured the bubbly and grabbed a strawberry. She placed the bowl and chocolate dip in the center of the bed, hoping her sister couldn't resist the temptation. There was nothing like chocolate for a broken heart!

"Oh, Rose. You're priceless, but believe it or not, I've already come to the conclusion that this latest challenge to my heart was not a mistake. Oh, I'll admit that it took a while for me to come to this earth-shattering conclusion, but now I know why I waited so long, and why I could never consummate my relationship with Brick. I must have known somewhere in the back of my mind that he truly wasn't the one. This has all been incredibly scary for me. Since the moment I met Colin, he's made me feel like the little girl who fell into the lake, completely out of control of my emotions."

"That was a pretty big bag of 'bricks' that you've been carrying around emotionally, you know. It was a full load. Seriously though," Rose said, draining her glass, "you know, today's woman is carrying a brand new bag filled with new attitudes, and a whole new set of rules that have cast aside all the old ones."

"Well, with all the crying I've been doing these past few days, I developed a few new bags myself," Kady teased. "You know, I've always wanted more than a physical relationship, not that it wasn't completely wonderful," Kady sighed, holding her glass out for a refill, "but I've always wanted true love, where we respect each other and where there's friendship, kindness and good will, toward others as well as ourselves."

"You go, girl. You do know what this means? You're in L.O.V.E, love." Rose quipped, happy to see her sister recovering her spirit.

"Oh, I know you'll think I'm mad, but remember when we were younger and we fantasized about knights in shining armor…Well, Colin made all my fantasies come true," Kady said, popping a chocolate-covered strawberry into her mouth and savoring the memory.

"That must have been some kinda night!"

"No, silly, you know what I mean. He's all those things, a good person, kind and decent to all the people he meets. More importantly, he proved to me the other night that my wants and needs come first, and...yes, yes, yes it was great, and worth the wait!" Kady said, throwing a pillow at her sister.

"Just how great was it, huh?" Rose said, holding up her hand, "No, no, spare me the details. I was only kidding. Honestly, Kady, I know that you've waited a long time, not wanting to give in to the whole sexual revolution thing, but, honey, real love is not giving in, but the balance of two people supporting each other in their strengths and weaknesses. Sometimes it's exhausting, and sometimes it's divine madness."

"Egad, Rose, when did you become so philosophical?"

"Right after my third glass of bubbly, kiddo!" Topping off their drinks, Rose held her goblet up into the air. "Let's make a toast. To love...Ain't it grand!"

Glasses clicked as they downed their final drop of champagne. Kady was relieved that she had confessed to Rose, and a sense of calm filled her.

They lay back, each lost in her own thoughts and eventually dropped off into an exhausted slumber.

THIRTEEN

A full day and hopefully an entire night lay ahead, and Colin had no time for daydreaming. There were a lot of things to do before his guests arrived. His housekeeper had been gone for the past week, but his home was still clean enough for company. It didn't take Colin long to drag the lawn furniture out of the garage and give it a once-over with the hose and a rag. Since he used his gas grill on a regular basis, all Colin had to do was throw on some new foil and flick on the switch. Running a grocery check list in his head, he knew that a quick trip to the market was in order.

Colin opened the screen door to the mud room and took off his wet sneakers. He had spent weeks putting in the solid oak flooring and was meticulous about keeping it clean. He stepped up into his kitchen and searched for a pencil and note pad. Gilly, his housekeeper, made sure everything was put away neatly; therefore nothing was ever where he left it.

"Damn," Colin said, tearing a scrap off a paper bag. Checking his cupboards and new Sub-Zero refrigerator, he made a list. "Six white potatoes, sour cream, a loaf of French bread, a half a dozen steaks and the makings for a big garden salad," he wrote, hoping that would be enough food. After all Kady did say she was bringing dessert. He smiled; he could only hope!

Colin grabbed sunglasses and wallet and headed toward his bike that was resting on the side of the house. The trip would not take long with his new Road Cycle. Colin had spent hours cooped up with his book revisions, and he was in desperate need of some outdoor exercise. His foot was finally getting back to normal. Peddling through the old, established neighborhood with its manicured lawns and multi-colored flower beds was just what he needed to work the kinks out of his legs and clear his head. Colin had a lot on his mind, most importantly figuring out how to strengthen his relationship with Kady.

The route led him by Lincoln Park where he recalled their first date. Colin desired Kady physically—there could be no doubt—but there was a larger awareness growing inside. Something more permanent, a bond he was just beginning to recognize as friendship and love. What he felt for her was powerful, dizzying, and sometimes exhausting. He knew he cared for her deeply and was drawn to her spiritual strength as well as the kindness she'd shown toward others. Her volunteering at Lakeview was one more thing they had in common. Colin also knew it was important that Kady understood and respected his career choices. He loved that fact that her Catholic upbringing instilled good, solid values. She was, at her core, a true old-fashioned girl, a throw-back to another time, a time Colin honestly believed was a better one then the one in which they lived. Her dedication to her family and religion was unquestioned, yet it never stood in the way of her becoming her own woman.

And what a woman! He moaned, thinking of her sweet lips and luscious curves.

Suddenly Colin hit a rock, his bike wobbled and he nearly crashed into a curb. He knew at that moment that he did not want an affair and was positive that Kady did not want that, either. Yet he was uncertain about how to handle this strange dance of relationships; the coming together, as well as interacting apart, the holding on, the letting go, never allowing their relationship to become a power struggle, but learning the steps together so they might dance for eternity. Now he just had to figure out how to do the dance without losing his balance.

Treasure Island was the ultimate in shopping. If they didn't have it, they'd get it. If they couldn't find it, then it didn't exist. That was their motto. Although it was more expensive than the well-known chain stores, Colin felt it was well worth the extra hole it left in his pocket. He could do one stop shopping and have all his needs met.

Colin got off his bike and locked it on the lamp post in front of the store. A blast of freezing air hit his face as he entered the air-conditioned store. He grabbed a cart that was specially designed for the baby boomer with a bad back. He remembered reading that in the advertisement when the store first opened. It always made him laugh when he pulled out the blue plastic-coated handles that were raised a few inches higher than the standard equipment. The manufacturers claimed that it placed the pressure points of pushing the light-weight cart on your upper forearms instead of the lower back. It was politically correct, and Colin wondered who or what they would cater to next.

Taking the torn piece of paper from his back pocket, Colin re-read his list and scanned the shelves for the items. Head bent, he was not watching where he was going, and suddenly found himself crashing into another cart. It had come from the opposite direction, yet it somehow ended up on his side of the aisle.

"Sorry," Colin said, looking up.

"Oh, Colin, I didn't know you shopped here. My, isn't it a small world!" cooed his new neighbor, in her phony I'm-so-sweet Texan accent.

Colin had become a little suspicious of all the places they kept running into each other. Last night it was the Thai take-out place, the weekend before it was the cleaners and cash station. No matter how much Colin varied his sched-ule, his neighbor seemed to be there. Recently, she'd taken to greeting him first thing in the morning as he opened his front door to collect his paper. He wouldn't have minded except he usually went out for the *Tribune* in his boxer shorts, and now he was forced to dress before his first cup of coffee. His neighbor was an attractive nuisance, but a nuisance just the same.

"Renae! How nice to see you again," Colin said with forced sincerity.

"Reenie, Colin. My friends call me Reenie," she corrected. Her smile was framed by collagen lips and a bleached bright smile.

"Of course. Well, I'd like to stay and chat, but you know," Colin said holding up his list. "Gotta finish shopping, I'm having a barbecue this afternoon."

"Barbecue? Oh Colin, are you having a party?" she asked, deliberately leaning over pretending to peer at his torn list, exposing a great deal of cleavage.

He knew that fake tits were all the rage, and while his ego was impressed by her not so subtle invitation, his eyes preferred the real thing, and Kady's were definitely real!

"Yes, it's a family thing. I'm just having family over. Well, like I said, see ya around," Colin said taking off with his cart like it was a Formula One car in an Indy five hundred race. He made his purchases in record time.

Colin had hoped that the final pages to Willa's family diary would have arrived by now. Since it was Saturday there was still a chance for a late delivery. When they arrived, he hoped they'd contain enough information to clear Daniel's name and finally tie up all the loose ends. Colin suspected that the outcome of Larken's story would play an important role in helping Willa move on with her life. When he had dropped off the first translation a few weeks ago, he knew that she was anxious to get to the bottom of the mystery between her dreams and clearing Daniel's name. Finally it came over a week ago and he had brought it with him the night he'd gone to Kady's apartment. After reading all the transcribed pages, both he and Kady were surprised by what they'd discovered. Kady had promised to ask her father and aunt about their ancestors' past, so Colin assumed that Willa was now aware of the family link.

Kady was having second thoughts, not about her love for Colin, but about the way she'd acted at the nursing home. It wasn't like her to act so bold. She had finally faced the fact that she would not have given herself so completely to Colin had she not been truly in love. She'd once read that sexual love is natural, but marriage is not. But Kady knew she wasn't cut out to handle an affair. Was that all Colin wanted? Or was he ready to form a bond that went beyond desire? Was she his one love? Kady knew that she was a woman who needed the stability and security of a permanent relationship. Now that her old friend self-doubt had returned with a vengeance to play around with her heart, she wasn't sure how to handle this next step with Colin. Tension built as she drove to his house.

The graystone Victorian looked warm and inviting as she pulled along the front curb. She noticed the loving care that was taken to rebuild this illustrious old lady to her former self. The decorative gingerbread carpenter's trim had been restored and painted a gleaming antique white, while the small stone porch and wide set of stairs sat proudly, inviting one within. Like Colin's personality, the house radiated warmth and shouted welcome. So why was she afraid to go in?

She drove to the side drive and parked her car behind Henry's. The back porch screen door flew open, and a huge dog who looked to be part boxer, part Labrador came running out. With large paws, drooping brown eyes and a long, drooling tongue, it jumped at her window, barking a greeting.

"Why hello, big guy. How are you?" Kady yelled over the noise as she rolled down her window.

"Ryder, Ryder, come back here, you big galloot, don't scare off my guests," Colin shouted, running after the dog, "Sit, good dog; sit," he commanded, pulling him down so Kady could get out of the car.

Seeing her hesitate, Colin said, "Hi, Kady. I promise he won't hurt you. He's a real softy. He loves to have company. Come on boy; let's give her some breathing space."

"Oh, I'm not afraid; he's just a little bigger than I am. I wonder, could you hold him back while I take the dessert out of the back seat?"

"How'd you know he goes crazy at the smell of food? That's his only vice. I can't keep anything on the counter or table while he's in the room. He jumps up and grabs it. He's so fast, that by the time I catch up with him, the food's gone. I've taken to locking him in the mud room when I'm preparing anything that I can't hold down."

"That type of reaction is a common trait in dogs this size and breed. You might want to ask Henry for some tips on to break Ryder of the habit."

"Speaking of Henry—both he and Willa are in the house enjoying the air conditioning. Let me help you with this," Colin said as he took the large tray from her hands. Ryder lopped along, licking at Kady's bare legs as they went inside.

"Hi, honey," Willa and Henry greeted them as they got up from a solid mahogany table covered with a wide assortment of food. A tray of jumbo shrimp rested in the center. Each shrimp had been delicately covered with bacon, topped with an olive and placed on a bed of small cream cheese sitting on rye crackers. A watermelon boat filled with every imaginable fruit was placed to its left, and a mouth-watering spinach salad sat next to six twelve-ounce steaks.

"Come sit down," said Henry. "We're literally holding down the fort so Ryder doesn't get at the food before we get a sample."

"Hi, Aunt Willa, Henry," Kady said, nodding to them both. "Henry, I thought for sure you'd have a few good training tips for Colin."

"Well, I told him about using a squirt gun or a good old fashioned nip on the snout with the newspaper, but seems like he's got his own ideas—"

"—Cruel, it seems cruel," Colin interrupted. "I'd never treat my kids that way, and Ryder's just a young pup. When I picked him out at the pound, he was scared of his own shadow. They told me that when he gets a little older, he'll grow out of this. Now, what can I get you to drink, Kady?"

"Anything cold and nonalcoholic will be fine. I can't believe you made all this. I thought this was supposed to be a barbecue," Kady said, glancing around at all the food on the table while taking in the eclectic blend of lovely antique furnishings.

"Your aunt supplied all the goodies. The steaks are my contribution," Colin explained.

"I love your house," said Kady. "It's fantastic."

Kady knew that original Victorian homes usually had large kitchens and big cupboards. Colin took advantage of all the space by restoring and refinishing the beautiful honey colored tiger oak cabinetry with their cut glass door knobs. He also added a spacious island with Corian tops. An old cupboard that had been whitewashed and hand painted with farm animals stood in one corner. It was a great room for large families or entertaining.

"Thanks. Would you like a tour? It's not much, but it's home," Colin said, taking a soda out of the large refrigerator with wood paneled doors.

"I'd love one," Kady replied, following him through the arched doorway.

Colin had turned the dining room into a beautiful library and work space. The home office setting was enhanced with rich grains and textures. An antique grouping made of cherry wood radiated with the same warmth as the decorative trim and spacious shelves. Colin completed his executive suite by sumptuously pairing it with a classic brass-finished, nail-headed trim chair. The oxblood leather blended with the rich tones of the wood.

"I like to write in this room, so I took some artistic license with the windows in order to take advantage of the view across the street."

Kady's eyes traveled to the park-like scenery.

"When my muse strikes, I end up spending a lot of time in here. Someday I want to have a family and be a hands-on kinda dad, not some guy that my wife and kids never see. So I figure this way I can be in the hub of activity and still take care of business."

Even with her experience as a teacher, Kady knew that sometimes it was impossible to keep kids under control. Thinking back to her boisterous childhood and the loving sounds that filled her family home, Kady asked, "Never having grown up with brothers and sisters, are you sure you would be able to write with all the noise around you?"

"Oh sure. When I have readings with large crowds, I have to concentrate very hard to weed out all the voices that are clamoring to be heard. It's a technique that I made a point to learn early on in my career. I'm confident I can work with my own children."

"Speaking of readings, I just got another package from my friend Michael. I haven't told Willa yet. I hope this is the last installment. I know how anxious your aunt is to clear up this mystery."

"Yes, she is, and I want to thank you, Colin, for helping my aunt. I know as much as she's loved communicating with Uncle Dan, it's time for closure. She hasn't been herself lately. I'm very glad that Henry has been with her through all of this. I know she can count on him just in case we stumble on any surprises."

"You're right. Henry's great. He's from the old school, a guy you can always count on," Colin said, leading her toward the vestibule.

Kady was thankful that she had found a man cut from the same cloth as her father's generation. She was certain that Colin wouldn't bolt and leave her no matter what the circumstances. He was a man of his word.

"The mosaic is beautiful, Colin. Did you restore this yourself?" Kady asked, pointing toward the floor.

"No, as a matter of fact the tumbled marble was all intact when I purchased this place. It was the first thing that caught my eye—you know, the workmanship. It's quality all the way. As you can see, I carried the mosaic theme around the border of the area rug. Most of the denatured moldings and hardwood floors were in pretty good shape, too. All I had to do was strip down to the original finish and find the beauty beneath," Colin said, staring at Kady.

Feeling a little uncomfortable, Kady said nothing. However, she couldn't help but feel the warmth of his gaze. Colin took Kady's elbow as he turned her toward the parlor. The furnishings were sparse and masculine.

"As you can see, I don't spend much time in this room. But I figured someday my wife will want to leave her imprint on this room."

Again he made a reference to having a wife, and Kady wondered. She couldn't imagine anyone other than herself taking that place in Colin's heart. The grandfather clock ticked loudly.

"There's also a large clothes closet down the hall. Let me show you the second floor. I've only had time to complete one bath and my own bedrooms."

They walked up the tapering dark oak stairway. On the left was the master bedroom. The wood floors were polished to a glossy sheen and covered with a classic hand-tufted William Morris rug. A mission style armoire concealed his TV and stereo center creating a perfect marriage of form and function. A large mahogany bed dwarfed the room.

"This was such a large house when I bought it that I decided to convert the master bedroom and nursery into one large suite and still have enough space for family and guests."

"I sure hope you have an accommodating wife. There are an awful lot of rooms to fill." Kady walked toward the long, low, mahogany bureau with a large mirror on the opposite wall. The glass was beautifully etched with a paisley design. She leaned over, running her fingers around the cut work of art. "This is beautiful, Colin."

He looked at their reflection in the mirror and said, "Not as beautiful as you." Taking her into his arms he playfully teased Kady's lips, and she felt the now familiar tightening in her breasts. His green eyes darkened and were filled with longing. "I've wanted to do this all day," Colin said, his deliciously sensuous kiss melting away her resistance.

She ran her hands over the hard muscles in his forearms, then, standing on tip toes, she wound her arms around his neck, pulling him closer. Colin groaned, deepening their kiss, sending them both to romantic oblivion.

"Kady, Colin! The charcoals are ready. We've put the steaks on," Willa called from below.

"We'll be right down," Kady breathlessly answered as they slowly drew apart.

Kady helped her aunt bring out the food, setting the grass cloth place mats on the glass tabletop while Colin and Henry manned the barbecue. Colin had placed the gas grill right under a huge old maple that offered shade to the entire Paver brick patio. "Hey guys, how much longer?" Willa asked.

"Depends on how well done you want these puppies," Henry responded, looking around. "Gadzooks," he said under his breath as Ryder came out the back door barking, followed by Kady carrying a tray of iced tea.

"Anyone have a thirst for something cold?" Kady asked, handing everyone a glass then setting the platter on the white plastic tea wagon that held their salad and bread. Willa admired Colin's beautiful English garden and pointed toward a cluster of American beauty roses.

"Kady, have you taken a look around Colin's yard? Oh Colin, I'm envious of all this wonderful space you had to work with. You must tell me the name of your gardener. He's done a wonderful job."

"Sorry to disappoint you, Willa, but you're looking at him," Colin replied. Colin didn't have a full-time gardener since he preferred to be outdoors whenever he could. On the occasions when he was out of town for any length of time, he hired a high school student to trim the bushes and cut the lawn. One of the previous owners had transformed the yard into a small scenic park with many perennials that needed little maintenance. Colin enjoyed taking care of the yard, feeling it worth the effort when he could sit back and watch the golden sunsets from his own backyard.

The beauty of this natural setting entranced Kady. She walked toward a row of pink-centered white peonies that ran along the edge of his fence. Their fragrance was hard to resist. Kady bent down and suddenly felt a spray of water soak her navy silk blouse and bare legs.

"Oh my," Kady squealed trying to jump out of the way.

"Sorry," said a sugary sweet little-girl voice from the person who had just ruined Kady's outfit. "Did I get you a little wet?" The question was asked by a grown woman who didn't look one bit sorry.

The woman was dressed in what Kady labeled a Beverly Hillbilly off-the-shoulder crop top and the shortest shorts Kady had ever seen. Kady just stared. Daisy May's clever smug grin vanished, and she dropped her weapon.

Colin had just noticed the commotion along his fence and went to rescue Kady from his nosy neighbor. Kady felt Colin's arms on her wet shoulders as he came up from behind.

"You OK, honey?"

"Hey Colin, everything's fine. Your family member just got a little too close to my hose. I didn't even know she was there."

"Oh, hi Renae. Seeing as how you battered my guest, I guess I better introduce you before she sues you for damages." Colin accompanied his comment with a friendly smile. "Kady, this is my new neighbor Renae Trianymen." Kady was always at a loss for words around women like this.

"Colin, Kady! Time to eat," Henry called, placing six perfect medium filet mignons and baked potatoes on the hard plastic plates that Willa was helping him fill.

"Well, I don't want to spoil your little get-together. See ya around, honey." Renae winked as she wiggled away, still trying to stake her claim.

"C'mon, let's go get you a towel," Colin said, putting his arm around Kady. "Ignore her, sweetheart. She's like a little hamster on a wheel. She's doing a lot of peddling, but getting nowhere."

Kady smiled, relieved with his handling of the situation. Colin could never understand women and their territorial attitudes, especially knowing that he had made it quite clear to Renae that he just wasn't interested.

As Colin's guests finished up their meal, dusk settled over the back yard. They sipped the last remnants of the wine and watched the sun set in a blaze of glory.

"Always loved a barbecue," Henry said patting his bulging tummy. "Now I could use a little snooze."

"Oh, no you don't. We're gonna work off a little of this delicious meal by helping Colin clean up, and then he's promised us another séance," said Willa. "Right, Colin?" Willa was excited to start the reading, hoping they would soon discover the truth behind her dreams.

After all the dishes were placed into the dishwasher and all the food was put away, Colin went into his library. He retrieved his notes and returned to pull the drop leaf table into place.

I hope you don't mind if we have the reading in my kitchen. I've never conducted a séance in my home before, and this is the only place where we can all sit together."

Henry and Colin pulled out chairs for the women as the three sat down, but Colin remained standing, gathering the rest of his paperwork that was stacked neatly on the counter top.

"This is perfect, Colin. We're all quite comfortable," Willa said with a wave of her hand, speaking for everyone.

"Thank you, Willa. I've given our last reading some thought and realized that we've been presented with small pieces of a puzzle. I also think it might be the right time for me to present you with a psychic chart. Earlier this week, I put together all the information we've gathered," Colin said, handing each of them a typed page with all the points that had been discovered. "Please review the facts and let me know if I've missed anything. Then we need to keep this information fresh in our minds when we communicate with Daniel and the spiritual guide. This will enable us to be more in tune with their energy pattern and give us a more precise reading." Colin sat down and gave everyone time to look at the detailed list of events. "Does anyone have anything to add?" Colin questioned.

"No, Colin. I think you've covered everything," Willa said.

"Now there's just this one last piece of information," Colin said, handing Willa the final pages of the translation and the actual diary.

Hugging the book to her chest, Willa exclaimed, "Oh Colin! When did this arrive?"

"Late this afternoon while I was out grocery shopping, so I haven't had a chance to look it over, but I thought you might like to do the honors and read it out loud to all us before we begin our séance."

Willa leaned across her chair and gave Colin a big hug. "Oh, you naughty boy. You've kept this from us all day. I'm so excited that I could jump right out of my skin," Willa cried.

"Wouldn't want that now, would we?" Henry asked. "Probably a good thing you waited, my boy. Here, sweetheart, dry your tears." Henry handed Willa another pristine white handkerchief, and she dabbed at her tears. "Guess I should have bought stock in this company a while back."

"Aunt Willa, would you like me to read the diary?" asked Kady.

"Oh, honey, would you? I'm afraid I'm just a little too emotional." Clearing her throat, Kady began:

May 1836

I know I must speak of that horrible night. I cannot
block it from my mind and perhaps by writing it down I
will be able to exercise its ghosts.

On the night that I gave myself to Napayshni as his
wife, we were discovered by his half-brother Inteus. We
did not know that he had followed us to our secret
meeting place. It was dark and stormy as he came upon
us in the dead of the night. He burst into our tent raging
with hate and caught us unaware with no weapons to
defend ourselves. He attacked us, and with a vicious
thrust of his spear, sank its blade into Napayshni's chest,
stealing his life. Blood poured from his wound, and I
tried to stop the flow with my hands but could not.
Inteus then erupted with a violent fury and attacked,
ripping me from Napayshni's side. He threw my body to
the ground, holding me down with his foot, as he
slashed Napayshni's scalp. He screamed victoriously,
and grabbed the healing shield from Napayshni's
belongings.

I cannot erase the feeling of my beloved's life blood
from my mind. The memory haunts me; it is still so
horribly clear. With the rain pouring overhead and the
thunder fighting to be heard through the clouds, Inteus
dragged me out into the night. Throwing me over his
shoulderm he climbed onto his horse. He raised his head
and howled into the moonless night that the Mystic
Healing Shield and the wicked woman were now his.
Inteus' voice bellowed with hatred, and I was frightened
beyond belief. Never before had I witnessed such an
evil force spewing from within one of God's creatures.

Suddenly there was a great rush of rain that blinded our
sight. The sound of booming thunder pierced the air.
Then a spark of jagged lightning hit us with a force so

strong that I felt the earth shake, and the ground beneath us split open. Inteus' horse reared, throwing us both on to the ground and into darkness. Instantly, I was free to escape. I smelled burning flesh but did not stop as I rushed through the muddied earth, hoping that I was not being followed. I ran for what seemed like miles when I finally realized that the rain had ceased. The only sounds that remained were that of my own footsteps and the pounding of my heart. I took shelter in the crevasse of a hollowed old tree, remembering how Napayshni told me that his tribe considered the mighty oaks their friends. I gave thanks to both our gods for my lucky escape. The angels in heaven watched over me as I slept through the night.

The thunderous sounds of horses' hooves shook me from my deep slumber. Suddenly there were soldiers swarming the forest near my nest. I was still so afraid. Then one of them spotted my footprints in the wet earth and found me. At first I was so frightened and cold that I could not speak. The leader of the troops ordered his men to build a fire and offer me food. Only then was I able to relay my plight. The captain, who called himself Joseph, offered his assistance to help me find Napayshni.

When I was rested, Joseph helped me upon his horse and for two days we searched for our campsite. On the third day we stumbled upon the charred remains of a rider and his horse. The Mystic Healing Shield had been spared. I knew then that Inteus had been thwarted by his gods, for the lightning that struck and the smell of burning flesh that I remembered was his. That evening we found our tent, and the soldiers helped me bury my beloved with his healing shield on the land that overlooked the great lake.

When the soldiers asked for my help, I told them that I was willing to do whatever I could. They needed to find the Waushanee tribe and were prepared to barter or battle for the lives of the white captives. To my surprise, I discovered that Captain Joseph Deloré was the husband of my good friend Marietta Asunda. He had been searching for his wife for the last six months. We both prayed that she was still alive. I told them what I knew of the tribe and gave them directions. Captain Joseph did not think it wise for me to return with them to the village, for we feared reprisal once the great chief found out that both his sons were dead. I also knew that the elders of the tribe would blame me for their deaths. I was sent with a missive back to the fort, and the Captain assured me that he would arrange for my return home.

The very next day the soldiers laid siege to the village. The handsome captain rescued his wife, Marietta Asunda, and all the other captives. Two weeks later I said goodbye to my good friends and boarded a train that took me to New York.

The trip was long, lonely, and dusty. Then on November 7, I was able to get passage home on a cargo ship owned by A. B. Kinschbaum & Co., compliments of the United States of America's government. I was finally going home. I look forward to returning to Ireland though I know my life there will not be easy. And though I have lost my beloved, he has given me the greatest gift possible. Every time I feel the flutter of new life inside my body, I am reminded of him. All we shared, our hopes, our dreams will be realized in the eyes of our child. My pregnancy has been difficult, but I am hopeful for that moment when I shall hold our baby in my arms and witness the living legacy of our divine love. After all that I have lost, I still do not regret my journey. For I will always be reminded of my beloved, all we shared, our hopes, our dreams, and how he gave his life for me and our child.

Captain's entry in English:

May 11, 1836

Born, female child to passenger Larken O'Hara, who died while giving birth, father unknown.

"Oh my," Willa sighed between her tears as she handed Kady a tissue. "Honey, it looks as though we Daileys are more American than we could have ever imagined."

Kady's emotions were in a complete state of confusion. Not only had she discovered her Native American heritage, but she had been presented with proof that her great-great-great-great-grandmother Larken was psychic. Mr. Tonto was real, she thought, and he had a name, Napayshni.

It had grown dark, and Colin could see the toll these revelations had taken on Willa and Kady.

"Would you like to postpone our séance for another time? I know this has been an awful lot to take in," Colin gently offered.

"No, Colin. As difficult as this has been, we must proceed," said Willa. "Daniel and I have waited far to long too rest for even one moment more."

"Willa, honey, you may be ready to continue, but I sure would like a break," said Henry. "How about a cup of tea before we begin if it's not too much trouble, Colin," Henry said. Henry knew that Willa was pushing herself too hard and needed a respite from the tumultuous journey they had just taken.

"No trouble at all. As a matter of fact, I believe Kady brought dessert. I think we could all use a little pick-me-up."

"Let me help," Kady said as she and Colin got up from the table. Their eyes met, and he reached for her hand.

"How are you holding up?" he whispered, drawing Kady into his arms, giving her lips a brief kiss.

"A little shaky, but I agree with Aunt Willa. It's time to get to the bottom of this."

"OK then. You get the dessert out of the fridge, and I'll grab the paper plates," Colin said, squeezing her fingertips lightly.

They ate the strawberry icebox cake in relative silence, lost in their own thoughts. Colin suspected that what lay ahead could prove to be even more emotionally charged than what had already occurred.

"Henry, you were right. A little chamomile tea and a bit of cake, and I feel like a new woman," said Willa. "Can we begin now, Colin?"

"Yes, Willa. It's time. I don't think we need to go back to my psychic chart. However, I will need the original journal."

Willa, who had kept it in her lap for the last two hours, reluctantly handed it to Colin.

"Now I would like you all to concentrate on remembering the words written in the diary and envision a shaft of silver white light with large wings binding and protecting us within its love. Let's take a deep breath…in and out…That's right, now once again…good."

Colin said a short prayer and placed his hands on top of the book. He closed his eyes and immediately descended into a trance-like state. Suddenly the temperature dropped. His body froze motionless, and slowly, very slowly, all the air seemed to leave the room. It almost appeared as though Colin were suffocating.

Kady desperately wanted to scream, "Stop this!" She was concerned for Colin's well being. She felt trapped and wished she could escape. Colin's body became rigid as he placed his hands on the table in front of him. His head violently jerked backwards, his shoulders arched as he attempted to stand, but then, just as quickly, he sat down again and began to speak.

"Willa, I know that this has all been very hard on you, and that during the last years of our life together I closed myself off to you and the world. But understand I felt I had failed you. Nothing is more devastating to a man than to feel that he no longer can contribute to his family. The shame and emptiness I experienced after my business failed drained the life out of a once proud and fierce man. I was trapped, no longer in control of my world. I would like your forgiveness."

"I'm frightened."

"It's OK, Willa. I'm here," Henry said giving her shoulder a squeeze.

Willa grabbed his other hand for support, and cried out, "Oh my love, there is nothing to forgive. I understood your pain." Willa started to sob uncontrollably.

"Napayshni, your great-great-great-grandfather, healer and keeper of the Mystic Healing Shield, stands beside me here on the other side. We have joined together in an attempt to right the injustices we experienced while on earth. We spirits have enlisted our descendants to help in this quest."

Calmer now, Willa interrupted, "Napayshni, was that you who came to me in my dream?" Colin drew his shoulders back and assumed a more rigid posture.

"Yes, my child. I also appeared to Kady because of all my descendants, she is the one who is most like my beloved Larken. Willa, I heard your husband's call from beyond the grave, and we became linked to this path here on earth. Do not be afraid. Our nation's hoop was broken and scattered, but a new trail was traveled by our ancestors. It is called the white man's trail. I want you to know that the love bond on earth continues in the spirit world and that my only child Beathag was raised in an orphanage when my beloved Larken died on the ship. Beathag married Kenneth Corndonagh, and they were parents to your grandmother Ceitidh. Your heritage is one of strong women. To complete the circle, the truth must be heard and the shield returned to a place of honor."

"Henry, I'm feeling very strange," said Willa. "It's as if there are cobwebs in my head, and I'm very frightened."

Colin's eyes opened suddenly, somehow aware of Willa's distress. "Willa, don't be afraid. Your spirit directors are channeling into your energies. It's not unusual for this to happen when one or more people have psychic gifts. There's an ectoplasmic aura surrounding all of us that becomes stronger the more often we meet. It's perfectly safe." Colin once again closed his eyes, slipping back into a trance.

"Willa, it is Daniel. Please don't shut down because of your fears. Remember where we spent our first anniversary. Do not forget that the truth lies with the lark perched upon the golden swing. And now, Kady, you must trust in your power, for only you can help Colin find his way."

Colin's voice gradually became faint, until he whispered, "Happy Fiftieth anniversary, my love."

"Oh my. He remembered," Willa exclaimed tearfully, sobbing into Henry's shoulder.

Colin shut down, body and soul, for a few minutes as he tried to regroup. There were still so many unanswered questions, and he could not get over the strange feeling of being boxed in. Saying another short prayer to the spirits for their help, Colin opened his eyes.

"Whew, that was one of the most difficult readings I've ever experienced. I'm sorry if this was upsetting to you, Willa."

"Oh, no. It's quite all right, Colin. I've always known there would be no easy solution. I felt from the beginning that Daniel's spirit was troubled. I just never fully realized the guilt he carried with him."

"Willa, I still can't get over the feeling of being trapped—or suffocated—whenever Daniel's spirit was present today. Can you shed some light on this? It's very disturbing to me."

Willa took a deep breath, knowing that she had never before revealed this information, "Yes, Colin, I believe what you were feeling was Daniel's spirit being trapped. I'm sad to admit that during the last three years of his life, Daniel never left our house."

"That makes perfect sense. I suspect he feels ultimately responsible and needs forgiveness to love himself once again. We need to pray for him," Colin answered bowing his head.

After a moment of silence, Henry spoke. "Well kids, I know that it's still early for you young folks, but I'm not used to keeping such late hours. I think it's time to take my little lady home. It's been quite an evening for her." Everyone was in agreement as Colin and Kady walked them to the door, wishing the older couple a good night.

"Willa, I'm afraid we'll have to get together one more time to say goodbye to Daniel's spirit."

"I know, Colin, but I still feel that there's something missing. What do you suppose they mean when they speak of this singing lark and a mysterious shield?"

"I don't know Willa, but Kady and I apparently are involved. Who knows? Maybe it will come to you in a dream, and then we can have closure."

"I hope so. Take care, you two," Willa said giving both her niece and Colin a hug.

As Colin and Kady walked back toward the parlor, Colin turned to her. "Are you too tired to stay a while?" Not waiting for her answer, he gathered her into his arms. "I've been waiting to be alone with you all day."

He kissed the pressure points on her forehead, her eyelids, the sides of her mouth, settling in the center of her sensuous, full lips. She had never felt so safe and secure. It was like coming home. His kiss made her feel like spreading her wings and flying over this entire new world that he had introduced into her life.

"Let's go upstairs," Colin whispered, lifting her into his arms as they ascended the stairs.

Although the revelations of the séance were overwhelming, Colin's touch reminded Kady of how much she longed for their bodies to once again be joined.

Kissing her with an overwhelming hunger, Colin sought out the pattern of her lips. His tongue moved to gain entry, and their mouths joined in a frenzy of lust. His hands searched, caressed, massaged, as she tugged the shirt from around his waist. He spoke only to say, "Honey, let's take some of these things off."

Kady's insides were rippling, for he had unleashed in her a sexual energy that bordered on chaos. Her only words were, "Can we shut off the lights?"

"Sweetheart, I've already seen—"

"—Yes, but that was in the dark," Kady whispered.

Slowly Colin raised them both from the bed, "Come here," he said as he guided her toward an antique mirror. "Now close your eyes. Don't be afraid. Trust me."

From behind, Colin gently removed her silk blouse, letting it drop to the floor. Then he slipped the straps of her bra off onto her arms and slid his hands down to her breasts. Kady gasped and her eyes opened, transfixed on their image.

"See, you're beautiful."

Kady's swollen breasts and erect nipples reflected in the mirror. For a moment neither of them moved.

"No, I'm too top heavy," Kady responded.

"You're perfect. See how they spill out of my hands," Colin said, gently fondling a breast in each hand as his thumbs fondled her nipples.

Kady's shock began to dissipate as his hands continued exploring while he kissed along the side of her neck, across her shoulders, and down her back. This sent a current of electricity across her skin. Closing her eyes again, delighting in her newly aroused sexuality, she thought, If this is a dream, please don't ever let me wake up.

Turning her slowly in his arms, Colin removed the rest of her clothing, then his own, while leading them to the bed. Lips locked and naked, Kady boldly ran her hands over his behind. Then he turned, guiding their bodies as he pulled her on top of his bulging penis. Rocking back and forth, he allowed her to adjust to his size. Kissing her senseless, he rolled her onto her side and stroked the tops of her thighs. He quickly separated her legs and firmly placed his hands upon her labia, caressing her throbbing clitoris. Kady began to writhe and moan with desire.

"Please... please," she begged.

"Not yet, sweetheart," Colin said as his erection threatened to burst. He wanted to touch, taste and feel all of her. His lips kissed a path to her mound of aching flesh. His tongue slid onto her clitoris while his fingers continued to probe every imaginable hidden area, in and out, pressing, seeking her hot spot.

"Oh no!" she screamed, tossing her head side to side as he plunged his tongue deeper into her vagina.

Colin shuddered, knowing he could not hold out much longer. He suddenly raised up and with one powerful lunge buried himself deep inside.

Colin felt Kady tighten around his swollen erection, creating a friction neither wished would ever stop. Every forceful thrust made Kady dizzy with pleasure. Sweat glistened between their bodies as they rhythmically moved up and down. Their oncoming orgasms exploded as they both screamed with abandoned cries of passion and pleasure. Kady gasped for air as she experienced contraction after contraction.

Colin lay back against the mattress, pulling Kady gently into his arms. Exhaustion took over their satiated bodies, and they both fell into a deep slumber.

FOURTEEN

*T*he harsh sounds of a telephone ringing woke Colin from a sound sleep. "Uh...hello," he slurred, mumbling into the receiver.

A high-pitched voice whined over the wires. "Is this Colin O'Dannaher?"

"Do you know what time it is?" Colin barked as his mind and body became alert.

"Why yes, sir. It's after midnight."

"Well, who the hell are you, and what do you want?" Colin said, lowering his voice as the naked body beside him stirred.

"I'm calling for Sister Agatha at Lakeview nursing home. I'm sorry to disturb you sir, but she said to tell you that this was an emergency."

"An emergency?" Colin was skeptical that anyone would wake him in the middle of the night.

"Why yes, sir. It seems that a Mrs. Jewel St. Jude is dying, and she is calling for you to help her soul rest in peace."

There were times when Colin had been asked to assist and comfort when someone was close to death and afraid to die. This was, however, the first time he had been called out in the middle of the night. "Yes, of course. I understand. Please tell Sister Agatha I'll be there as soon as I can."

He rolled over onto his back, placing his arm over his eyes as he tried to assimilate all his thoughts. Kady breathed softly as she slept. He longed to take her into his arms and rekindle their lovemaking, but his sense of duty to a distressed soul came first. He pulled back the covers and proceeded to get up. He had only met Mrs. St. Jude once, but he remembered her pain and understood her fear of the unknown.

Colin dressed quickly not bothering to shave. He took one last longing look at Kady's exposed sleeping form. The sheet had fallen from her shoulders exposing her luscious breasts. Colin hungered for one last taste. He bent over, taking her sweet nipple into his mouth. Kady flinched at the chilled wetness of his tongue. Half asleep, she groaned and rolled over on her side. Colin stood up, letting out a frustrated sigh, and covered her enticing body.

He drove to the nursing home as the silence of the moonless night reflected his mood. He wanted to howl, for his mind and body yearned for Kady. Consciously, he was aware of the dark streets, devoid of all traffic; subconsciously, he replayed every breathless moment of their lovemaking. It did not take him long to reach the home. The parking lot was empty; only a few cars from the midnight shift lined the curb. Colin slid into a spot right in front of the building. He checked for signs that would show time restrictions, knowing that he could be here for hours.

The silent corridors echoed his footsteps. Colin signed in with the night nurse and followed her directions to Mrs. St. Jude's floor. This was where the sick received around-the-clock care.

Directly outside the room he was greeted by Sister Agatha who immediately noticed his unshaven face, "Oh, Colin, I'm sorry to have gotten you out of bed, but I didn't know what to do or how much time she had left. I'm so glad you've come. Poor Mrs. St. Jude is so restless. She's been calling out your name for hours. One minute she is quite lucid and the next she returns to a fetal position, staring out at nothing. The staff nurse tells me she hasn't eaten for days. The doctors don't give us much hope. It could be a few days or a few hours. I hate to see her so tormented."

"That's OK, Sister. I'm happy to help. Can you fill me in on her background?"

"Well, we don't have much except for her health records. They are quite extensive, due to the fact that she's been here for years. I believe she's one of our oldest residents. Sister Agatha pulled a chart out of the plastic holder nailed to the door. "Let me see now," she said running her fingers down the page. "It says she was brought here some-time in the late sixties. She came over from the hospital at the University of Chicago. Born 1907 means she's eighty-four years old."

Turning the page she continued, "She suffered a stroke about ten years ago, had a successful triple by-pass. Oh, here. This might be of help. It says she was treated for lung cancer due to the second-hand smoke she was exposed to during her career as a jazz singer. Looks like she was married, but her husband's deceased, and she has no children. That's about all I can tell you other than the few rumors that have circulated over the years."

"That won't be necessary. I think I'll let Mrs. St. Jude tell me anything else she wants me to know. Thank you, sis-ter," Colin said, entering the room.

The sight of the tiny frail woman lying upon the bed broke Colin's heart. Her aura and demeanor reflected defeat. She appeared listless, emotionally vacant, and lost in her own world. Still Colin felt compelled to communicate with her.

"Hi, Mrs. St. Jude. I hear you've been asking for me."

At the sound of his softly spoken words, Mrs. St. Jude's eyes fluttered, and she woke from her trance-like state.

"Oh, Mr. O'Dannaher, I knew you would come. We've been waiting for you," she said holding out her hand.

"Who's here with you, Mrs. St. Jude?" Colin asked, feeling another presence in the room. The spirit, however, gave no indication of wanting to be heard.

"Why, it's Willy. You remember him, don't you? From your last visit? He came to me in a dream last night."

The pressure from her grasp increased, and Colin had an impression of a young woman swinging on a velvet swing. Colin tried to hold his concentration while still being recep-tive to the spiritual energy in the room. The image changed and the young woman was now holding out a gun.

Suddenly Colin blurted out, "It's time, time to free my soul." Colin rubbed his eyes as if to clear the vision, feeling that he was about to unravel a deep dark secret locked in Mrs. St. Jude's past.

Taking a deep breath, Mrs. St. Jude slowly began to speak. "Many years ago when I was young and foolish, I had dreams of becoming a star. I was willing to take any kind of job that came my way. I was a waitress, a dance hall singer and a barmaid during prohibition. I worked hard and still lived hand to mouth, barely having enough to pay my rent. Then one night, I was performing at a little tavern in Old Town when I met this handsome young man. He offered me a job singing at The Velvet Swing, one of the most popular night clubs in the city. Needless to say, I was ready and willing to accept his offer. He said he was the owner of the club, and he would make me a star. I believed everything he said to me. He was so charming and convincing."

"Willy was so good to me," she continued. "He showered me with gifts, took me to fancy restaurants, opened up a whole new world to me. Then one day he told me he loved me, and I believed him. We became lovers. At first our rendezvous were limited to his office upstairs of the club, and my apartment. He was always very secretive about his life away from The Velvet Swing, rarely speaking to me about anything but business. He was, I thought, a very private man. On our first year anniversary, he picked me up in his brand new maroon Packard and drove me to 666 Mohawk. There, to my surprise, was this beautiful graystone that he had bought for us. He called it our little hidey hole. Oh, we were so happy there. He knew how much the security of having a roof over my head meant to me, and so a few weeks later he gave me the deed to the house and told me that he'd put it in my name. I loved him so much that I believed him when he promised to marry me. He said to be patient until he could earn more money. You see, he told me that he was holding down two jobs and wouldn't always be able to see me on a regular basis. I didn't care because the time we shared was so special. Thanks to Willy, my career finally took off, and I was able to headline under my own name, Jewel Monroe. I was the star at The Velvet Swing. You should have seen it; there were standing room only crowds every night. It was all so grand. I sang my songs in this little yellow, sequined outfit, perched on a swing, so I became known as The Lark...I...I." Seeing her falter, Colin reached over and poured her a glass of water, placing a straw in her cup.

"Try to take a few sips of this. You'll feel better," Colin said. He helped her sit up. As he touched her frail shoulders, bringing her closer to the drink, suddenly he recalled the earlier images and could feel even stronger mental energies in the room.

"Thank you. Please, I need to continue."

He suspected Willy's spirit was urging her to complete the story. She regained a little strength and waved the cup away.

"I was feeling on top of the world until one day after rehearsals, I came out the back stage door and a boy approached me. I thought he was a bit young to ask for my autograph, but sometimes youngsters sneak in. All of a sudden, he started yelling and screaming at me to stay away from his father because his mother was threatening to kill herself if I didn't stop seeing him. As I looked into the tears running down the boy's face, I saw Willy as a young man. 'What's your name, son?' I asked, not wanting to believe my eyes. He puffed up his chest and shrieked, 'William Chaddack Junior! My dad owns you and this club. Leave him alone, or I'll kill you! You're just another of his bad women who make my mom cry.' I was so shocked. I had no idea Willy was married. I would never have carried on with a married man. I felt dirty and cheap and ran home crying. Looking back now, I can see how I conveniently ignored all the signs. He was so sincere when he charmed. I didn't want to return to the small town I had come from. I was restless and in my youthful ignorance thought I could better myself. He offered me the chance I was waiting for, to get out of the life I was headed for. I guess I ended up there anyway," Mrs. St. Jude said, taking a deep breath.

William Chaddack Junior. Why did that name sound so familiar? Colin thought to himself. Mrs. St. Jude slowly continued.

"When Willy came home that night, I confronted him. At first he lied; then when he saw that I would not believe him, he flew into a rage and hit me, knocking out my front tooth. When he realized what he had done, he fell to his knees and begged my forgiveness. He promised never to hurt me again. I wouldn't believe him. He wasn't the same man I had fallen in love with. I didn't know this man who was abusive and a liar. I screamed 'Leave me alone, and don't ever come back!' You see, I could never take another woman's husband. The very next day, I quit my job and went to work at another club for less money, but I didn't care, even if it meant losing the roof over my head."

"Weeks later, I met Angelo St. Jude, an older gentleman who was kind and truly cared about me. Thank God, I finally found true love with Angelo. His faith in God and inherent goodness saved me. He was a locksmith who owned his own business. At first we were just good friends, but he took my mind off the heartbreak of Willy's betrayal. He came to the club every night and made sure I got home safely, no matter how late I worked. Then one evening, I came home and found that one of my windows had been broken. Angelo immediately changed all the locks in my house. I was so frightened."

Mrs. St. Jude became very agitated and Colin asked if she would like for him to call for a nurse. "No, no, I must finish," she said as she reached out for Colin's hands and resumed her story.

"A few nights later, after Angelo had walked me home and said good night, I entered my house. I could smell the faint odor of tobacco in my living room. I was still very apprehensive because of the broken window, so I was terribly scared when I noticed the rear door lock had been pried open.

Suddenly, I heard a noise in my upstairs bedroom. I ran to the bureau in my parlor and took out a gun Willy had given me. The house was pitch black, and I heard footsteps, but I couldn't see anything. Then I crept, quiet as a mouse, searching for my telephone. Just as I was about to dial, a large hulking shadow descended down the stairs. You must understand—I feared for my life. I panicked. May God forgive me, but I fired the gun three times, up into the darkened stairwell. The intruder lurched forward in agony and tumbled down the stairs head first.

"I dialed the police, yelling my address, 666 Mohawk. 'Please,' I yelled, 'help! Someone has broken in.' I then heard moaning. With the gun still in my hand I inched my way over to turn on the light. I screamed. It was Willy I had shot. Crying, I ran to his side cradling his head in my lap. 'What are you doing here?' I asked, 'Why didn't you call out to me?'

"At first he didn't answer. I thought he was dead, but he must have just been unconscious. I started to shake him, begging him to still be alive. He began to mumble. I think he was delirious from the fall because all he kept repeating was, 'Hide the shield, make sure no one finds the shield...'and then he died in my arms."

Crying, she could no longer speak. Colin held her slight form as he tried to calm her with reassuring words. "It's OK. He forgives you, and he knows that you loved him. Talk to him; you can do it. You've been sending him telepathic messages along with your prayers. He hears you; tell him you forgive him...and then forgive yourself," Colin said, patting her back and rocking her in his arms.

When her tears subsided, Colin rang for the nurse. Colin's senses were screaming. He didn't have the whole picture, but he suspected that the shield was an important piece of an even larger puzzle. He wanted to ask her if she had found it, but feared she was to weak to continue.

The nurse came in and suggested a sedative. Mrs. St. Jude shook her head.

"I need just a little more time with Colin. I'll be all right. Please leave us...I have to complete my story before I can rest."

"Are you sure? I can come back later," Colin said, torn because he wanted to hear the rest of her story.

With a feeble motion, she held up her hand, "No, Colin. The end is near, and we need your help or Willy will be eternally damned. Let me continue...

"When the police came, I was arrested for Willy's murder. His wife hired a well connected lawyer and made sure I could not post bond. She even tried to take my house away from me. I don't blame her; she was betrayed. I would have acted the same. He was not a good husband. Angelo used all his savings for my defense. I was acquitted, and the judge ruled it self-defense. You must believe me; I would never have killed him." Colin patted her hand, reassuring her. "When I was released from prison, Angelo St. Jude and I were married, and we lived out the rest of his life in the house Willy had bought for me. Angelo was a good man, and I tried to make him happy. Although Willy had lied to me, I'll always be grateful to him for my house.

"Did you ever figure out what Willy meant by 'hide the shield?'"

"No. When I came home from jail, I searched the house from top to bottom. I never found anything. And now Willy's spirit is calling for help...but first I must find the shield so Willy may find peace. Please help me, Colin."

"I'll give it my best shot," Colin answered.

"Willy's here, you know. I'm so afraid...for both of us...you must help me! I was culpable too. He was a married...Promise me you'll find the shield!" she said.

The tormented Mrs. St. Jude collapsed from exhaustion.

Colin pressed the call button for the attendant. The nurse gave Mrs. St. Jude some medication while Colin continued to hold her hand until she dropped off to sleep. He rose from the bed and walked to the nurse's station. Colin was emotionally drained, but he knew that he had to clear his head and think.

Sister Agatha took one look at Colin's weary face and handed him a cup of black coffee. "It's late, Colin. Why don't you go home? Mrs. St. Jude is resting easily now, thanks to you."

"I'm happy to have been some help. I'll just finish this up and be on my way," Colin said draining his cup and throwing the empty styrofoam into the trash can.

Slowly, dragging his feet, Colin walked to his car. Before starting the engine, he laid his head on the steering wheel and closed his eyes. He prayed to God and called on the help of his spiritual guide.

Suddenly his energy returned. It was as if the caffeine had just kicked in. He raised his head as it all became so clear to him. He felt an inexplicable urgency. He must find Mrs. St. Jude's home. That must be the connection, he thought, trying to remember the address she called out. "I've got it," he said out loud thumping his hand on the steering wheel, "Six-six-six Mohawk."

Colin started his car and drove back to Lincoln Park. It was not far from his house. Thinking of home reminded him of Kady as he pictured her lying naked in his bed, awaiting his return. So lost was he in the image that he almost missed the street.

He headed back west again and found Mohawk. Turning left, he drove down two more blocks and slowly looked for the exact address. The homes were old and dilapidated. The neighborhood screamed for loving homeowners to restore them to their original glory.

He pulled up to an old gray, abandoned Victorian home that was ready to fall apart. Colin rubbed his eyes, exhausted from the long hours spent at the nursing home, and stared at the numbers on the crooked frame.

Rolling down his window for a closer look, Colin said out loud, "It can't be," as he realized the similarities to his own home. Even the painted carpenter's gingerbread trim, although it was rotted and the paint was peeling off, looked terribly familiar. The hairs on the back of his neck stood on end as his eyes swept over the small front porch with the wide set of stairs that was half hidden by overgrown shrubbery.

The more he looked, the more he realized that the house was an exact replica of the home he had purchased and was now living in. Colin wondered if it would have the same hidden compartment behind the fireplace. It dawned on Colin, "That's where I must look, if only I can get inside."

Walking around to the trunk, he reached in and pulled out the set of tools he always kept on hand when he was working on a construction sight. He grabbed a crowbar and flashlight, turning the rubber cylinder back and forth to make sure it worked.

Quickening his pace, he walked up the long, cement sidewalk, trying to avoid stepping on all the cracks. High bushes grown out of control partially blocked his view of the wooden entrance that was listing on its side. The only occasional sound was that of a solitary owl hooting for its mate. Gingerly he placed his foot on the first step. As the rotted wood gave way, Colin jumped back just in time to save himself from an accident. He looked up, squinting in the darkness, trying to locate another entrance when he spotted a sign on one of the windows. Turning on his flashlight, he focused the beam and read, "No Trespassing. This house is consigned to the wrecking ball of the Matthew's Demolition Company." At the bottom in small print was their slogan: "You employeth, we destroyeth."

Very funny, Colin thought. A home wrecker with a sense of humor. Colin decided to try his luck at the back entrance and made his way toward the rear of the building. What lawn there had once been was now torn up with gapping holes. Large rocks and fallen bricks were blocking the way. It took all of his concentration to avoid injury and find a clear path. He located the three cement stairs that led into the back porch and was thankful that they were still intact.

Although the entrance had been boarded up, Colin cautiously pried it open, removing the rusty nails.

Setting the board aside, Colin realized that he was now standing in the mud room. Warm, musty, damp air greeted his senses as he inched his way toward the step up that would lead him to what was left of the kitchen. His flashlight scanned the spacious room that had once been designed to accommodate the hub of family activity. The cabinets had been torn from the wall, and electrical wiring stuck out from the outlets causing him to wonder if all the electricity had been shut off. He didn't want to trip over an open wire and get electrocuted.

Making his way through the dining room, Colin took note of further destruction. All the carved cove moldings had been ripped off the walls, leaving large gaping holes with insulation hanging out. He glanced toward the area where the enclosed vestibule should have been, but there were no doors left standing to indicate the exact location of the entrance. Sweeping his light across the room, he saw the staircase leading up to the second story. He hoped that the original solid oak steps wouldn't be rotted.

Colin took the stairs two at a time, feeling his way toward the top. To the right he knew he would find the small bathroom but doubted that the antique claw foot tub and fixtures still remained. To the left was the master bedroom and what he hoped would be the end of his journey. Colin's excitement grew as he raised his flashlight, skimming the area where he knew the doorway opening should be. The beam of light landed on a door, the only door left standing. There appeared to be an original cut glass doorknob still attached. Colin wondered how the scavengers missed this highly prized hardware.

Curbing his rising excitement, he gingerly opened the door, surprised that it was still on its hinge. The doorknob stayed in place. "Bingo," he said out loud. Sure enough, the bedroom was an exact replica of the one in his home. The fireplace still remained standing, but pieces of the floorboards had been torn up. Colin focused the beam of light in front of him as he made his way forward. A gaping two-foot hole in the center of the room went right through to the floor below. Making a large arch, Colin walked around it cautiously, wondering if the wood would hold his weight. It held, as renewed energy coursed through his body. Colin could feel the end in sight. The fireplace looked identical. He crawled awkwardly into the chimney, entering slowly so he could maneuver his body into a standing position.

The cool brick pressed against his spine. Although he was not claustrophobic, the space was tight. Colin held the crowbar steady in one hand and gripped the black rubber coated cylinder with the other. He heard the flapping of wings and a rumbling. He hoped that he had not disturbed a bird's nest above. His eyes followed upward. "Damn," Colin spat as chunks of mortar and bits of bricks tumbled onto his face. Unexpectedly, he lost the grip on his flashlight. As it fell to the floor, it flickered and went out.

Even though Colin could not see through the darkness, he was not about to give up. He blindly guessed his way toward the storage box. "Got ya," Colin said into the darkened room. He deftly lifted the heavy crowbar, hitting the rusted lock with one clean swoop. Colin flinched, raising his hands to protect his head as broken pieces of metal fell all around him, landing on the floor at his feet. He had dislodged more than the lock, and a sudden large crack split through the air as more crumbling brick plummeted down. Now Colin felt caged in and trapped, but he had come too far to give up.

Steadying his nerves, he stretched his hands upward pushing the box open. He reached inside and found a canvas sack. Quickly, he shoved it out the hearth's opening.

Wanting to escape the small enclosure before anything else fell on him, Colin crawled once again on his hands and knees in search of his flashlight. "Damn, damn, double damn," Colin swore as he heard the echoing sounds of it rolling away. Carefully he edged his way toward where he hoped the flashlight had landed as the aged oak tore up his hands.

Suddenly he heard the roar of hundreds of pieces of wood splintering and cracking in the silence of the night. Crying out into the darkness, he reached out to grab on to something —anything—but found nothing. The two-foot hole had now become large enough for a man to fall through. Colin's body tumbled through the opening, crashing down. Landing on the first floor below, he lay sprawled and unconscious.

Kady tossed and turned with the violence of her dream. Breathless and trembling, she felt someone shaking her awake, and for a moment Kady was disoriented, not recognizing her surroundings. She turned to Colin, only to find him missing from the bed. The room was dark as she sat up shivering, trying to figure out what had caused her to wake up so suddenly with feeling of dread. Slowly the mental images returned, and she remembered the frightening journey.

Something had happened to Colin. She had seen it with her mind's eye, and with a sense of alarm she knew he was in danger. She could see him lying on the floor in his own house.

Leaping out of bed, she ran to the other rooms, opening every door and cupboard she could find. They were all empty. Only the sound of her labored breathing echoed in the house. "Remain calm and think," she demanded of herself, and she returned to Colin's room and sat on the bed. The room became colder. She grabbed the shirt that Colin had thrown on the floor the night before. She rubbed her arms trying to get warm.

Suddenly another telepathic vision emerged. Colin was falling, falling through a hole in his bedroom. Then the mental picture faded, and the name Matthew's Demolition Company flashed in her head. What could that mean? she wondered. The yellow pages. I must check the yellow pages, she thought, once again running through the house, turning on every light she passed, searching for a phone book.

Checking the library, she rummaged through all the shelves and finally found it in the bottom drawer of Colin's desk. She flipped through the pages, found the number and dialed, only to hear an answering machine announce that their offices were closed and wouldn't re-open until seven a.m. She grabbed a pencil and paper off the desktop and jotted down the address. Without warning, the grandfather clock in the hallway struck six a.m. She was running out of time.

Back in the bedroom, Kady threw on her crumpled silk shorts and blouse and rushed out of the house.

There was very little traffic this early in the morning, and Kady arrived in less than fifteen minutes at the Matthews Demolition Company. Sprinting to the door, she found it locked. Just then, she heard a truck pull up and a workman got out of his pickup.

"Can I help you, ma'am?" the burly young man offered. "The offices don't open till seven."

"Oh yes, please," Kady breathlessly answered. "Are there any houses scheduled for demolition today?"

"As a matter of fact, we got three going under the wrecking ball today."

"Three!" Kady squealed. "Are there any scheduled for 270 Magnolia?" Kady asked, giving him Colin's address.

"Not that I know of. Would you like to come in while I check the books?" he asked, opening the door to the office. The air-conditioning had been turned off for the night, and the room smelled of coffee and stale cigarettes. "Is there some kind of problem?" he inquired.

"Well, yes. As a matter of fact, I think you're tearing down the wrong house. I know, 270 Magnolia has just been newly renovated."

"We don't usually make mistakes like that, ma'am. Let's see. Here are the addresses of what's going down today. I don't see any notes about changes." He said pointing with his dirty index finger to the bold black markings on the old tasteless Farrah Fawcett pinup calendar tacked to the wall. "Are you sure about the address you gave me?"

"I'm pretty sure. Can I just check those addresses again?" Kady asked, shaking her head when none of the numbers seemed even remotely similar.

"Would it help if you saw a picture?" he asked, handing her three photos. Kady thumbed through the first two without recognition. Picking up the third photo, her hand trembled as she saw a house that looked remarkably like Colin's.

"That's it! That's the one!" she cried, trying to hold her hand steady. It was Colin's house, only it wasn't. The difference was that this place looked much older and was falling apart. But the similarities were definitely there, and it scared her to death. "You're sure this isn't 270 Magnolia?"

"Positive," he said, taking the photo from her hand and turning it over. "See, this says 666 Mohawk, and it's due to come down in less that twenty minutes," he said checking his wrist watch. "I don't think you can make it there in time."

Kady was already out the door. He looked out the office window, admiring her sprinting figure. Then he shook his head and said, thinking out loud, "Great looking chick, but one crazy broad."

Kady wished Rose could see her now as she sped through the neighborhood streets, barely stopping at the signs, thankful she had made all the lights with no cops in sight. She pulled up in front of the old dilapidated house and jumped out of her car running and screaming at the top of her lungs toward the crane that was just about to hit its target. "Stop, stop!" she yelled, waving her hands in the air.

The man seated in the cab hollered back, "Move it or lose it, lady. We've got a job to do." Neither could hear each other, as the noise from the bulldozer and wrecking ball were deafening.

"No, no, you can't! There's a man in the house. There's a man in the house!" Kady cried, putting herself right in the line of fire and hoping that he wouldn't swing the big black ball in her direction.

The man in the machinery thought, What's with this dame? She must be crazy. After another ten minutes of shouting at her, he realized that he was going to have to call in the cops. There was no other way to get this nut off the property. After all, he had a job to do. Shutting off his engine, he radioed to the other bulldozer that there was a problem. He took off his hard hat and jumped down from the cab.

"Thank God you stopped! There's a man in the house. Did you hear me? There's a man in the house!" Kady frantically shrieked.

"Lady, where did you escape from? There's no one in this damn house. It's been vacant for months."

"Are you sure? Did you check?" Kady questioned, trying to look and act calmer now that she had his attention.

"Look, babe, we've got our orders, and this place is coming down. Now do I have to call the cops, or are you gonna leave under your own steam?"

"Please, please just let me check the house. Please, what have you got to lose? If I'm right you could be accused of manslaughter," Kady begged, tears welling up in her eyes.

Right now, I definitely want to brain this broad, he thought, but I can't stand to see a beautiful dame cry.

"OK, OK. But you gotta put on a hard hat. I don't wanna get in trouble with the union," he said, walking off to his car.

Relieved, Kady closed her eyes and leaned up against the house, telling herself that she was not going to cry. Minutes later, a big yellow hat was thrust on her head.

"Here," he grunted, "let's get this show on the road. I've got a job to do." Kady took a deep breath and ran after his burly form. "Watch your step. A lot of this wood's rotted," he mumbled. Kady cautiously followed, trying to keep up. They entered through the back porch.

"OK, lady, see anyone here?" he said, checking the small closet and proceeding up to the kitchen.

The destruction was devastating, and Kady had a hard time recognizing any similarity to Colin's beautiful home. Suddenly she wondered if she was on a wild goose chase, or if maybe she was crazy. What if Colin had received an emergency call from his grandmother and just forgot to leave a message? Slowly they picked their way through what was left of the kitchen.

"Let's check the library," Kady suggested.

"Library? There ain't no library in these kinda houses. You sound like you've got a few screws loose," he mumbled shaking his head. There was an old, ripped tarp piled up in one corner of the parlor and he walked over to it. "See, no boogie men here, either," he sarcastically said, kicking at the pile of rags.

Kady walked over to the vestibule, tripping over an empty can of paint, and suddenly she remembered the large walk-in broom closet behind the stairwell. Slowly making her way through the debris, she located the closet, or what was left of the closet.

"Oh my God!" she cried seeing a foot sticking out at an awkward angle. She pulled open the door, dragging planks of rotted wood away from Colin's listless body. "Call an ambulance! Please, call an ambulance. Colin's been hurt."

Two hundred thirty pounds of sweating flesh pushed his way through the small opening. "Lady, lady, is he still alive? Don't move him. I'll go get help," he answered, moving quicker than she would have thought possible. Tearing out of the house, he ran, shouting at his co-workers to call for help.

"Colin, oh my darling," Kady sobbed seeing the coagulated blood on his scalp. Using her CPR skills, she checked for a pulse. After feeling a strong beat, Kady sat back on her knees stunned. "Dear God, what should I do? Action, I must take action," she told herself trying to calm her fears.

She ran over and grabbed the old tarp, then she slowly began to check his body for broken bones. Kady knew that she could not move him before the ambulance arrived, and she covered his body with the large canvas rag hoping to ward off shock. His left arm hung limp from his side, and he whimpered at her touch.

"It's all right, darling. Help is on the way," Kady said, brushing bits of wood and dirt from his face. She glanced up and saw the hole and knew that the ceiling must have collapsed from the weight of Colin's body. The wood was rotted, and the hole was about four feet wide. She was amazed and thankful that he was still alive. Looking down at his battered face, she placed a light kiss on his lips, and his eyes fluttered open.

"Don't move, Colin, please don't move, I'm afraid you might have injured your spine."

"Oh, God, I hurt," Colin moaned, closing his eyes again.

"Stay with me!" she cried. "Colin, stay with me. I don't want to lose you," Kady knew it was better for him to be alert.

"You won't ever lose me, honey. I'm here to stay," Colin whispered. Moments passed, and Colin's lips moved again. "I found the sack, Kady. It was in the house. Get the sack." The excruciating pain caused him to black out again.

Kady did not want to leave Colin's side, but she looked around the closet and into the outer room, seeing nothing but total destruction. The sounds of the siren blared as the paramedics broke their way in through the front door.

"Here! We're over here!" Kady yelled as she moved aside for the men to enter. They checked for broken bones and quickly splintered his arm and foot before placing him on the stretcher. Then they maneuvered the cot through the narrow hallway. Kady silently watched, paralyzed with fear, praying to God that he would be all right.

"Are you the person that found him?" one of the men called over his shoulder. Kady nodded. "You best follow us in your car. The police are gonna want a statement."

Just before Kady left she glanced back into the closet and saw what appeared to be a canvas sack. She bent down, afraid to pick it up. Then she looked up again into the hole and realized that this must have fallen through the opening with Colin landing on top of it.

"Hey lady, you better clear outta here. That ambulance is takin' your boyfriend away," Kady heard the construction worker yell as she grabbed the dusty sack and ran to her car.

For almost two days Colin had been unconscious, delirious and moaning one moment, quiet and subdued the next. Then, forty-eight hours later, Colin suddenly woke up, looking straight into the concerned eyes of Kady, who had never left his side.

"Hi," Colin whispered.

"Oh, Colin, you're awake. Thank God you're awake," Kady stammered, jumping from the bed.

"Hey wait a minute. Where am I?"

"You're in the hospital. Let me call for the nurse."

"No, no. Let me get my bearings before you send in the troops." Colin winced as he tried to sit up and stop Kady from pressing the nurse's call button.

"You're in pain. Let me call for some medication. You'll feel better."

"Take it easy. I can hold out for a while. I'm sure they put some of that stuff in this," Colin said, jiggling his IV and slowly taking note of the cast on his left arm and the metal brace on his ankle.

"But, Colin, we've all been so worried," Kady said.

"Come here, honey," he said reaching out to take her hand. "Tell me everything that's happened. I don't remember much of anything," Colin said, touching the white bandage on his forehead.

Kady cradled his right hand gently in hers. She was so happy that he was conscious that tears began to well up in her bright blue eyes. She wasn't sure where to begin.

"Hey now, don't go getting all emotional with me. Rumors of my demise have been greatly exaggerated," Colin said, using his thumb to wipe the moisture from her face. "I'm gonna be just fine. Now start from the beginning and tell me what the heck happened."

"Do you remember the barbecue at your house with Henry and Aunt Willa? You know, the night I slept over?" Kady said hesitantly.

Colin looked puzzled for a moment; then a big smile spread across his face. "I believe the whole damn house would have had to fall on me in order for me to forget that," he replied.

Kady blushed momentarily and continued. "Long after we'd fallen asleep, I awoke suddenly from a terrible dream to find you gone."

"How many days ago was that?" Colin questioned.

"Two. You've been here since early Monday morning. Today is Wednesday."

"That long, huh?" Colin rubbed his hand over his unshaven face. Beneath his sprouting beard he was deathly pale.

"Yes, darling, you've been in and out of it for days, and we've all been so worried. Your poor grandmother is beside herself. The doctor finally sent her home with a sedative and demanded that she get some rest. She promised to come back later tonight."

"As soon as I get all this clear in my head, we'll call her. Now how did I get here?"

"Like I said, I was having this dream that you were falling, falling through a whole in your bedroom floor. But it couldn't have been your bedroom because I was lying in your bed and you weren't there."

"Oh yes, now I remember. I hated to leave you, but Sister Agatha called me some time after midnight about a woman I had seen during my last visit to the nursing home. Mrs. St. Jude, a woman from the Lakeview nursing home, was dying. She had been asking for me all night. Do you know her?" Colin asked.

"Yes, of course I do, but that still doesn't explain how you ended up in that dilapidated old house."

"Well, when I went to see Mrs. St. Jude, she told me the most amazing story about her life with a man named William

Chaddack. He was her lover, and years ago, she'd accidentally killed him."

"My God," Kady gasped.

"That's only part of it, Kady. In the later years of her life, he kept coming to her in a dream, repeating over and over his dying words. 'You must find the shield; you must find the shield.' She was haunted by his demand." Colin paused, grimacing in pain. "Could I please have some water?"

"Oh, honey, I think I better call the nurse. You're still hooked up to the IV, and I don't think you can drink anything yet."

Kady rang for the nurse, who was surprised that Colin was so alert and coherent. Kady mentioned that he had been awake for at least fifteen minutes asking questions.

"You should have called us, miss. The doctor must be made aware the moment the patient regains consciousness."

Colin gave the woman a huge smile. "Nurse, don't be mad at Kady. I'm the one who wouldn't allow her to call. I needed to find out how I'd gotten here in the first place, and if it's OK with you, I'd like her to finish the story."

"All right, young man, but I need to check your vital signs. Then I'll be back with the doctor and some pain medication. I have a feeling you'll be needing some." She proceeded to complete her task and left the room.

"Colin, shouldn't you wait for your medicine?" Kady asked.

"I don't want to be so groggy that I can't figure out what is being said, so I'd just as soon wait to take the darn stuff. From what you tell me, I've lost days of my life, and I really need to piece them together." Colin was getting agitated, and Kady longed to ease his mind.

"I still don't understand how you ended up knocked out on the floor of that old house," Kady asked

"Mrs. St. Jude begged me to help her find this hidden shield. You know, Kady, a shield. Sound familiar? I felt there must be a connection. She had mentioned her old address and I knew I had to go there."

Kady shook her head. "In the middle of the night?"

"Yes. Believe me, Kady, nothing would have made me happier than to return home to you, but I felt compelled to find that old place." Colin paused, taking a deep breath and realized that his ribs had been bruised too. "I feel like I've been hit by a Mack truck."

"Well, it wasn't exactly a truck, but I'll tell you later just how close you came to being crushed. Please continue."

"When I left the hospital, I drove straight to 666 Mohawk. It wasn't difficult to find; it was only a few miles away from my home. As I pulled up in front of the place, I was stunned. The house was a carbon copy of my own. Suddenly the name William Chaddack registered in my mind, and it all began to make sense. The similarity in the houses couldn't have been a coincidence, and I became aware of the connection. There was no doubt in my mind. I knew were the shield was hidden."

"Connection? What connection?" Kady asked.

"When I was renovating my home, I found a secret compartment built in the wall behind my fireplace. Inside he found a native American peace pipe, a ceremonial war bonnet, and the deed to my house showing William Chaddack as the original owner. Simply holding the artifacts in my hands I felt intense psychic vibrations. I had no idea what it meant, but my curiosity and been roused. I felt as though I were Nancy Drew's older brother, so I hacked my way onto the UCLA Library site to see if there was any information on missing Native American artifacts."

Suddenly Colin remembered something. "Did you find the bag?"

"What bag?" Kady questioned.

"The canvas sack. Did you see it? I found it in the house. Was it there?"

"Yes, yes it was. The bag was lying in the rubble underneath you. I found it after the paramedics took you away. I was so worried about you that I hadn't given it a second thought."

Colin winced in pain.

"Should I get the nurse?" she asked.

"No, there isn't much left to tell, but you must bring me the burlap sack. Promise me you'll bring the sack."

"Of course I will," Kady said.

"You started to tell me about some information at the UCLA Library."

"Sorry. I'm having a little trouble focusing, but now I remember. Back in 1939 there was a break in at Navy Pier and several priceless native American artifacts were stolen." Colin's speech became slurred. "Kady, I'm sorry, sweetheart, but I'm gonna need that medicine sooner than I thought. Could you please call..." Colin asked closing his eyes in pain. Kady immediately summoned the nurse, who came rushing in with a syringe.

"Would you step outside, please?" the nurse asked pulling the curtain closed. Kady stood outside Colin's room. She was exhausted and leaned against the wall.

"Now turn over, and here we go. My, you lasted a mite longer than I thought. You've got a stubborn young man here, miss," she called out. "But he's mighty handsome, even with that big old bandage on his head," the nurse said, trying to distract Colin from the needle she had just stuck into his rump. Colin immediately closed his eyes waiting for the pain to subside.

The nurse pulled the drape open. "He'll likely be out for a few hours, miss. Why don't you go home and get some rest?" the nurse asked, noticing the circles under Kady's eyes.

"I think I will," Kady whispered, tiptoeing over to the bed. She leaned over, kissed Colin on the forehead, and looked upward. "Please, God, let him be all right."

Kady returned to an empty home. Rose was filling in for Kady at work and Patti took over Rose's tour guide position.

Her entire family had offered to pitch in and help when Kady had called them two days earlier from the hospital. They had all offered to spot Kady so she could get some rest, but she politely refused, causing the family to be concerned for her health. It took both Willa and her mother to explain to the rest of the Daileys why Kady needed to remain at Colin's side until he recovered from his unconscious state.

The first thing Kady needed to do was call Colin's grandmother and then her Aunt Willa. They were both grateful to hear that Colin was conscious and on his way to recovery. Willa and Edna agreed to meet Kady at the hospital that evening. With parts of the puzzle still unsolved, Kady was concerned that another mediumistic reading would do permanent injury to Colin's health.

She would not allow any harm to come to him. His body needed to heal, both mentally and physically in order to recover properly. But she also knew that he would rest much easier knowing that they had solved this mystery. She lay down on her bed with her mind spinning out all the possibilities until she fell into an exhausted sleep.

Kady slept fitfully for a few hours, then showered and changed into a soft peach skirt and blouse. Getting into the car she briefly remembered seeing construction in the northbound lanes on her way home from the hospital. She decided to take Lake Shore Drive, knowing that she could avoid the traffic. Kady had not been outside for a few days. She rolled down her windows, letting in the fresh air. She took a few moments to enjoy the sunset. It reminded her of Colin and the wonderful times they had shared watching the sun go down.

Driving by the lake, she saw beautiful blue water and the rhythmic motion of the waves. It calmed her inner thoughts, and she was able to assimilate all the things that had happened in the last week. Bit by bit, she ran them through her mind. Some of the pieces fit, yet something was still missing.

When Kady arrived at the hospital, she unconsciously searched for parking, driving around and around before finally noticing that all the lots were full. Exasperated, Kady was about to circle the parking lot one last time when she saw a familiar face. It was Napayshni pointing to an empty space that Kady had not seen. Warily, she pulled in and got out of the car. As quickly as he had appeared, he vanished. As she headed for the hospital she felt compelled to look back one last time. Sure enough, Napayshni stood next to Kady's car, pointing to the back seat. Kady turned and walked toward him.

For the first time, she came face to face with her great-great-great-great grandfather. A sense of calm replaced her previous anxieties. He smiled and glanced at the sack that lay upon the rear seat. Kady instinctively knew what she must do.

Colin's hospital room was filled with people who seemed to be all talking at once. Kady did not want to interrupt, so she quietly walked in, placed the bag in a corner, and waited for someone to notice her.

"Oh, Kady. It's so wonderful to see you," Edna O'Dannaher said, turning to giving Kady a hug. Then before she knew it, Henry and her Aunt Willa also greeted her. Kady was a bit overwhelmed, and she looked over at Colin whose color had returned.

Colin shrugged his shoulders and said, "Hey, what about me? Don't I get a hug, too?" Kady shyly walked over to the bed and bent down. With his good hand, Colin pulled her forward and gave her a searing kiss.

"So that's the way the wind blows," Henry quietly commented.

"Now, Henry, you leave these two young people alone," Willa said, giving Henry a poke in the shoulder.

"It's OK, honey. Sit here," Colin said with a smile, patting the side of the bed as Kady sat down.

"We've all been waiting for you. Colin has some amazing news," Willa said.

"Kady, when I first told your Aunt Willa about my meeting with Mrs. St. Jude, she had no reaction," said Colin. "That is, until I mentioned the name Jewel Monroe."

"Jewel Monroe," Willa said with disgust. "She was the bane of your Uncle Daniel's existence. Her lover Willy was none other than William Chaddack of the Chaddack Boiler Company. That man did more to ruin your uncle's life than the tragedy at Navy Pier itself."

"Willa, you couldn't be more right," Colin interjected. The room fell silent as Colin continued.

"Kady, just before you arrived, your aunt gave me some valuable information that helped me understand the psychic connection between your great-great-great-great grandfather Napayshni, and your Uncle Daniel's unrest." Colin reached for the control at his side and slightly raised his bed. Kady instinctively helped him with his pillow, bringing a collective smile to Edna, Willa, and Henry.

"Kady, if I'm not mistaken, you have something for me." She walked over to the corner, picked up the bag, and handed it to Colin. For a moment it seemed as though time stood still. From the large burlap sack he removed a handsome buckskin pouch decorated with four silver studs. Then came a pair of moccasins embroidered with flowers and a horse's head, with a rattle of deer hooves resting inside them. Colin reached in one last time and pulled out a small shield made of cedar bark, ornamented with gold beads and thread, woven in the design of herbs entwined around a half moon.

"Oh my," Willa exclaimed, grabbing her heart as she sank down into a chair.

Kady ran to her aunt's side, "Aunt Willa, are you OK? Should I call a doctor?"

In a shaky voice, Willa slowly said, "Thanks, honey, but I'll be all right. Just give me a second. I'm not a hundred percent sure, but I think I've seen these things before." A fine sheen of perspiration beaded her forehead. "I'd swear these are the same artifacts that my Daniel's men were accused of stealing years ago from the museum at Navy Pier," said Willa. "Colin, where on earth did you find these things?"

"I believe this is the shield your Uncle Daniel and our great-great-great grandfather wanted us to find. Kady, until yesterday I don't think I'd ever told you that I had discovered some native American artifacts and the original deed to my home in a secret compartment behind the fireplace."

"Well, then, if I'm not mistaken, both sets of artifacts were taken from Navy Pier at the same time, and the only link between them is William Chaddack.

"Why would William Chaddack steal these things if he was already a wealthy man?" Kady questioned.

Colin looked up from the shield. "Tell her why, Willa."

"Kady, William Chaddack's company had been in competition with Uncle Daniel's company for years. He terrorized the men who worked for us a number of times, and one night he came to our house drunk, threatening to kill us both. He was furious because Chaddack Boiler Company lost their bid to work on Navy Pier to us. His family had enormous political clout, so when the accident happened at the Pier, he was the one hired by the city as an expert in boilers to head the investigation. It was his testimony that led to the demise of Uncle Daniel's business."

"Can you remember anything else?" Colin questioned.

"I don't know if this has any significance, Colin, but I remember reading about his murder in the newspaper," said Willa. "It made the front page."

"Wasn't he killed by his lover?" Edna interjected.

"That's right," Colin said, "and, as we all know, his mistress Jewel Monroe was accused but found innocent of his murder. However, I didn't know until the other night that she was a singer whose stage name was 'The Lark.'"

Kady gasped, "My God, Colin, that's the psychic message Aunt Willa and I both received."

Colin continued, "Jewel St. Jude, a.k.a. Jewel 'The Lark' Monroe, summoned me to Lakeview nursing home two nights ago with the hope that I would be able to help William find eternal peace. He had sought forgiveness and wanted the truth to be known so his spirit might finally cross over. But to me the most important thing she told me was that Chaddack had insisted, with his last dying breath, that she find a mysterious shield. It was then I remembered where I'd seen the name William Chaddack. It was on the deed hidden behind the fireplace in my home with the other native American treasures. Willa, I contend the reason William Chaddack had the shield was that he was the one who broke into the Pier that night, sabotaged the boiler, and stole the artifacts. Add to that the restlessness of his spirit, and it's obvious to me that he was the link between the boiler accident and the stolen goods. After all, who had the most to gain from the accident? William Chaddack and the Chaddack Boiler Company!"

The absence of sound weighed heavily in the room as the importance of Colin's discovery dawned on each of them. Suddenly the temperature in the room dropped.

"My, it's gotten chilly in here," exclaimed Edna, breaking the silence as she reached for her sweater.

"No, Grandmother, what you're feeling is the cosmic energy of a renewed soul. William's spirit came to Mrs. St. Jude begging her to find the shield because he was locked in the vibrations of retribution. While on earth he had allowed himself to become obsessed with power and money. He has come here tonight to express his deepest regrets to all those injured by his thoughtless actions."

Willa placed her hand to her heart as all eyes focused on her. "To err is human, to forgive divine. If God can forgive him, so shall I," she said, overcome with emotion.

Everyone in the room was moved by Willa's compassion and capacity for forgiveness. "We may have kept his spirit from suffering eternal damnation," she said, "but his redemption rests in God's hands."

"Willa, I feel Daniel's spirit has also joined us, but it no longer carries its suffocating burden." Colin closed his eyes, "He wants you to know that the Mystic Healing Shield did indeed belong to your great-great-great-grandfather Napayshni, medicine man of the Waushanee tribe. He asks that you please return it to a place of honor." Colin glanced at Kady.

"As partners in the spiritual world, Daniel and Napayshni tell me they are eternally grateful to all of us for our help. Daniel says always to remember that it was forgiveness that ultimately freed their spirits. Being aware of your spiritual heritage enabled you to believe in Willa's dreams and Kady's premonitions. We have all proved that love can show us the way."

Colin paused as Daniel's message became more personal. "Willa, Daniel wants you to know that his love for you knows no earthly boundaries, and he shall wait patiently until the time that God reunites the two of you in the kingdom of heaven." The climate in the room returned to normal as everyone sat in silence.

Willa turned to Colin, "Oh, Colin, I don't know how to thank you. At long last I feel Daniel's soul at rest." She turned to give her old friend Edna a hug. "God knew what he was doing when he let you raise this wonderful young man."

Edna sniffed, looking around for some Kleenex. Henry pulled two freshly laundered hankies from his pocket, one for each woman.

"I'm always prepared," he said giving Colin a wink. Henry stood up, "Well, girls, this has been a night none of us will ever forget. What do you say I treat you two psychic sisters to some coffee and desert over at Poppin Fresh Pies. Besides, I think it's about time we leave these two lovebirds alone."

A smiling Edna and Willa linked arms with Henry and slowly left the room. They had all been through an incredible emotional journey, each one of them courageous in a special way. Their willingness to open their minds and hearts to the spirit world had, in the end, brought peace and forgiveness. Having faith in God and believing in life after death allowed them the opportunity to see the greater picture.

Colin and Kady sat alone on the bed. Kady looked so vulnerable, so lovable, that Colin thought his heart might burst. With his one good arm, he pulled her into his embrace, kissing her with all the passion that he had been holding inside. A floodgate of emotions poured through Kady's body as he deepened his kiss. Her happiness and relief was so evident that she began to cry.

"Hey, that's the first time my lips have reduced a woman to tears," Colin teased as he pulled back. Kady gave him a weepy smile, as he knew she would.

"Colin, I can't thank you enough for all you done for me and my family. I love you, Colin O'Dannaher. You're amazing." As she pointed to the shiny metal brace on Colin's leg, she began to chuckle, "Come on now... a girl's got to be able to recognize a suit of armor when she sees it."

Colin smiled from ear to ear. "I love you, Kady Marie Dailey, and now that you're no longer afraid of your psychic gifts, what do you say you and I become lifelong partners on a psychic team?" Colin looked lovingly into her questioning eyes, uncertain of her answer. "You know, we could become the Nick and Nora of psychic phenomenon."

"Oh, Colin, I'll be part of any team you're on," Kady said leaning in. Colin raised himself up on the bed, taking her into his arms. As their lips met, two spirits in heaven and two hearts on earth joined in a moment of perfect bliss.